Andrew Towers grew up and lives in Hartlepool. He studied English Literature at University College London before graduating with an MA in Creative Writing from the University of East Anglia in 2007. His short story, 'Jellyfish', won the *Guardian* Short Story Award in 2010. He has worked as a cleaner in a Unitarian holiday hostel, a call-centre helpline assistant and, currently, a bingo caller. He used to share his home with two Russian Dwarf hamsters called Jeeves and Wooster, but they passed away in quick succession in May 2013.

Top of the House

Andrew Towers

corsair

CORSAIR

First published in Great Britain in 2015 by Corsair
This edition published in 2016 by Corsair

1 3 5 7 9 10 8 6 4 2

A CIP catalogue record for this book is available from the British Library.

ISBN: 978-1-4721-1918-6

Printed and bound in Great Britain by Clays Ltd, St Ives Plc

Papers used by Corsair are from well-managed forests and other responsible sources.

MIX
Paper from
responsible sources
FSC® C104740

Corsair
An imprint of
Little, Brown Book Group
Carmelite House
50 Victoria Embankment
London EC4Y 0DZ

An Hachette UK Company
www.hachette.co.uk
www.littlebrown.co.uk

For
My late grandpa, Michael Towers
And
My new nephew, Michael Malone

Contents

Contents

Kelly's Eye

The monkey statue glittered with a light sheen of frost. Its eyes shone like pieces of quartz. It rose triumphantly out of the polluted waters on its thick, cylindrical pedestal, frozen in lotus position and holding a deep bowl between its folded legs. Impervious in its cold constitution of solid bronze. On the front of the bowl was a plaque, and the front of this plaque read:

MAKE A WISH FOR THE MONKEY

Attached to the harbour barriers to its right was a little information board, stamped in the corner with the emblem of Deerpool Borough Council (a minimalist depiction of a roe ferrying a large rat on its back over crudely drawn impressionistic waves).

THE LEGEND OF THE MONKEY

Legend has it that during the Napoleonic Wars, fishermen from Deerpool witnessed the wreck of a French warship on their coastline. The only survivor was the ship's mascot – a monkey whom the crew had dressed in French military uniform. Believing the monkey to be a Frenchman, the townspeople tried and executed the primate in the town square.

In 2005, Deerpool Borough Council erected this statue to commemorate the legend. Some say that if you throw a coin into the monkey's lap and make a wish, your wish will be granted.

All proceeds go to Deerpool District Hospice.

I reached into my faux Dolce & Gabbana handbag (only a knock-off from the covered market, but I was rather attached to it. Black 'leather' with a zip-top, wrinkled with stylish folds and buckles, and a little golden chain, gratuitous but pretty, dangling from a loop in the leather on one side). I scrabbled around the crumbs and loose extra-strong mints at the bottom until I found a penny.

Fingering the face of our monarch, I wished my current favourite wish – that I would one day own a real D&G handbag. Handbags give a feeling of security. Especially to those who own only enough valuable belongings to fill one. There's something comforting in knowing that every material thing I care about is nestled on the crook of my hip. Of course, then there's the accompanying anxiety that one day I'll have it snatched away from me.

I threw the penny into the monkey's bowl. It landed with a gentle clink, resting atop probably around twelve pounds fifty-worth of hopes and aspirations of other wishing, dreaming townspeople. I don't believe that wishes are granted – much less that they're granted by a begging inanimate primate perched in a cesspool. But it doesn't stop me wishing.

That morning, I was in a Per Una Enchanted Romance sleeveless drape jersey dress, accessorised with an open-weave tassel scarf from the Indigo Collection and KG Horatio court shoes. I'd tucked my penis carefully between my legs and hoisted up my Dreamgirl Spanish Fly Knit thong to keep it resting snugly along the line of my bum crack. Though I say it myself, I'm rather well endowed, and this was no mean feat.

My outfit was a lovingly constructed ensemble. I didn't 'pass' as female – I knew this. Even if I shaved off my stubble and made some attempt at disguising my broad shoulders, the prominence of my brow and the resonance of my voice would give me away. Besides, if I presented an entirely convincing female facade, I wouldn't feel quite the thing. I liked hovering there, in a space of ambiguity. It made manifest my relationship to the town. I didn't quite fit. For all that I'd grown up there, lived, loved and worked there for forty-seven years, I stood a little outside, veering unpredictably from full participation in Deerpool's singular social rituals, to gawping in bewilderment at the goings-on.

The clouds were threatening to disgorge snow, and I was quite unbearably cold, the goosebumps standing to attention like eager sea cadets on my pale forearms. The sea cadets, as it happens, were drilling not far away – a fact that broadcasted itself on the strains of amateur trumpet calls and the sound of synchronised marching and 'Hup! Teeeeention!'s hitching a ride on the harsh November wind. As I approached the lock gates, an unbearable, dual-toned alarm began to screech and the gates clamped shut. A boat was coming through.

This was just perfect. Now I would be there for at least ten or fifteen minutes. I would be late for my appointment with Divvy Karen. And she doesn't like to be kept waiting. So I stood watching the grey water gush from the harbour into the lock pool, breathing deep the scent of sea kelp and raw sewage, the water levels gradually evening out. The lock gates stirred like great black sea creatures awakening and stretching, and slowly, lazily parted, as though one was going for a morning shower and the other to make breakfast. As they drifted apart they revealed a tiny speedboat, buzzing impatiently to be out of the playpen of the harbour, eager for a jaunt on the open waves. A desperate little craft, white with black stripes along its sides in the shape of lightning strikes, too ostentatious for its size. It motored through the gates indignantly, churning up an insignificant tumble of white bubbles in its wake, like farts in bathwater. At the helm was a small man with a shiny face and a red beanie hat too large for his head. The name on the side of the boat was:

BARBARA

I wondered idly who this 'Barbara' was.

Perhaps she was the shiny beanie man's ex-wife. A current girl-friend. A younger sister who'd died of leukaemia. A prostitute he'd paid for one lonely night on a business trip to Norwich with whom he'd fallen in love but never seen again. Perhaps she took all his money and stole his watch and his debit card and the Frusli cereal bar he'd bought for the train trip home, but he couldn't bring himself to be angry with her. She remained forever a spec-tacular Venus on a clamshell in the otherwise still and shallow waters of his unremarkable imagination. Perhaps that's why he bought the speedboat – to look for her.

Perhaps it was just the make of the boat.

One Little Duck

As the gates slowly closed I paced in a small circle, crushing barnacles that had fallen off the hulls of boats they hoisted up on to the concrete dock. A large red and white sign perpetually announced: 'KEEP OUT. BOAT HOIST IN OPERATION.' Though they only hoisted boats twice a day at the most.

The hoisting apparatus, though, was a constant and rather ominous presence on the quayside. Thirty feet tall, at least, and made of unfriendly-looking blue steel, it straddled a square of water bitten out of the jetty to the right of the lock gates like the archway entrance to Neptune's kingdom. Near the bar that ran across its top, it was slung with enormous sturdy cables, to which were attached thick leather straps. These could be lowered into the water to fish out a boat and suspend it over the gravel shore for a five-star 'makeover' – a fierce hosing down with a spray of antiseptic saltwater.

The barnacles were easy to crack and flatten beneath my Horatio courts – the soles of the shoes were still in good condition, despite the fact I'd purchased them from the Salvation Army. Quite a find, if I do say so myself. The shells of the tiny creatures lay in little piles on the concrete slabs, served up in a *jus* of sludge and saltwater, garnished with a green seaweed and sewage jelly. I knew that they were still alive inside their crusty casings, gulping in their last breaths of seawater. I was squashing the tiny life of each one I stepped upon.

Behind the barriers, the water of the harbour looked frigid and lifeless. At this time of year, its only occupants were the stubborn shoals of half-drowned rubbish chucked into the water by lazy humans. In late March would come pods of jellyfish of all sizes. The water would heave and pulse with them. Seagulls would call constantly like abandoned babies. At the moment, though, the water and the air were silent, dead and still. We'd barely had Bonfire Night, and already the spectre of winter had drifted in to haunt the town.

3

One Little Flea

Beside the lock gate, Don was painting with watercolours. His straggling strawberry-blonde beard was smeared at the tips with the chartreuse he was using to shade in the waves. His works of art were spread out over the ground in a miasma of washed-out colour, greyer and waterier even than the washed-out weather. There were at least fifty pictures – all A5 in size, most of ships and lighthouses and choppy water and looming cumulonimbus-laden skies. There was one, however, of the monkey statue, which was quite startlingly realistic. It was about the size of a postcard. The shading was so detailed – he must have used a very fine brush – that you could almost feel the cold, dimpled texture of the bronze. He'd captured perfectly, too, the cheeky sparkle in the statue's eye – the one that made me sometimes think that it was a metal husk, inside which was squatting a child, peering out through bored eyeholes.

'Greetings, Don,' I said, beaming my best art critic's grin.

'Don't tread on 'em,' he said gruffly, finishing off a pale purple background wash on a larger canvas. My attention was captured as much by Don's paintings as by the small tattoo he sports in the very centre of his brow. It is a small round black circle and resembles nothing so much as a bullet hole. Was it a tattoo, though? I wondered. Could it be a birthmark? Back in 1990, Don won one hundred thousand pounds on a scratch card. He was in the *Deerpool Chronicle*. Last year, he was in the *Chronicle* again – the story this time was that he'd spent it all on booze, drugs and loose women, and now had to eke out a meagre living selling average artwork. This wasn't entirely true. His artwork was above average.

'Never,' I replied. 'Never never. Anathema, to defile such keenly observed artistic achievements. I particularly like the way you've captured the lettering on the hull of the *Persephone*. What a marvellously brisk day it is, don't you think? How much for the monkey picture?'

'More than you could afford, yer scruffy meff,' replied Don.

I laughed heartily at this urbane observation, then lurched forward and snatched his pot of brushes and scampered towards the lock barrier. He came after me, tiptoeing through his pictures and wrestling me to the ground. He clawed at my hands where they clutched the brush pot, trying to prise my fingers loose from his property.

'Ha ha!' I cried in triumph, 'I have your brush pot!' Not the most inventive of triumphant cries, I acknowledge this, but it seemed to enrage Don quite wonderfully, for he drew back his right arm and planted his fist into the centre of my stomach, knocking the wind from me. The blow sent the pot shooting out of my grip to roll wildly towards the lock barrier, scattering brushes in its wake.

We wrestled for some time on the damp, fishy concrete, barnacles poking into parts of our anatomy both bony and fleshy, until our interaction proved almost homoerotic and I'm not ashamed to say I became slightly aroused.

Before Don could sense my erection and become even more enraged, I kicked him smartly in the knackers and disengaged myself. I then grabbed the monkey picture, shoved it down the front of my Freya Faye underwired plunge bra (thank goodness the paint was dry), scrambled to my feet and dashed over the lock gates, skidding slightly on the wet metal. I made it over just before the wailing alarm began to sound once more and the gates swung open to admit another boat into the harbour. Don was left standing forlornly amidst his paintings, shaking a fist in the air and threatening loudly to 'knack me' when next we met.

I suddenly felt incredibly elated, and broke into song:

> *Who's a scruffy meff, now,*
> *Who's a scruffy meff?*
> *Not me, not me:*
> *You're a scruffy meff!*

I sang to a little improvised tune, dancing a few steps on the gravel. I call this my 'Maurice Dance', and perform it only in moments of supreme personal triumph. As I hopped and skipped, I was vaguely aware of several chavs filming me on their mobile telephonic whatsits from the other side of the lock.

'Dance for us, Maurice!' they shouted. 'Do yer tranny dance!'

One of them sang a song, to the approximate tune of 'My Old Man's a Dustman'.

> *Maurice is a tranny,*
> *He wears a tranny's hat,*
> *He fucked your fuckin' granddad,*
> *Now whadya think of that?*
> *HEY!*

I took a bow and turned away.

I walked through the car park towards the stretch of chalky wasteland that lies between the Marina and the back end of the town centre. An elderly gentleman in a Reebok cap was sprinkling his Mini Metro with a watering can. Perhaps he expected it to grow into a Cadillac. Through the misted window of a large

9

Vauxhall Astra, I could see that the front two seat covers were in the design of dogs, pictured on the fabric as though they were sitting in the seats. The driver's side was a Dalmatian, the passenger's a golden retriever.

They had their paws over their eyes.

4

Knock at the Door

I was, it transpired, precisely on time to meet Divvy Karen down by the 11 O'Clock Shop. We had arranged to meet there at 11 o'clock. Things like this amuse us.

It was Sunday, so I was confident she'd be wearing her Sunday leggings (black and tight enough to severely restrict the circulation to her legs) and tormenting some cornered innocent with stories from her youth.

Sure enough, as I approached, I spied her sitting on the low brick wall by the shop's front entrance, her legs sprawled out over the pavement so that passers-by had to step over them. Beside her on the wall was perched a nervous androgynous adolescent in gothic get-up, his/her hands on his/her steadily bouncing knees. It was hard to tell whether his/her white face was down to the layer of ghostly white face powder or Divvy Karen's alarming monologue.

'Me mam ye see, she nearly didn't 'ave me, 'cos they gave 'er a barium meal when she was sixth months pregnant, and that's radio-active, 'cos they didn't believe she was 'avin me, and she told them, she said "Don't you kill me baby inside me with that barium meal," but they gave 'er it, and three months later she 'ad me. My uncle used to sit me on 'is knee and tell me to touch 'im, but it wasn't bad or owt 'cos 'e'd been burnt wi' bitumen and 'ad to 'ave 'is bollocks removed. 'E used to chloroform me auntie for sex, till she sewed 'im up in a sheet one night. Me dad 'ad to cut 'im out and me uncle ate glass, 'cos 'e couldn't stand to be without 'er, but 'e didn't die or owt and now 'e can't speak 'cos 'e's 'ad 'is nerves all removed.'

'If . . .' the teenager ventured in a small voice, 'if your uncle had no testicles, why did he need to chloroform your auntie for sex?'

A perturbed look shadowed Karen's face and she made a small, helpless sound, as though her entire perception of the universe had been shattered.

I sat down beside Karen on her other side and lit a cheapy tab.

'It's okay,' I said to the trembling teenager. 'You can go now.' He/she nodded in relief and scurried away towards St Aidan's Church Corner.

I puffed serenely on my tab. Then I lit another tab and tucked it between Divvy Karen's lips. It seemed to calm her.

At this point I should mention that Divvy Karen has not always been a Divvy. 'Divvy', after all, is a subtle classification. It lies somewhere beneath the heading 'Idiot' and is more pejorative than 'Numpty' but less wounding than 'Knobhead.'

Divvy

Pronunciation /dɪvi/

Noun (slang) (Plural **divvi**)

1. A person of sub-standard intelligence, eccentric
    appearance and poor communication skills

    ('You divvy, that was a brand-new can of shaving foam.'

    'Are you calling me a divvy? You absolute knobhead.')

    (Abbreviation: **div**)

    ('What a div!')

Verb (**divvy, divvies, divvying**)

('What are you doing divvying about over there?'

'If you don't stop divvying with that group of numpties, I
will come over there and twat you one.')

Nor is it a title of which I'm particularly fond. But it seems to
have stuck, and everyone who knows her now uses it, to Karen's
apparent indifference. It originated at Deerpool Comprehensive.
I was her English teacher, you see, from Year Nine through to
GCSE. She was never really a social animal – the other children
were fond of throwing things at her at any available opportunity
(toilet paper, sausage rolls, staplers). And in the year following her
brain-damaging drug overdose, I noticed the 'Divvy' slowly
establish itself, like a parasitic mite getting comfy on the back of a
hedgehog. Now it just lives there as part of her name.

'All right?' I said. Which is our usual greeting.

'Yeah, all right,' she said. 'All right?'

'All right,' I said. 'All right?'

'All right,' she said.

A middle-aged lady in a power suit stepped over her legs.

'Y'got ten pence for the bus?' inquired Divvy Karen, looking
up plaintively into the lady's gaunt face. The lady ignored her and
strode on. 'Cowbag,' said Karen.

5

Man Alive

I gave Karen the Cornish pasty and iced bun I'd purchased from Greggs on the way to meet her.

'Ta,' she said, gratefully. She balanced the pasty on her skinny knees and laid a hand on it, as though blessing it before beginning to eat. Divvy Karen is, it has to be said, oddly proportioned. Her upper half is almost emaciated, her arms often bare (as she favours vest tops and enjoys cutting the sleeves from her other garments), but her arse is large – bulbous and peachy, and only accentuated by the tight black leggings she favours. She has an endearing habit of tilting her head to the right and gazing up with her great blue eyes, and I've often thought this must skew her view of the world. Divvy Karen, it has to be said, sees things the rest of us can't.

The one-armed-bandit players in the bingo arcade – those mesmerised old birds who sit perched for eight hours or more pecking with bony fingers at the 'spin' buttons on the Rainbow Riches – call her Gollum. Their cruelty cuts me to the quick, although I can't help but think that in a way it's apt. I remember a time before all this. Before Chunky waved the precious golden ring of Class A drugs in front of her, and she began to metamorphose slowly into this wide-eyed, pitiful, pale creature. She used to wear her hair in pigtails. She sat at the very back row of my English class, and she would peer at me as I taught, listening with her head tilted slightly to the right, her right pigtail bouncing against her shoulder as she joggled her knee beneath the desk.

She was absolutely hopeless at literacy. I remember my dismay the first time I read one of her essays. From the handwriting, spelling and grammar, you'd think it had been written by a three-year-old. It was odd, given her brilliance with numbers. Her Maths teacher, Mr McGee – Duke – was a close companion and confidant of mine, the only other staff member I could trust at that place. He assured me she was quite an exceptional mathematician, though I don't think I truly believed it, until he staged an after-school 'arithmetic show' in his class – mine the only invite. He launched equations, algebraic formulae and long divisions at her like tennis balls in a batting cage, and every one of them she whacked right out of the court. I was astonished.

To this day I refuse to think that I had anything to do with her disintegration. She was seventeen and out of school before I ever touched her (or she me). It sounds as though I'm being defensive, I know. But the school really was wrong about the nature of our relationship. There was something about her. From the moment I saw her, I knew that I'd found a kindred spirit, and I think she knew the same thing. The other students used to tease her mercilessly. Throw things at her – calculators, shatterproof rulers, food and the like. Spit at her. There was very little discipline at Deerpool Comprehensive – approaching a *Lord of the Flies* sort of situation, I'd go so far as to say. She'd turn up at my classroom ten minutes into lunch break, covered in flakes of sausage-roll pastry, mucus and chewing gum, and I'd let her take refuge. I'd give her paper and a pen, let her scribble down equations. We talked a little, too. About maths (though I understood little of what she said). About her Aunt Neenie. About my mother.

Now, on the wall outside the 11 O'Clock Shop, she passed me a tenner.

'The pasty cost one pound forty-nine,' I said, 'and the iced bun was eighty-five pence.'

'Seven pounds sixty-six change,' said Karen, without a discernible pause. I counted the money out. Karen helps me out in matters of mental arithmetic. Even the simplest problems stump me like an amputated leg. Karen's number-crunching skills, on the other hand . . . Well.

'Karen,' I asked, nonchalantly, 'what's the square root of five thousand one hundred and ninety-eight, divided by twelve, times nine, plus seven, minus two?'

'To what decimal point?' she asked.

'Erm . . . three decimal points.'

'59.073. Rounded up.'

'Get *outta* here.'

Karen got up and began to make her way down the street. I pounced on her and tugged her back down to sit on the wall.

'Not literally?' she asked.

'Not literally,' I said. 'Would you like a watercolour painting of a monkey statue?' I dug into my bra to retrieve the stolen painting.

'Yeah,' she said. 'Go on then.' She took it, studied it for a second and then stuffed it into the Almart bag at her feet. 'Got summat to tell you,' she said, smacking her lips and blinking several times in quick succession, her large, lizard-like eyelids flicking forward to moisten her protruding eyeballs.

'Go ahead,' I said.

6

Tom's Tricks

'Was round Chunky's last night,' she said.

Her voice is rather high and nasal, her accent broad Deerpudlian. A unique accent, often miscategorised as 'Geordie' by those who live south of Middlesbrough. If your ears, however, are attuned, through long residence in the area, to the subtleties of inflection that distinguish a Sunderland lad from a native Sedgefielder, then you can easily detect the idiosyncrasies that give Deerpudlian its singular melody. A slight resonance at the back of the throat during long vowels. A barely lilting, meandering tunefulness that grows more pronounced as an uninterrupted utterance progresses. A strange but not unpleasant tightness around the 'e's, reining them in awkwardly but attractively, like a grandmother's torso-lette reins in her stomach fat.

'Oh,' I said, breaking eye contact and lifting my nose high in the air. 'Round Chunky's, were you?'

'Yeah,' she said.

'Yes?' I said.

'Yeah,' she said. 'I was round Chunky's, and he gave us a bit of speed, like.'

I sighed. The spasms of despair and disappointment at Karen's drug use had over time, through overexposure, weakened to clenches in the abdominal region, similar to constipation pangs.

'Karen,' I said, sagely, launching into an oft-repeated lecture, 'haven't you learnt your lesson about Chunky's speed? I wonder what rotten unmentionable he cut it with this time. Caster sugar? Rat poison? Splenda? Kettle lime? Dandruff? The sherbet from inside those flying saucers . . . ?'

Apparently it was Bar Keeper's Friend that brought her so close to death that one frightening evening a few years ago. According to the neurologists at the Nuffield, the solvent caused 'permanent deep white-matter abnormalities'. Before then, she actually made a species of sense when you spoke to her. Now you had to think laterally to understand her, most of the time. Though miraculously, her aptitude for numbers remained untouched.

'. . . Yeah, like,' she interrupted, 'let me tell me story, marrah.'

[**Marrah**

Pronunciation /ma-ra/

Noun (slang) (Plural *marray*)

1. Good friend, mate, chum or treasured acquaintance.

   ('Ta, marrah, I'll see you tomorrow, then.')]

'. . . So he give us a fiver and tells me to get twenty cheapy tabs from the shop round the corner.' A 'cheapy tab' is an inexpensive cigarette, incidentally.

'And what did you say?' I asked, looking up at a perfect formation of cumulus clouds overhead.

'I said, "Get yer own cheapy tabs, yer dirty meff."'

[**Meff**

Pronunciation /mɛf/

Noun (slang) (Plural *meef*)

1. A person of sub-standard intelligence, eccentric
   appearance and poor communication skills
   ('You meff, that was a brand-new can of shaving foam.'
   'Are you calling me a meff? You divvy.')]

'An admirable insult,' I said. 'And what did he say to that?'

'He said, "I'll kick yer 'ed in". And I said, "I'd like to see yer try, yer meff."'

'An excellent comeback,' I said.

'Anyway,' she said, ''e really was goin' to kick me 'ed in. So I offered 'im a shag.'

'Oh, Karen,' I said, 'we've spoken about this.'

'I knar,' she said. 'I knar.'

'Your body is sacred, Karen. Sacred.'

She looked down briefly at her twig-like arms, deflated breasts and overstuffed sausage thighs. Then blinked at me, deadpan.

'But 'e was goin' to kick me 'ed in. I thought I'd rather shag 'im than 'ave 'im kick me 'ed in.'

'You needn't have done either,' I said. 'You could've come and found me.'

I intensely disliked Karen's association with Chunky. Not only because it was so physically unhealthy in so many ways. Chunky seemed to think he had a hold on her that won out over mine. True enough, I couldn't provide her with drugs on tap in exchange for sexual favours. But I cared about her well-being in ways for which he lacked the capacity entirely.

'Yeah,' she said now, dismissively. Then, 'Well, 'e took me into the kitchen. You know 'is kitchen?'

'Yes,' I said. 'I know his kitchen.' I'd seen the surprisingly pristine classic decor of his kitchen several times, forced to venture into his lair to drag a near-comatose Karen home and to safety. And that one dreadful evening, of course, when we had to take a detour via A&E.

'And 'e pulled down me leggins and sat me on the long counter.'

'Most unhygienic.'

'And 'e was gettin' me ready, you know. Feelin' me down there and that.'

'Yes, yes. I get the picture.' I really couldn't stand to hear much more of this. Karen, though, seemed oblivious to my discomfort.

'And then after a bit I felt somethin' dodgy.'
'Dodgy? In what respect?'
'Like, radged . . .'

[Radged
Pronunciation /radged/
Adjective (slang)
1. Unacceptably, unconventionally and otherwise
   inexplicably 'wrong'
   ('The meff spends all his time looking at road maps of
   the Cotswolds. He's radged, he is.')
2. Disconcerting and unpleasant
   (There's not even any loo roll in here. This is radged, I
   tell you.')]*

'. . . Like . . . Really radged. Down there. Turned out . . .'
   '. . . Oh, Karen. I'm not sure I want to . . .'
   'Turned out it were a kiwi fruit.'
   Well. That wasn't quite what I was expecting.
   'A . . . a kiwi fruit.'
   'A kiwi fruit, yeah. 'E was runnin' it over me down there. Over
me . . . you know. And me . . . you know.'
   'Yes, I have a vague idea.'
   '. . . Flaps.'
   'Yes.'
   '. . . And that.'
   'Yes.'
   'Yeah.'
   'A kiwi fruit.'
   'Yeah.'
   'Peeled or unpeeled?'

---

* There is, by the way, no noun or verb equivalent. The concept of 'a radge'
is unheard of, nor can one 'radge' someone.

'Peeled.'

'Ah. What did it feel like?'

'. . . Sting-y.'

'I should think so. The kiwi fruit has enzymes which slowly digest tissue. It's why your mouth often stings after eating them.'

'Mingin'.'

'Yes. So . . . what happened then?'

'Well. After 'e'd . . . run it over me . . . you know.'

'Yes.'

'. . . Flaps.'

'Yes.'

'. . . For a while, 'e sort of . . . put it . . . inside me.'

I took a moment or two to process the conversation so far. There was a distinct possibility that I'd got entirely the wrong end of the stick. I stared for a moment at the fibreglass butterfly stuck to the front wall of the house opposite.

'He put a peeled kiwi fruit inside your twat?'

'Yeah.'

'Are you all right?' I asked.

'Why aye. Come out in a bit of a rash on me chest, like.'

'You think that might've caused it?'

'Yeah. Too much of a coincidence.'

I crossed my legs and pursed my lips. If I'm honest, I was a little disappointed. I'd been planning to regale her with the dramatic tale of my wrestle with Don and triumphant acquisition of the monkey painting. She'd rather trumped me with the kiwi fruit. And I had to admit, I was intrigued.

'Did you get it out?'

'Eventually. Sat on the bog and relaxed me muscles.'

A bus rumbled by. Through the window, a middle-aged, blonde-bobbed woman gave us a disappointed look. I held up two fingers at her, knuckles outwards.

7

God's in Heaven

'Can I stay round yours tonight?' she asked. 'Worried Chunky might come round the 'ostel.'

I didn't much like the idea of Karen staying at the hostel, though since her aunt threw her out there seemed little other option. She could have stayed with me on a permanent basis – I'd offered. Apparently she wanted her independence. I suspected she rather wanted the freedom to flit between me and Chunky, but I didn't question this from fear of losing her entirely.

'Why?' I asked. 'Why would he come round the hostel?'

She looked at her feet, biting at her bottom lip so furiously that I was afraid it might start to bleed.

'Well . . .' she said.

'Well?' I said.

'Well . . .' she said, '. . . 'e said 'e was gonna kill me.'

Christ on a wholegrain cracker.

'This is his twelfth death threat this month.'

'Nah,' said Divvy Karen, her face growing progressively paler. 'He really means it this time.'

'How do you know?'

She shifted her buttocks restlessly and lifted her top, twisting her torso around to expose the small of her back.

'Good grief,' I said. Bile rose in my throat.

On Divvy Karen's lower back, just to the right of her spine, was a long, relatively fresh . . . 'gash' would be the wrong word for it. It was more like a tear. Like someone had taken a blunt object – most definitely blunt; the wound wasn't clean – dug it into her flesh until it burst and then dragged it six or seven inches across, parting the reluctant skin and tissue raggedly in its wake. It was crusting slightly at the edges, but its centre was still moist, raw and gooey. There was, in addition, something in the centre of it. Something thick, black and glistening. What on earth? The wound couldn't have started to necrotise in this short time, could it? It almost looked like . . .

'What did he use?' I asked, in disbelief.

'A Staedtler Triplus Fineliner,' she said.

I swallowed back the bitter remnants of my breakfast.

'There's ink in the wound,' I said, standing up and shucking off my 10 denier Secret Magic Shape Support Tights. I then fished in my bag for a mansize Kleenex (something of a concession, for a transgender person, though I'm forced to concede that I still have man-sized nostrils). 'Hold still,' I commanded. I then clapped the Kleenex to the wound and wrapped the tights tightly around her waist, holding the tissue in place. We would clean it when we got back to the flat. 'What precipitated this calligraphic attack?' I asked.

Karen winced.

'He wants his lucky charm back.'

8

Garden Gate

And then I remembered the troll doll.

A fortnight ago, there had been a large jackpot evening at the town's biggest bingo hall – the Pentagon. Chunky, as I learned from Karen, was unable to attend. He's a tattoo artist, you see, and apparently he was scratching artwork into the arm of one of his best Ecstasy suppliers – a touch-up of his baby daughter's fat face on his bicep. Now, Chunky had desperately wanted to attend this jackpot evening, and was chagrined that the supplier would accept no other slot for his appointment. Chunky therefore sent Karen to the bingo in his stead. And being a frighteningly super-stitious individual, he gave her his trusted bingo talisman – a tiny troll doll with wilted green hair – to ensure her win. She was instructed, upon pain of death ('a massive knacking, and then death,' as Karen relayed his words), not to lose it.

This troll doll, you see, was Chunky's bingo mascot. He visited the bingo about once a fortnight – always accompanied by this foul plastic homunculus – and never failed to win at least a tenner, sometimes substantially more. Other customers were bitter about his amazing track record, and cries of 'It's rigged' echoed in the wake of every one of his winning shouts. But Chunky insisted it was the troll that made the magic happen. Once, he'd tested its power by leaving it at home. Sure enough, that evening he didn't win a sausage (literally – that night's prize was a year's free meat from Cameron's Butchers). This only cemented his conviction that the troll was a miracle charm.

Per Chunky's instructions Karen held the troll doll clamped between her teeth the entire evening it was in her care. This, apparently, was necessary in order to secure the win. As fortune would have it, Karen did indeed win Chunky the two thousand pound jackpot full house. I know, because I was there. But as staggering misfortune would have it, at the evening's end she couldn't find the doll.

I was initially worried she'd swallowed it without realising, though nothing showed up in the toilet bowl in the following days, and we were forced to admit that she must have dropped it somewhere in the bingo hall.

She looked up at the sky, her big eyes shining with tears.

'I'm scared,' she said.

And she was right to be. We'd searched on our hands and knees beneath bingo tables for that troll doll for nigh on an hour, though it was nowhere to be seen. Chunky would want it back, for sure.

'Can't we just buy another little green troll and mess up its hair a bit?' I proposed.

Karen looked at me like I was insane.

''E'd know,' she said. ''E's had that troll since 'e was three years old. Got it from Northallerton Market, apparently. There's all sorts of marks and stuff on it that only 'e knows. We'd never fool 'im.'

'Shit.'

She began to tremble.

'Listen,' I said, 'it's possible that one of the cleaners has found it and given it to Barnie on reception to put in Lost Property. Let's get along to the Pentagon and see.'

She stood up, sliding the pasty deftly out of its greasy paper packet and taking a huge bite.

'Yeah,' she said. 'Why aye.'

9

Doctor's Orders

The decor of the Pentagon's foyer is just traditional enough to retain some of its original tacky charm, but modern enough to approach a measure of sleekness. The walls are marbled orange and glisten like boiled sweets. They're the sort of walls you want to lick, or take a giant crunching bite out of. The walls in which the front doors are set are mirrored, which gives the foyer the illusion of being bigger and more imposing than it actually is. Six fruit machines stand sentinel against the walls, three opposite the main doors and three on a small raised platform against the right-hand wall, each with its own tall purple plush-cushioned stool. They are the newfangled, computerised kind – touchscreens bulging with a selection of different games:

THE X FACTOR
MAX'S MILLIONS
IRISH FIELDS OF GOLD
MONTY PYTHON'S GOLDEN GRAIL
HAMMER HORROR SLOTS

These bleep and trill, merrily advertising their jackpots to anyone who will listen, or simply singing to themselves. The smell of sugar paper and strong mints oozes out of the long red dusty curtains bunched at the side of the mirrors and the vaguely unpleasant carpet, pale beige in colour and splattered with a pattern of little red spots, like a meningitis rash on pale skin.

There is a small reception desk sandwiched between the two groups of fruit machines, and behind this desk, as always, sat Barnie. He was typing on the monster of an old-fashioned computer with one determined forefinger. He'd propped up the keyboard with a stapler turned on its side.

'Tally ho, Barnacious-ness,' I said, startling him somewhat and causing his knee to hit the underneath of the desk, dislodging the keyboard from its stapler-supported position and sending it crashing down on to the floor.

'Maurice!' he said. 'Haven't seen you in yonks!'

I eyed the stapler bemusedly.

'Oh,' he said, 'takes the glare off the keyboard if I use that to balance it.'

Barnie is a good bloke, all told. He once let me leave a Mars Bar milkshake behind the front desk to finish later, even though one's own food and beverage is forbidden inside the hall. He's a large gentleman in his mid-forties, with slicked-down dark-brown hair thinning at the top to show his creamy scalp, giving the effect of someone having splatted a large Cadbury's Creme Egg on the crown of his head. He suits his Extra Large uniform and carries off the starched white shirt, moss-green waistcoat and mustard-yellow bow tie like he was born to it.

Now, his look of friendly greeting dissolved into one of horror as he stumbled to his feet.

'But Maurice,' he said, 'I thought you were . . .' he lowered his voice and spoke through an unattractive grimace, '*barred*.'

'Yes,' I said, with confidence, 'I was indeed barred. For one week. Precisely one week ago to this day. Please check the system if you doubt my integrity.'

'No, no,' he said. 'I believe you. No one ever tells me anything in this place. Welcome back. Hello, Karen,' he shouted. Karen was pressing all of the buttons on one of the new Irish Fields of Gold fruit machines, and remained oblivious. When she pressed the 'Rules' button, it played a leprechaun sound bite, '*Ah, go on. You win, you win*', in a chirrupy Southern Irish accent. She paused, thought for a moment, and then pressed it repeatedly, cutting it off each time after the '*Ah*'. The effect was a pained-pleasured sounding '*Ah-ah-ah-ah-ah-ah*', like a soundtrack from a leprechaun porn film. Lepreporn.

'Since you're here,' said Barnie, 'can I show you the draft of a letter I wrote? Check it for grammar. That sort of thing. You used to teach that stuff, didn't you?'

'And swore I never would again,' I said, with disdain.

'Please,' said Barnie. 'Just cast an eye over it.'

I sighed and held out a hand. 'If I must.'

He gave me the letter.

Cock and Hen

Customer Service Dept.
Almart Supermarket
Palace Retail Park
Deerpool
BSZ 2RQ

Barnie Reynolds
C/O The Pentagon Bingo
Palace Retail Park
Deerpool
BSZ 2RY

November 12th, 2014

To whom it may concern,

I am writing in regard to the matter of the shopping trolleys which keep being left round the back of our building upon numerous occasions.

I will say it in one sentence.

IT HAS HAPPENED AGAIN.

I ask you to refer back to letters 1, 2, 3 and 4 you have received from me on this subject, which, if you are any sort of responsible conglomerate, you will have kept on file. It saddens me to have to write again, but what was once a molehill is now quite frankly a mountain.

I have requested upon numerous occasions that someone come around to collect these trolleys that keep being left there. However, on the first two occasions it took OVER A MONTH for anyone to respond to my complaint, and on the second two it took JUST OVER TWO MONTHS, which is a disintegration rather than an improvement upon the situation.

THEY ARE BLOCKING OUR FIRE EXITS AND CREATING A SERIOUS HEALTH AND SAFETY HAZARD.

They have also been USED BY HOODLUMS in the causing of trouble, namely running and bashing the trolleys against the side of our building.

In the past, I have been so polite as to request that a member of your staff come to remove the trolleys. Now I am afraid that I am reduced to DEMANDING that you send someone round in a timely fashion to remove the offending trolley.

IT IS NOT OUR RESPONSIBILITY TO REMOVE THESE TROLLEYS AND RETURN THEM TO YOU, AS HAS BEEN CONFIRMED BY YOUR GENERAL MANAGER AND AREA MANAGER.

If you should fail to collect this trolley, I will have no qualms in contacting the City Council to gain advice on a further course of action.

Yours sincerely,
Barnie Reynolds
Senior Team Member, The Pentagon Bingo, Deerpool.

Legs Eleven

'It's fine,' I said, clenching my teeth against a tide of detailed feed-back I knew would serve only to hurt him. 'Forceful but not aggressive.'

Barnie gave a beaming grin.

'That's what I was going for,' he said. 'I've contacted Almart on Facebook, too. Left several messages on their page. Still no reply. Are you on Facebook yet?'

'Ah – I still don't really . . . have a computer.'

'Oh, it's marvellous. Marvellous. You update your status, you see, to whatever you're doing at that time. Last night I wrote, "Having a lovely evening in with Mr Brown Ale and Mr Vodka.' It got twelve "likes".'

I was about to ask him what 'likes' meant, when I remembered our reason for being here.

'Barnacious-ness, my man,' I said, 'do you recall having had a troll doll handed in to you as Lost Property at any time during the past week?'

He screwed up his face in deep thought.

'Troll doll,' he said, contemplatively. 'Troll doll, troll doll, troll doll, troll doll . . .'

I waited with bated breath, until his eyes lit up with a spark of memory.

'Tiny little thing?'

'Yes.'

'Ugly face?'

'Yes.'

'Ratty green hair?'

'Yes!'

'It's in Lost Property.'

I nearly slumped to the ground with relief. My mind had been conjuring all sorts of medieval scenarios featuring me and Karen, Chunky and a length of rusty barbed wire.

'Oh, Barnie!' I cried. 'You've no idea how happy you've made me, you marvel of a man.'

Barnie beamed.

'Never let it be said that I don't know the whereabouts of everything that enters my domain.' He crossed to the cupboard beside the doors to Booksales and unlocked it with a small silver key. After rummaging around for a minute or two, he let out a sneeze-like huff of frustration and slammed shut the cupboard door. 'Maybe I left it beside the computer.'

He hurried to check the area around his computer. As the search lengthened, my heart rate sped up accordingly. He ducked down to check the floor beneath the desk. Then he disappeared into the walk-in cupboard behind the desk for several moments. A flurry of muffled thumps bled through the door, and he emerged looking somewhat flustered.

'I'll find it,' he assured me. 'It's somewhere. I know it is. I've seen it.'

I approached him and laid a hand on his shoulder.

'Barnie,' I said, 'it's imperative that you find this troll. My life, and Karen's, may very well depend upon it.' I squeezed his shoulder for emphasis.

Barnie nodded.

'Come back tomorrow. I'll have found it by then. I promise.'

Then the phone on his desk rang. He snatched up the receiver with excessive force and hit himself with it in the right eye. Quickly, though, he manoeuvred it to his ear and spoke.

'Good afternoon,' he said, in a clear, confident tone. 'Pentagon Bingo, Barnie speaking.' Here, he left a long pause, cupping his palm over the mouth end of the receiver to shield it from sound. To me, he whispered, 'Always leave a pause after the name. It's called "Letting the name *land*."' He exposed the mouth end again and continued, 'How may I help?'

I looked at Karen, who was still battering the fruit machine without mercy. Perhaps we should stay and play the free books now that we were here. We might even win a fiver for a cup of coffee and a doughnut. Just then, my thoughts were invaded by a screechingly commanding voice.

'Maurice!' it said. 'Is that you? Gerrover 'ere!'

Monkey's Cousin

It was then that I spotted Neenie settling herself onto one of the fruit-machine stools opposite the doors.

I made a farewell gesture to Barnie, who was telling the phone receiver all about this evening's book prices, and approached Neenie's stool.

'Hiya, kiddeh,' she said, as I drew near. She didn't turn to look at me, though I knew she was scrutinising me in her peripheral vision. A fruit-machine player is always on the lookout for lurkers. They constantly scan their surroundings, protecting their bubble of luck with hawk-like awareness, waiting to swoop and peck to death any little sparrows who want to alight on their perch.

'Hi, Auntie Neenie,' I said. 'You all right?' Neenie is not, in fact, my auntie, but Karen's. She has, however, one of those large, M&S blouse-draped, dandelion-clock-haired presences that compel everyone to call her 'Auntie'. She turned to look at me, simultaneously attempting to feed a twenty into the note accepter. It drooped like a piece of damp toast each time it approached the glowing blue aperture. Eventually she gave up.

'Cowbag,' she muttered, stuffing the note back into her purse and drawing out another, crisper twenty. She whistled through her teeth, quietly and tunelessly. 'Yeah, ta, kiddeh,' she said to me, at length. 'I'm all right. You've got to be, don't yer?'

'This is true.'

'This one's being a cowbag already.' She motioned to the machine with a nod of her head. 'Took five hundred off me last night, and it's not give me a thing back.' Five hundred might seem an extortionate amount, but it was run-of-the-mill for hard-core players like Neenie. These weren't your garden-variety, convivial, ten-pence seaside-arcade fruit machines, either. These were true one-armed bandits. As addictive as meth amphetamine, and just as expensive a habit. They were a pound a spin, and paid out five hundred pound jackpots. And they fed a variety of addicts as diverse as the sallow-cheeked inhabitants of a crack den. There were the young men who hopped from club to club on a tight schedule, staying only as long as they were winning and moving on as soon as the flow of cash dried up, convinced they were operating on a schedule and a system driven by something other than sheer luck. They thought they were professional gamblers, though their beaten-up Honda Civics suggested otherwise. Then there were the ones who couldn't afford it, but coasted along for a while on sporadic large wins that they fed directly back into the machines. I recall once watching a young man and woman who can't have been more than nineteen or twenty taking turns to feed pound coins into a fruit machine while the other one sat in the car with their near-newborn baby. They were there all through the afternoon session – five hours or more. Then there were the ones flush with cash, who played partly out of boredom and partly because it was a convenient way to launder ill-gotten gains (one doesn't need to pay tax on winnings from gambling). Neenie fitted most snugly into that category. She had a great deal of disposable income from several business ventures around town, some legitimate, some more shady. The bandits never had her over a financial barrel, though that's not to say she wasn't as addicted as the rest of them. She was emotionally involved. And that, more than anything, smacked of true addiction.

Over her M&S print blouse (a similar pattern to that on the Pentagon's carpet, but blue), she was wearing an enormous white cardigan, no doubt self-knitted. Beneath her plain black comfortable slacks, her white trainers glowed incongruously, propped carefully on the metal footrest bar of the tall purple stool.

Neenie is one of those people who look as though they might be someone else in disguise. Like their obesity might really be padding, their hair a good-quality wig and their clothes from the rack in Harlequin's Costumier's. The skin of her face looks slightly too tight for the bones – pinched at the corners, stretched around the eyes and tucked under the chin like an ill-fitting latex mask. She never seemed to age – hadn't changed an iota, in fact, since I first encountered her at one of Karen's parents' evenings. She raised Karen (or at least made a go of it) from the age of around six onwards. Gossip in the staffroom was that Karen's mum had come under some scrutiny from social services around that time. Something to do with her involvement with Karen's dad – brought up on several charges of 'enticing a minor'. Karen was removed from the equation, for her own safety.

Neenie, as it happens, was one of the more ordinary frequenters of the Pentagon. As the moon draws the tides, the Pentagon, sooner or later, drew every outcast, every misfit, every penniless, musty-smelling tramp puffing on his harmonica on the street corner of society, into its mystical, slightly seedy orbit. And like a five-pointed star in a Hammer Horror film, it conjured up its own brand of devilry. Ordinary passers-by, clean-cut housewives dropping in for a one-off visit, tourists attracted by its bright lights, would become changed and possessed by its tawdry power.

Not that I'm knocking it. Never. It accepted me. It's the only place I've felt at home since my sudden and scandal-ridden disbarment from teaching. There are people here, you see, who burn with the same desires as I do. I might speak scornfully on occasion of hardened gamblers such as Neenie, but in truth, I am as bad, and worse. Every day I feel adrift and afraid, because of how little I have. How little I own in this world. You'd think it would feel like freedom, to have so few possessions weighing me down. It just makes me feel like a tiny boat without an anchor. The weight of expensive things is what tethers us to land. A longing to be rich doesn't have to stem from greed. For me, it's all about knowing I'll be okay. If I could strike it lucky, just once, then everything would be all right. And I've always had a feeling in my bones that it will happen.

I like the Pentagon, too, because the people here have never judged me for dressing as I do. I never felt comfortable, you see, wearing the kind of clothes that truly felt right, in the stifling and judgemental atmosphere of the school. Duke McGee had understood me. I'd have him round for coffee a couple of times a week, and he'd never lifted an eyebrow at my lilac velour dressing gown or striped bow ballet slippers. But others were nosy and disapproving and just plain unpleasant in the face of unconventionality. When I'd been sacked, I'd decided – it was finally time to wear what I wanted. My mother was a classy lady, despite the fact that she was most definitely poor. In my five years of teaching, I'd used most of my spare cash to buy designer (or mock designer) outfits for her. We'd get the train to Darlington or York and go shopping. Those were good days. After her passing, I was of course left with all of those clothes. Even in my most desperate moments of destitution, I couldn't bring myself to sell them, so I made good use of them myself. Nor could I part with her beloved collection of Herb Alpert cassette tapes (though tapes would be impossible to sell nowadays, anyway).

Mum had a lot of oft-used phrases, but her favourite was, 'You make your own luck, Maurice.'

And I always took it as an instruction.

13

Unlucky for Some

I turned to check on Karen again, and jumped a little when I came face-to-face with Sheila. Sheila hovers in Neenie's orbit like a small, plump, pale moon. She gathers Neenie's winnings from the jackpot tray when they drop, and takes them to the coins-to-notes machine to be changed into twenties. Now, indeed, she clutched a thick bundle of twenty-pound notes – I estimated there to be about two hundred pounds worth. She handed them to Neenie, only the slightest hint of regret and envy creasing the corners of her eyes.

'Ta, chuck,' said Neenie. 'Not even half of what I've put in over the past hour.' She paused, and then inhaled deeply. 'Can you smell fish somewhere about?'

Sheila tipped her head back until it lay right flat back. She breathed in a great lungful of air.

'Don't think so, Neenie,' she said. 'No fish.'

'There is bastarding fish,' said Neenie. 'Somewhere.'

'It'll be that one who works 'ere. Gabby,' said Sheila. 'She has sex on a morning and then comes in without washing 'er tush.' Sheila pulled her trousers out of her arse crack. 'Got a wedgie,' she muttered.

'Thanks for sharing,' said Neenie.

The cold November light was slicing through the glass of the entrance, turning their grey perms an unearthly silver. Every so often a blast of frigid wind pushed open one of the inner doors and licked around them, setting their hair and their cardigans trembling.

Neenie had yet to acknowledge Karen's presence. It was, though, only a matter of time.

Sure enough, only seconds later, Karen broke away from playing imaginary piano on the plinth next to the other set of fruit machines and sidled up to Neenie, her head bent even more dramatically to the right than usual.

'Lend us a tenner,' she said, in her most pitiful tones. She widened her eyes in a masterful imitation of a kicked puppy.

Neenie ignored her.

'Please, Auntie Neenie,' said Karen. 'Lend us a tenner.'

Neenie's eyes never left the revolving reels on the screen. Eventually, she turned to me and said, in an icy voice, 'Take her away from me.'

I longed to defend Karen's corner, but I didn't feel it my place. Instead I stood silently, unsure how to proceed. Neenie and Karen hadn't spoken since April 2009, around the time her allegedly inappropriate relationship with me was exposed. Surprisingly, it wasn't this that drove Neenie to disown her. Neenie had a zero-tolerance policy on drugs, and when Chunky had turned up one evening at their respectable detached house in the Fens to demand fifty quid for speed, Neenie had hit the roof (quite literally – Karen told me Neenie'd thrown an ornamental rabbit so hard in Karen's direction that when she had ducked, it had bounced off the sofa cushions and crashed into the ceiling, shattering into several pieces and knocking out the light fitting, plunging them both into darkness).

'I have it on good authority,' said Sheila, 'about Gabby and 'er tush.' She put another ten-pound note into her bandit.

'You have sex with 'er yerself, then?' asked Neenie.

'That's below the belt,' said Sheila. 'I'm not a rug muncher.'

'Sorry,' said Neenie. 'I don't want you to think I'm being thing-ummy or anything.' Then she turned to me. 'Sorry, Maurice,' she said. 'I didn't mean owt by it. You're one of them, aren't you?'

'A rug muncher?' I asked. 'No. I'm not a "rug muncher".'

'No,' she said. 'But you're in the same group, aren't you?'

'Loosely.'

Very loosely indeed. I don't know precisely what Neenie thought I was. She didn't seem to be able to distinguish between a lesbian and a Lebanese, let alone a lesbian and a transgender person. I'd thought for a long time in my youth that I was a cross-dresser, though as I aged I began to feel that perhaps this label did not quite fit. I frequented bars (there's a wonderful one called the Rainbow Trout just outside Middlesbrough), and educated myself. I knew I didn't feel entirely like a man. I was happy with my name – it felt like 'me', despite the fact it was typically mascu-line. I longed for feminine things and felt happy only in women's attire, but had no desire for surgery to achieve a female physique. Chicken fillets in the bra and carefully tucked privates would do. I suppose the umbrella term would be 'gender queer', and in my mind, this is what I was. Though 'queer', to Neenie, would be a term of insult rather than empowerment, so I could hardly tell her this was how I identified myself. So I offered no explanation. And why should I? I was just Me. And if people saw me as odd, well. Bugger them.

'She makes me angry, that Gabby,' Neenie went on. 'How can anyone have such a huge body and such tiny pin legs?' She mimed a large circle and then dangled her index fingers down to illustrate Gabby's feeble limbs. '*How?*' she asked again. '*How* does someone get themselves into that state?'

I hadn't a clue, so I remained quiet.

Neenie was playing Fields of Gold. She needed three silver pots to go for the jackpot.

'You had the Pots yet?' I asked.

'Nope,' she said. 'The cowbag. It's a cowbag, kiddeh.'

'Yes,' I said. 'It's a cowbag.'

'That it is, kiddeh,' said Neenie. 'That it is. Cowbag, isn't it, Sheila?'

'Cowbag,' she agreed.

'And the staff don't give a shit.' She turned to Sheila, her eyes gleaming with righteous fire. 'Remember last week when you had that water infection and hallucinated a pencil up my nose and that little bastard cockney man played your credits off your machine? They didn't give a shit.'

She fed in another twenty and hit 'Autoplay'. Then she leaned over, fed a twenty into her second bandit and selected Egyptian Treasures. She pressed 'Spin' twice in quick succession, and won two fifty-pence coins for a line of coffins and a pound for half a screen of frightened explorers. Their faces popped out of their squares, their hats lifted off and they screamed, their tongues sticking out and waggling and their eyes boggling. Then she went back to her main bandit and fed in another tenner. Her autospins had won her a mere five pounds fifty pence.

'Fields of gold,' she said, bitterly. 'Fields of shite. That's what they are.'

'That's what they are,' I echoed back, softly. 'Fields of shite. Indeed.'

'Maurice,' she said, almost angrily. 'Listen. I need you to do me a favour.'

'Certainly.'

'I've lost six hundred today. I can't afford it. Not with the way the business is taking a dive.'

I was carefully non-responsive. To hiss in sympathy would cast aspersions on her bandit habit. To reassure her that it was okay would be to make light of her predicament. Either way, she'd bite my head off.

41

'It's that bastard fish woman,' she said. 'She's taking all my customers.'

Neenie owns a beauty salon, you see. It offers mainly nail treatments, though she does stretch to massages and fake tan, if the client requests it.

'Bastard fish woman?' I asked.

'Yep. That bastard fish woman with her bastard feet-eating fish. I haven't had a customer in three days.'

'Oh,' I said. I'd walked past the shop on Cathedral Street. One of those trendy new age, alternative treatment places. Tanks full of tiny wriggling fish called Garra rufa. You paid to sit with your feet in the tanks and have the dead skin nibbled away by their tiny mouths. I'd looked through the window – seen rows of customers ankle-deep in the shimmering, animate water, shivering and grimacing at the vaguely disgusting novelty of it.

'But it'll be okay. I've got a plan.'

'A plan?'

'A plan. You're going to go to the Sea Life Museum, and get two or three fish. Now listen carefully. They're called bristlenose plecos, and they'll be in the tanks near the starfish at the back. They eat Garra rufa for breakfast. So you're going to steal two or three bristlenose, and then make an appointment at the bastard fish woman's place. I'll give you the money. When you're there, with your feet in the water, put our secret weapon into the tanks. They'll eat those tiny blighters down to the bone. Then we'll see how smug she is at the working men's club on Thursdays.'

'Fine,' I said. 'Fine. But you'll have to give me the money now.'

With a pinched face, she peeled a twenty off the bundle in her lap and gave it to me. I stuffed it down the front of my bra.

'We're going to play bingo,' I said. Then I took Divvy Karen's hand and led her through the arcade to Booksales.

'See yer after,' said Neenie.

'Yes,' I said. 'See you after.'

A strange farewell, that – Deerpudlian to the hilt. So many times I've heard it and said it, and I've never been sure *what* exactly I will see someone 'after'.

After the Apocalypse, perhaps. I keep feeling it's going to come soon.

14

Valentine's Day

'Six lots of frees, please, Trish,' I said. Trish tore off the bingo books and plonked them onto the counter. The free books are silvery-edged, each with five pages, each containing six bingo tickets. The paper, I think, always feels slightly warm and dusty, as though they've just spewed out of a photocopier. The prize money on the free ones is paltry (five pounds lines, ten pounds full houses), but it's 'summit for nowt', as they say around here.

'You all right, Maurice?' asked Trish. 'Thought you were barred.'

'Yes,' I said, patiently. 'I was barred for a week. Today's my first day back.'

'Ah,' said Trish. 'Well done, chuck. Good to see you.'

I threw Trish a friendly salute over my shoulder and proceeded into the hall, Karen close beside me. We threaded our way across the vast hall, past the cash-bingo caller's podium and mainstage, through the maze of fold-down cushioned red chairs, to take our usual seats near the bar.

God, I'd missed this place.

The hall smelled of jelly beans, mushy peas and Magner's Pear Cider, but beneath it all was the faint whiff of tobacco – the lazy ghost of the days before the smoking ban still hanging around, propping up its ethereal feet on the upholstery.

The walls of the massive hall were all the same gleaming, boiled-sweet orange as the foyer. They were called, by the cleaning staff, 'the Oranges', which I've always thought appropriate and marvellous. 'Have you washed the Oranges this morning?' one might hear one cleaner asking another – quite redundantly, for it was always obvious when they'd been washed, as they gleamed far more brightly and juicily than ever.

I laid out our bingo books on the tabletop. One book was for me, the other five for Karen.

'Which dabber would you like this time?' I asked next. I removed the ten bingo dabbers from my Modalu lambswool cross-body bag and laid them out in front of the books. Divvy Karen sat down, looked at the pens intently and then selected one by pointing to each in turn while reciting the customary rhyme (one, I remember, that she and her schoolmates used to sing in the playground, clapping their hands together in incredibly skilled, lightning-fast configurations):

> *We are the Golden Girls*
> *We wear our hair in curls*
> *We wear our dungarees*
> *Upon our sexy knees*
> *I went to school one day*
> *Uh oh! The boy next door*
> *He got me on the floor*
> *He gave me fifty pee*
> *To go behind a tree*
> *My mother was surprised*
> *To see my belly rise*
> *My father jumped for joy:*
> *It was a baby boy!*

'That's an awful song,' I said.

'Nah it's not,' said Karen. 'It's about loss of innocence.'

Karen's finger had landed on the blue pen. She uncapped this, poised it above the far-left book and sat motionless, completely focused, waiting for the game to start.

15

Young and Keen

I hummed quietly along to the song playing in the background (someone asking us to 'Take a look at my girlfriend') and studied the magic-eye-esque geometric red and black patterns on the carpet.

At long last, the All Areas announcement boomed:

'Ladies and Gentlemen, your main session bingo game is about to commence. Please make your way into the auditorium.'

The hairs on the back of my neck stood up. I uncapped my dabber and placed the pen top carefully beside my book, my eyes trained on mainstage.

Mainstage has always reminded me of the landing pad of a UFO, with the belly of the spaceship hovering above it, banded by a dazzling circle of neon light, and casting a warmer, more flattering orange glow down upon the electronic lectern – the Random Number Generator itself – the microphone and the Master of Ceremonies, the mainstage caller.

And there he was. One second the stage was empty, and the next minute he was standing there, his small, square head just visible above the numbers console. He was a well-established caller in the region, and I knew him relatively well – we'd conversed numerous times over the years I'd been coming here.

His overlarge name badge read:

LEONARD OVERALL
HOST AND MAINSTAGE CALLER

It was shimmering gold with black letters, and covered nearly all of his right man-boob.

His presence was at first unremarkable, but as he removed the microphone from its plastic clip holder on the console, adjusted his stance and brought the mic to his lips, it quietly and slowly asserted itself, like a spirit materialising and taking corporeal form. Before he'd even said anything through the microphone, he managed to subtly distinguish himself amidst the sensory clamour.

He had little hair. A couple of chocolate-coloured tufts, just above his long, narrow ears, the lobes stretched-looking, as though someone had been pulling on them every day for years. They were the kind of ears you knew would be icy cold if you touched them.

We weren't close enough to tell, of course, but I knew that he would be wearing too much Lynx Chocolate body spray, the odour singing in counterpoint with the rank smell of his sweat, creating an unpleasant olfactory cacophony. I could see the sweat on his temples, too, collecting in the shallow creases on his forehead, sparkling in the follicles of his close-shaven upper lip. He was not seriously overweight, but the suggestions of love handles swelled beneath his loud yellow waistcoat.

Eventually, when he deemed it time, he flicked the mic on with his thumb and began to speak.

16

Never Been Kissed

'**What,**' he said, pausing until every one of the two hundred-ish people in the hall had acknowledged the word, '**do you call an orang-utan with a lot of facial piercings?**'

'*I don't know,*' chorused the audience.

He paused just long enough for optimum comic effect, and then delivered the punchline.

'**A punky monkey.**'

The audience released a warm, involuntary burst of laughter, just as an incontinent might let loose an accidental stream of urine. The stale, air-conditioned atmosphere of the hall soaked it straight up like a Tena pad.

'**What do you call an orang-utan who can disco dance?**' he went on.

'*I don't know,*' came the chorus.

'**A funky monkey.**' This time he barely paused for the laughter. '**What do you call an orang-utan with dyspraxia?**'

'*I don't know.*'

'**A clunky monkey. What do you call an orang-utan who's failed his exams?**'

'*I don't know.*'

'**A flunky monkey.**'

This time, he waited for the wave of laughter to dissipate.

'I suppose,' he said, pacing the small space of the stage now like a stand-up comic, **'you're wondering "Why all the monkey jokes?"'** There was a murmur of assent from the crowd. **'Well, Ladies and Jellyspoons, I'm almost too excited to tell you.'**

'*Get on with it!*' called a lone voice from somewhere near the back of the hall. A bingo addict growing impatient.

'That's what she said last night,' answered Leonard, without missing a beat. Another wave of laughter. **'No, I'll tell you, Ladies and Jellyspoons. The monkey jokes are in honour of something huge we've got coming up.'**

Something huge? Unlikely. I suspected the art of exaggeration was heavily in play here. Some five-pounds-off promotion, or the like.

'One month from now, Ls and Js, on the fifteenth of December – and mark that date in your diaries, because you'll not want to miss this – is Monkey Night at the Pentagon Bingo. What does this mean? Well. This means we'll be celebrating the legend of the Deerpool Monkey with a night of primate-themed games and frolics. There'll be costumes, Fun and Theatre, all sorts of special shenanigans. But what you'll really care about, Ls and Js, is the special Super Link Game, in which the Pentagon links up with all the other clubs in the North East region. This game will be played at the very beginning of the night, before our early session, in all our outlets. And what are we playing for, Ladies and Jellyspoons? Ha. Well. Appropriately, we're playing for a monkey.'

A murmur of puzzlement and disapproval passed through the hall. A monkey? What could this mean? Leonard interrupted the muttering.

'Yes – a monkey. But no ordinary monkey. This monkey will be made of . . . solid gold.'

For perhaps half a second after Leonard said 'solid gold', the atmosphere in the hall changed. The collective energy of five hundred imaginations, simultaneously picturing a glittering monkey made of solid gold, seemed to charge the very air with an unprecedented static crackle.

'A monkey made of solid gold, and twenty-five pounds in weight. Twenty-five pounds of solid gold, my lovelies, is worth five hundred thousand pounds. I repeat, five hundred thousand pounds.'

In the counting house of five hundred Deerpudlian imaginations – including mine – five hundred thousand pounds worth of crisp, fragrant fifty-pound notes were counted into bundles and stacked in front of them like hot buttered toast at an Emperor's breakfast table.

It wasn't unusual to play for high-worth items instead of prize money. Last summer the Pentagon gave away an entire kitchen suite on a large promotional evening – white goods, toasters, crockery, the lot. Holiday packages were common, too, and very occasionally a car. But this monkey was a world apart from all that; this monkey would be life-changing.

And then, as though he hadn't just announced the biggest event in North Eastern British bingo since Lorraine Kelly allied herself with Mecca, Leonard went on with the business of the session.

'Before we begin, a quick reminder – those wanting to go on our Stockton coach trip next Monday, put your name down with Barnie in reception. It's twenty pounds for your seats and bingo tickets, to be paid up front. And now, without further ado, let's get down to this afternoon's bingo. Your first number is . . .'

A hush fell over the hall, so dramatically that those unaccustomed to the routines and rituals of bingo briefly panicked about sudden deafness.

Each number is called twice, so that there's no confusion

between thirteens and thirties, seventeens and seventies, and so forth. Something like this:

'Two and one, twenty-one.' A moment's pause. **'Eight and nine, eighty-nine.'**

And all around you, the tiny, scuffling, scratching sounds of felt tips against rough paper, like forest creatures stirring in the undergrowth.

They don't do the novelty calls any more. 'Legs eleven', that sort of thing. Barnie tells me they're politically incorrect. Also, like everything, I suppose, bingo is continually striving to become cleaner, less cluttered, more streamlined. The frills and the fun are disappearing. Large corporations are smelting it right down and hammering it into nuggets of pure, glinting Gambling. Still, though, at least at the Pentagon, it manages to retain remnants of its dirty charm. The leaky dabbers. The ritualistic theatricality of the audience interaction. Barnie – still manning reception after twenty-five years. Customers like Karen and me.

There are three rows and nine columns on a British bingo ticket. Each ticket contains fifteen numbers, randomly dispersed apart from these rules: each row contains five numbers, and column one contains only numbers between 1 and 9, column two numbers between 11 and 19, and so on up to column nine, which contains numbers between 80 and 90. In many bingo halls, including the Pentagon, the tickets are sold in sets of six – therefore every number from 1 to 90 will appear once somewhere on those six tickets – and all six tickets are played at once. The game is usually structured in three parts – first, players aim to mark off any line of numbers across. The first person to do so shouts, and wins the line prize. The same is repeated for any two lines across on any one ticket. And then for the full house. The tension element arises with the hard and fast rule that if the caller gets out even part of one syllable of the following number *after* you have your claim, your chance to claim the prize is gone.

Karen is a dab hand at the game. The numbers are called out at a rate of at least one every two seconds and some experienced players can manage two sets of six tickets at once, or one set turned upside down to add a bit of extra excitement. But Karen, with her eidetic memory, grows bored if she plays fewer than four. I knew that as she played, rapidly locating each number and dabbing it off with a flick of her wrist, her mind was speedily recording precisely which numbers she needed on each ticket to achieve each line, two-line combination and full house and how far away she was from shouting for each prize.

Numbers fascinate and frighten me. They're like stars, or undiscovered sea creatures on the deepest parts of the ocean floor. When and how are they born? What do they get up to all day, floating around in their dark, theoretical atmospheres? Where do they go, when they no longer exist?

I can't get my head around them. But luckily, Karen can.

17

Often Been Kissed

As we moved onto the third page and I still hadn't won once, I laid down my dabber and looked around me.

I'm always amazed and entertained by the sheer variety of dabbing methods one can observe within a twenty-yard radius. For those unfamiliar with the customs and paraphernalia of bingo, I should explain that a bingo dabber is a large, chunky pen with an ergonomic, womanly shaped body and flat, spongy nib that, when pressed firmly to a bingo book, leaves a glistening wet corona of sticky, translucent ink over the number. Many bingo players delight in the staggering array of themed and novelty dabbers available from bingo halls and pound shops, the latest being the *Coronation Street* dabber, adorned with depictions of Ken Barlow, Sally Webster, Norris Cole and the late, great Jack Duckworth. Some players, for reasons of luck or taste, prefer to use a conventional felt-tipped pen or even a biro. Sheila, who was sitting just to my right, uses six different colours of felt tip, one for each ticket on her page. Not only does she use six different pens, but also six different marking styles. For the top ticket, she uses a green pen and places a little tick over the number. For the second ticket down, she uses yellow and a spiral. For the third, blue and a cross. And so on and so on down the page, capping and uncapping at lightning speed as she marks off each number called.

Each player will also, inevitably, have their Bingo Face. The look of intense concentration that paints the visage during a particularly intense game. Neenie clamps her top teeth over her bottom lip and closes her right eye. Sheila puffs out her cheeks, and keeps them puffed, until someone calls 'House', when she purses her lips and lets out the air in a startling raspberry sound. Karen wrinkles her nose and stretches her mouth into a horrible grimace. It's disconcertingly similar to her Orgasm Face.

Another fifteen numbers were called, and the shrill and urgent call of 'HOUSE!' erupted from the far left side of the hall, near Booksales. The usual rumble of disappointment swelled throughout the crowd and died down again as the young claim-checker – clearly a new lad, I didn't recognise him – dashed over eagerly to read out the serial number on the book.

'I'm off to the loo,' I whispered, easing myself out of my chair and letting the plush seat spring up *slap* against its equally plush back. Divvy Karen gave a barely audible grunt of acknowledgement.

I wove my way through the bowed heads towards the toilets, accidentally standing on the occasional cash bingo chip – little yellow plastic rounds, the size of tiddlywinks counters and bisected by half-inch-high finger grips. They are used to mark off the very fast cash bingo interval games, the boards for which are built into the structure of the tables.

When I reached the toilets, I quietly pushed open the door to the Ladies'. My high heels clicked loudly on the clean tiled floor. I checked the first cubicle. There was an unappealing turd floating in the bowl. I checked the second. No loo roll. I checked the third. Ahh. Just right. I entered the cubicle, closed the door behind me, pulled down my knickers, hoicked up my skirt and took out my cock.

By Christ, I was dying for a slash.

So great was my relief as I let loose a giant, arching stream of glorious yellow into the bowl that I barely registered the sound of the outer door opening and the quiet pad of feet cross the tiles to stop outside the first cubicle. A faint sound of disgust indicated the discovery of the turd. A 'tut' registered the paperless second.

I realised only as my forehead slammed hard against the porcelain of the raised cistern that I'd forgotten to lock the cubicle door.

I felt my hair swept aside, and hot, moist breath condensed on the back of my neck.

18

Key of the Door

'Might've known I'd find yer in the Lasses' bogs,' said a sibilant voice into my ear. 'Yer fuckin' radged pervert,' it added.

'Hello, Chunky,' I panted into the cold porcelain. 'Your stealth-bumming technique grows ever-more honed.' My words suggested confident defiance, though I knew to Chunky's ears they sounded forced. And they were. My heart was beating in my chest as fast as a hamster's. Chunky was capable of things horrible beyond contemplation.

He gripped the fleshy top of my arms with his vicious, spindly fingers and dragged me back out towards the sinks. Spinning me around, he planted one hand on the back of my head and smacked my face against the mirrors. Through the tears that sprang into my eyes, I made out the blood from my nose spread out across the glass. I tasted it when I licked my dry lips.

'Callin' me a poofter?' he said. 'I wouldn't touch yer with a ten-foot pole.'

He yanked my head backwards by my hair, until my neck was hideously cricked and I could see his menacing reflection in the mirrors.

Chunky is not a tall man. Nor is he bulging or bulky. But there's a wiry strength in his slender limbs. His large, blue, Irish eyes are unusually beautiful – prominent, wet and glistening, with thick, startlingly long, blonde eyelashes. How his eyeballs remain so moist is an absolute mystery, for he never seems to blink. His arms are covered in sleeves of tattoos, and his neck, most of his face and all of his bald head are similarly, intricately inked.

Before you picture the barbed wire, love hearts and tiger faces of one's stereotypical tattooed thug, let me tell you that Chunky's tattoos are highly unusual, expertly drawn and frighteningly cryptic. Across the front of his neck – from the bottom of his chin, over his Adam's apple down to his suprasternal notch – is a dissected frog, its flesh pinned back to reveal its curled, glistening innards, all intricately labelled in small, serif text. His right arm, from his shoulder to his wrist, displays the story of Little Red Riding Hood. Halfway down his bicep she encounters the wolf, and at the midpoint of his radius, the story veers suddenly from the track well beaten by Grimm and Anderson, as Red Riding Hood takes a hunting knife, eviscerates the wolf, her grandmother, the hunter *and her mother*, before climbing into the wolf's skin to embark upon what we can only assume would have been a reign of terror and bloody destruction, had his arm been longer.

On the upper bicep of the left arm is a haunting depiction of a ramshackle wooden hut – the roof falling in, the windows smashed, the door slightly ajar, only darkness visible inside. It stands in a vista of snow, and through this snow, in a trail down his arm to his wrist, are footprints. They begin distinct and solid, emerging from the door of the hut, evenly spaced and crisp. As they make their way down the arm, however, they grow messier. Haphazard. Other patterns appear on the snow – the marks of someone limping, struggling and stumbling. Until, near the wrist, where the tattoo ends, they stop altogether, near two or three crimson drops of fresh blood, stark against the snow.

It's his head, though, that is the talking point. Some tattooist of obscene talent has rendered his skull sawn open and the top half removed, his moist grey brain exposed from the ears upwards. It's a truly disconcerting effect, even when one gets close enough to realise that it's just a tattoo.

I was uncomfortably aware, from the faint chill on my backside, that my skirt and knickers were still around my ankles. Bile stung the back of my throat as I felt the polyester of Chunky's shell-suit bottoms squeak against my naked flesh. He tightened the Red Riding Hood arm around my neck, his monstrously decorated scalp sliding sweatily against my left cheek.

'Well, you have got your groin against my bare arse,' I pointed out.

He grunted in disgust, and let me go as if I were on fire.

'Pull down yer fuckin' skirt, then,' he said.

I scrambled to do so.

Fabric now safely separating our sensitive areas, he resumed the aggressive stranglehold.

Not for the first time, I noticed that Chunky smelled like plasticine. Almost precisely like plasticine. Though with something a little less chemical, a little more moist, a little more human to it. The smell of cheese is rather lovely if it emanates from a nice aged Gouda. On the other hand, if it emanates from a penis, it is as foul as it gets. Thus it was with Chunky's plasticine smell – not the odour itself, but its source, which made my stomach churn.

Clenching my hair even tighter, he drew my head back and pushed my face against the glass again.

'I've not been winning as much at the housey, lately,' he said. 'Wonder why that is?'

'I . . . I really couldn't say.'

'Yer really couldn't say, could yer? Well, I could. I could say that maybe it's because my *fucking* troll doll has been *fucking* lost by a retard and 'er sick tranny boyfriend.'

Chunky's superstition is staggeringly powerful. It seems to imbue him with a kind of primal strength, ancient and sinister, fuelled by the force of his unquestioning belief.

'Ah . . .' My nose began to slip and slide against my own blood and condensed breath on the mirror glass. 'Chunky – I can explain. We haven't lost the troll doll. We've just misplaced it. We can have it for you tomorrow.'

I believe I passed out for a brief moment, but when I came to, Chunky had begun to whisper, softly and almost tunefully, in my right ear.

'Thirty-three,' he said, 'listen to me.'

I felt warm, viscous blood trickling gently over my chin to pool in the hollow of my neck. Without pain from the wound site, it might actually have been comforting.

He kneed me from behind, crushing my cock and balls against the cabinets below the sink.

'Thirteen,' he said, 'don't make a scene.'

I swallowed and made a small sound of assent.

'Fifty-four,' he said, lowering his voice even more, 'Karen's a *whore*.'

Now that just wouldn't do.

'I really must ob—'

He kneed me again and I fell silent.

'Seventy-nine, you've lost something of mine.'

The taste of blood was beginning to make me feel sick.

'We haven't lost it – we've simply misplace—'

'Eighty-one, I've got a gun.'

My heart skipped a beat before I realised that he was probably bluffing. Though there *was* something hard and suspicious digging into the small of my back.

He kneed me one more time, which seemed unsporting, as I hadn't moved since he began to call his perverse 'game of bingo'. I spat out blood into the sink beneath me.

'Number ten,' he said, 'we'll meet again. Tomorrow. Two o'clock. The Pres-lash. If yer not there, I'll come and find yer.'

By 'the Pres-lash' Chunky meant that we should meet at the

Presley pub on Prince George Street. It was colloquially known as 'the Pres-lash'.

Then he paused meaningfully, before finishing with, 'And you tell that fuckin' divvy mate of yours' – he wrenched my head back by my ponytail so that I could look into his cold grey eyes – 'fuckin' Divvy Fuckin' Karen' – his breath smelled of prawn-cocktail crisps – 'that she's a fuckin'' – he clenched his over-abundant teeth together, his moist lips peeled back in a grimace, and spoke in a tone that would have chilled the hearts of lesser men – '. . . divvy.'

And with that, the pressure on my head and back disappeared. By the time I'd hauled myself upright and turned around, the sound of heavy footsteps on the tiles had faded and Chunky had gone.

I stood for several seconds, breathing shakily and pondering my next course of action. It seemed wise to look for some toilet paper. I ripped a long strip of it from the dispenser on the wall and pulled down my skirt again, examining my crushed genitals and checking for any permanent damage.

Just then, the door swung open again and an ear-piercing shriek registered the discovery of myself, knickers around my ankles.

My double-breasted True Decadence shell-print mac was ruined.

19

Goodbye Teens

I found Karen behind the Pentagon, squatting in the small alcove where the vents from the kitchen breathed out steady warmth and hamburger smell. On cold nights such as the one that fast approached, Karen often slept around there.

I tucked myself into the alcove beside her and pulled her into a loose embrace. Then I leaned back against the wall, my hair snagging against the brick, a warm vent blowing enjoyably up the back of my skirt. Karen sat down against a lower vent so that the hot, meaty air ruffled her uncombed locks.

'Sorry I buggered off,' said Karen. 'Scared.'

'It's okay,' I said. 'Long as you're safe.'

How did I get here? I wondered. Was it written in the stars – destined, right from the days when I'd stand shivering in the corner of the playground at primary school, watching the other children playing 'Speedy Gonzales' and terrified to join them, sick with the thought that I would be too slow and my Mexican accent inadequate? Or did I do it to myself? Was it all *my* fault? Had my life been a series of wrong turns I could have avoided? I didn't think it was my fault that I'd been fired from the school. That had seemed entirely out of my control. If it was fate, though, the one compensation was that it led to my relationship with Karen. As the wise yet troubled Robert Louis Stevenson once said, 'We are all travellers in the wilderness of this world, and the best we can find in our travels is an honest friend.'

Karen was such. I genuinely didn't know what I'd do without her.

'You all right?' she asked, touching her fingertips to my right eyebrow. I knew my nose injury was probably branching out to bear two plum-purple black eyes as fruit. 'Did yer get barred again?'

'No,' I said. 'But they're making me use the men's toilet next time.'

'Sorry,' said Karen. 'Is Chunky gone?'

'Yes. I have to meet him tomorrow. If we haven't found the troll by then, I don't want to think about what might happen.' I looked up at the grey sky. 'Do you know, Karen? When I was a little boy, we lived in the Fens. Not in the nice area, but not in the nasty area, either.' I realised then that I'd never spoken to Karen about my childhood before. I didn't think about it often. Not that it was unhappy. It just no longer seemed relevant to my current situation. Perhaps I'd been wrong, though. 'I was bullied terribly at school. I went to Deerpool Comprehensive, just like you did, and it was much the same back in my day. I wouldn't wear girl's clothes then – it seemed like too much trouble even to think about it. But I was still bullied. I was kind and articulate, and so the other children thought I was gay. I'd come home bruised and crying, and my mum would say, "Maurice, one day you will get back at those people by *living well*." She was a clever lady, my mother. She came from mining stock. Her grandfather was an electrician down the pits, and the whole family lived in pit-owned housing. When her grandfather died, their whole family had to leave the house, and they were left with nothing in the world.' I spoke softly, whimsically, as though telling Karen a fairy story. 'My grandmother (my mum's mum, that is) gave all their furniture to a council official in exchange for pushing them forward on the list for a council house. They picked themselves back up, but they never got to live well – not like my mum wanted. Not like she dreamed – never having to worry about money. I wanted to do that for her. And when I became a teacher, I thought I might do it. I thought that Mum and I could move to a little place in Durham, perhaps. Have holidays in nice places, like Edinburgh, or the Lake District. But then . . .'

'Was this 'ers?' asked Karen, playing with my Pandora charm bracelet. There was just the one charm on it. A little silver horseshoe.

'All of this was hers,' I said, looking down at my outfit. 'She did have nice clothes. That was one thing I got to buy for her, before the school gave me the heave-ho.'

Karen looked at me for a long moment, something touching and sincere in her eyes.

'You want to shag, then?' she asked.

'Yes please.'

I stepped forward, hoisted her to her feet and turned her around to face the wall. Her leggings were so tight I had to use the pads of my fingers to roll them forcefully down over her arse and thighs. Eventually, the fabric accumulated in a thick roll around her knees. I opened my ruined mac and wrapped it around her to protect her from the bitingly cold air, enclosing both of us in something of a shell-print cocoon. Then I stood, hitched up my skirt, took out my cock and pushed it inside her.

20

Getting Plenty

Fifteen minutes later, we sat on the dry yellow grass by the Pentagon, slightly apart. From this short distance, in the fast-encroaching darkness, the mirrored outer walls of the building made it look like an enormous aquarium, the colourful reflections of cars swimming across it like exotic fish.

Karen was pulling up her leggings.

'Can we do The Thing?' she asked, when she was finished.

I sighed. I was quite exhausted, to be honest, and not quite up for it.

'You want to do The Thing?' I asked. 'Right now?'

'Yeah,' she said. 'I want to do The Thing.'

'Fine,' I said, shaking off the post-orgasmic haze and scrambling to my feet. I crossed over to the half-bald patch of bushes separating KFC from the back of the Pentagon and dug around in the largest until I found my 1992 Yamaha tape player, wrapped in an Almart bag to keep it rain-proof. A quality vintage music machine. I've always maintained that the good old cassette tape produces the most resonant and soulful sound. Plus, I can't afford any new technology.

'Get ready, then,' I said, placing the tape player up against a support strut from the roof overhang of the Pentagon and turning the volume knob up to Max.

'Right,' said Karen. She launched herself around the corner and returned pushing the Almart trolley we use on these occasions. She clambered in with some difficulty, mounting it as though it were a restless horse. It kept slithering away from her on its loose, squeaky wheels, but eventually it hit the wall and this held it still enough for her to climb inside.

'Ready!' she shouted.

'Ready?' I shouted back.

'Ready!' she replied.

I pressed 'Play'. There were three seconds of crackling static, during which I hurried to the trolley, grasped the cylindrical handle with both fists and leaned my weight back on my left leg, like a sprinter on the starting block. The first drum beats of Herb Alpert's 'Tijuana Taxi' rattled forth from the speakers. I gave Karen 'The Look'. She gave me 'The Look' right back.

'Honk! Honk!' we both tooted along with the music, and that was the cue.

To the woody melody of Herb's xylophone, I set off, pushing with all my might, accelerating at a fast clip. The wheels of the trolley squeaked in joyful counterpoint to the Tijuana Brass.

By the time we'd reached the compound gates we were travelling at a dizzying eight miles an hour, I'm sure. I was rather getting into the spirit of things – endorphins had all but washed away my fatigue, and I was really going for it.

'Where would Madam care to go today?' I asked, somewhat breathlessly.

'Kindly take me to Tijuana, if you would please,' said Karen.

'But Madam,' I replied, charting a swerving course through four bollards, and thumping down the curb into the back of the Pentagon car park, 'we are already in Tijuana.'

'Are we?' she asked. 'I had not realised.'

'Why yes,' I said, 'this is a Tijuana taxi.'

'My gracious,' she said, 'so it is.'

Karen played the air xylophone like a virtuoso as I executed a magnificent handbrake turn, narrowly missing a badly parked red Lexus.

As the second 'Honk' of the taxi horn sounded from the player, I reversed some five feet with enthusiasm and began a wild zig-zag in the direction of the bushes. As I rattled along beside them at spectacular pace, Karen leaned out over the side of the trolley and grabbed one of the feral black cats that make their home in the shrubbery. She yanked it out by the scruff of its neck. The trolley very nearly overbalanced, and I had to use my full weight to keep it from toppling over. The cat did not seem happy. Its legs cartwheeled in the air as Karen clutched it, asking it quite loudly, 'Where can we take you, Madam? Tijuana?'

The cat squawked, more probably in protest than affirmative answer, and finally wormed free of Karen's grip, leaping spectacularly from her arms in such a bound that it cleared the end of the trolley. I barely managed to avoid crushing it beneath the wheels as I rounded the corner for the home straight, coming to a screeching halt in more or less the same place we'd started.

As the final 'Honk' sounded from the tape player, I collapsed onto my back on the grass. Some moments later, I heard Karen struggle out of the trolley, and sensed her substantial form deposit itself on the ground beside me.

I hoisted myself up into a sitting position, growing pensive as I slowly regained my breath.

'If we could go to Tijunana,' I said, 'just you and me, would you do it? Would you come with me?'

'Yeah,' said Karen, with more than a sprinkling of sarcasm in her tone.

'No,' I said, 'if we could really go. Far away, to Tijuana, and ride a taxi all day, with the wind in our hair and Herb Alpert on the radio, would you do it?'

'Course I would,' said Karen. She sat up, keeping her legs

straight out in front of her. I picked a piece of grass out of her hair. 'Doesn't matter, though,' she said. 'Never going to find that troll doll. Gonna get knacked. Both of us. Hate my life. Hate it. Can't be arsed. Can't be arsed. Can't be arsed.'

Something cold and tight gripped my chest. Then it moved down to my stomach and squeezed, making me feel slightly sick. Karen began to rock backwards and forwards on her haunches, mumbling repeatedly to the dry, dead ground, 'Can't be arsed. Can't be arsed. Can't be arsed.'

I watched, feeling numb and impotent. I wished I could offer her some words of comfort. But I didn't want to lie to her.

'Come on,' I said. 'We're going back to my place.'

21

Just My Age

The exterior of 'my' block of flats is as grim as its interior.

The building protrudes outwards parasitically from the fat, crouching body of the Presley – my local, and the roughest pub in town. The walls are inadvertently Mediterranean, flaking pale-pink plaster, eaten into at intervals by the ugly shapes of hard-edged brick, mottled brown like rotted teeth. Opposite is Ruby's night-club, whose blood-red neon sign winks into life around 6 p.m., drawing stilettoed sixteen-year-olds to its damp dancefloors like moths to a flame.

It isn't far from the Marina – one of the town's newest and most affluent areas – but as opposite to its squeaky-clean, tourist-baiting, Australian-inspired syntheticism as it is possible to be. I'm close enough to the water, though, to hear the rigging of the boats clank in the wind at night like the dry bones of skeletons.

I unlocked the main door, ushered Divvy Karen through and we clambered up the three flights of stairs to my floor, avoiding the suspicious stain trailing along the ragged carpet that hinted of a psychopath dragging his latest victim via the same route in a seeping bin bag.

We made our way through four doors, winding through three long, labyrinthine, moist-carpeted corridors until we came to my door. Number 79.

Inside, it was oppressively dark, so I felt oh my hall table for the two forehead-mount caving lights I kept there. My electricity was cut off months ago, after what I refer to as the 'npower Fiasco'. I may have missed one or two bill deadlines. I may have responded a little heatedly on a helpline to a brutally worded debt-collection letter. I may at one point – though the memory is hazy – have used the term 'incendiary device'. The whole misunderstanding was resolved with the police and the bomb squad, though I've yet to brave ringing up the call centre to demand reconnection, and I'm not sure I could afford to pay the bills now any more than I could then anyway. I stretched the elastic strap of one of the caving lights around my head and flicked the switch to activate the beam of clear white light, directing it so that Divvy Karen could see to attach hers.

'Would you like some edamame-bean salad?' I asked, as Karen made herself comfortable on one of the striped deckchairs at my five-pound Ingo IKEA kitchen table.

'What the fuck's that?' asked Karen.

'I believe it's a fancy name for soya beans,' I said. 'They were fifty pence per tub at Almart.'

'Give us one, then,' said Karen.

'Righty-o,' I said, taking the tub of salad out of the fridge – now merely a glorified food cupboard – opening the lid and setting it in the middle of the table. I hoped it hadn't gone bad. The beam from my caving light momentarily illuminated the piles of textbooks on my badly constructed pine mantelpiece, remnants of a previous life I tried hard not to think about. Still, I couldn't bear to hide them away in boxes. I still felt a painful stab of pride when I looked at the collection.

I took two forks out of my kitchen drawer, gave one to Karen, and sat down in the deckchair opposite her.

Karen swiped away a pile of the dog-eared papers that littered the kitchen table.

'Sorry,' I said. 'Having a sort-out.' In all honesty, I was searching through all my 'important papers' to see if I could unearth any money I'd forgotten about. Things were tight. Yesterday I'd gutted my junk-stuffed wardrobes, checking for things eligible for Cash Converters. There was nothing of monetary value, but I had found three more of Mum's old Herb Alpert cassette tapes, which had made the exercise worthwhile. Mum had loved Herb Alpert. She'd said that the chirpings and tootings of his Tijuana Brass had transported her somewhere bright and beautiful. 'Tijuana Taxi', of course, had been her favourite – the most joyful of all Herb's tunes. For my eighth birthday, she bought me a little toy car horn. When we were sad, or something unpleasant had happened, she'd put the song on the tape player and I would honk along with the horn parts.

It was just me and Mum, when I was little. Curiously enough, I'd never asked why Dad was absent. I had a feeling he wasn't dead, though there was no evidence to back this up. I supposed he was somewhere – just not with us.

'What's these ones?' said Karen, grabbing a pile of lined, handwritten sheets poking out perpendicular to and slightly beneath the 'Benefits' pile.

It was a pile of essays. The last pile of essays I'd brought home to mark, in fact. I'd never had the opportunity to return them. Karen's was amongst them somewhere, I was sure. Yep. She'd homed in on it – the rest of the sheets were now scattered on the floor around her chair.

'Give me that,' I said, gently.

Had it really been five years since I applied that grimacing 'Grrrrrreat work!' tiger-face stamp to the bottom of Karen's strange efforts? The red ink was smudgy around the teeth – it looked as though the tiger had just chowed down on a freshly mauled gazelle. Or whatever tigers hunt.

22

Two Little Ducks

may Favrit Hoby
by Karen Cholmondeley
class 10B, cet 4

may Favrit Hoby is gon te th housey wit me mam Th housey hal is
cald the pentigan an i pretned I was ateen te get in i wons cald
on to lines fer fifty ponds. i cald in 47 nummers wit 6 tcts an thr
wr 50 peepl in th hal wich men that may ods of wining wr 6
dvd bay 50x6 wich is 6 dvd by 300 wich is 0.02 which is 2
pcen but this is ownle if evrewon in the hal war plane 6 tickets i
went ons or twise to bingo wi Sheza an Dave but fers one time
they chuked us ot fer smelin of weed an then won time Sheza
acyoused me mam of lezing of wit th wuman from springs jim an
i stoped torkin te her

i lice th housey cos its ecsitin an wen ye get te swetin on on nummer
its mint its not raged or owt ye can sit an werk out the prbobibilitees
of winning or ye can memerise the nummers on yer ticet an were they
r an clows yer ese wile ye pley yea ther r a lot of oldees ther an
sum of them smel of wee But thers yung peple ther 2

an ye can get evn taped up if ye cum on a sunnay nit wen
evreywon plays the free wuns.

last weec i wen wit me mam but we cunt stay cos me mam had

72

brort me babby sister an she trayed te leev her wit the fat bloc at resepton wile we plade but he sed he cunt be held libel for a chile
its things lice this mayc me angre.

other things mac me angre lice I tork to me mentow bowt it but i down thinc they belev me i tole me mentow abowt the wun time me dad put me mams hed fays fers thru th telle but they dint belev me cos they sed thed sene me mam and her fays was fin, but i sed, it was shaterprewf glass an they sed, they dun yuse shatterprewf glass in telles and i sed, wel they mus hav in this wun also wen they say i won get a job becos of scivin an even tho i alredy have my maths GCSE an its an A star i won get ane other egsams don becos I don aply myself

and im SHIT.

at th housey i dun go on the frootes cos ther adictive an its a slipery slowp ther not like the frootes down seton carew becos thos wuns r manly ten pens wuns but thes r therty or fifte pens wuns an sumtimes a pond, wich can add up cwicly fer egsampel if yew spen 5 hors on a froote in seton carew spennin fifte pens every to minits youd spen senty fi ponds and if yew stade fer ten hors yewd spen a hunned and fifte and if yew stade fer thre dase youd spen a thosan and ety ponds i torced to miser terbuten bot the tely and he achly lisend te me i thin if i wos lowd te be taut by miser terbuten al the tim i wud be bete in jenral im goin to recwes this

miser terbuten has

bron har.

bron ays.

lon legs.

no berd.

a vos lac trever mucdunuld but hes not blac.

and he teches us insting thins he taut us about the derepewl munke. he taut us a song.

all yers lads an lasses get yers to the dyewns
  Cum an see the rajie man wots gon an been maruned
  the mere ses hes a munke but we sey is he ec
  its clere that hes a frenshman so wel ang im by is nec

An he dose the gitare parlene twity sed i sang flat Litle smac hed.
  parline twity this is a mesage to yoo
  YOO AR A LITLE SMAC HED
  Singed Karen Cholmondeley

i was goin te hav te go an stay wit ante neene but she hates me
that wer befor i teld me mentow bout the tele but afte i teld me
mentow bout when they let me watch them have sex on the eyeonin
bord me mentow ased me did they no yu wer ther, and i sed of
cors they did I was watchin gladaters on the sofa an he sed oh
so yoo wernt ther on the eyeoning bord an i sed no they wer, me
mam and dad wer on the eyeoning bord an I was on the sofa but
it wasn a vere stron eyeoning bord so they broc it
  wen I get older i wunt te cotino wit me hobe becos i don se
ane reson not te afte I hav cids i wil proble induse them to the
housey to ons they get to fifteen
  i don se that its as bad as goin to ladbrucs

23

The Lord Is My Shepherd

After we'd eaten, I proposed that we retire for the night.

'It's only five o'clock,' said Karen.

'Yes, but it's pitch black and it's freezing,' I countered.

She shrugged, and we made our way to the bedroom. Once there, we dived onto my single bed and entwined our limbs until both of us could fit. I dragged my ancient 15 tog coverless duvet, anaemic and translucent in the silvery moonlight from the curtain-bare window, and tucked it tightly around us.

'Your essays really were awful, you know,' I whispered into the blackness. I knew she wouldn't be offended. She was proud only of her maths skills.

'I knar. I hated English. Your classes were okay. You were nice. Hated writin'.'

'I always loved it. I loved studying it at university.' This was nice. Just talking to Karen. It felt like there were very few moments of peace in life, at the moment. I was always striving for something, or running away from something. But here, just now, despite the cold, this was nice. 'I thought,' I went on, 'that being an English teacher would be easy. I didn't realise it would be so complicated. That so many people would be . . . out to get me. Just in a comprehensive school. Why is that? Why are people so afraid of unusual but harmless things that they feel the need to try to destroy us?'

It had all started towards the end of 2008. I remember the day clearly, because it was the day we broke up for the Christmas holidays. It was lunchtime. I'd erected a small fibre-optic Christmas tree in the corner of the classroom, and Karen, as usual, was hiding from the bullies, helping me out with small tasks in preparation for my afternoon lessons. Today we were hanging tags on the Christmas tree. The top-set GCSE class was studying *The Strange Case of Dr Jekyll and Mr Hyde*, and on each tag I'd written a quote by Robert Louis Stevenson. My idea was that every student would take a tag and use it as inspiration to write an essay (in the end, an angry young boy from the bottom set called Christopher Callicut punched the tree and knocked it over, scattering the tags everywhere and damaging the fibre-optic lights so that they were stuck permanently on a sinister red).

As I was hanging a quote from *Treasure Island* – 'In the immediate nearness of the gold, all else had been forgotten' – the head teacher came into the classroom without knocking. Mr McCommon, the head teacher was called. He was average height, average build and lacked a personality. His name suited him perfectly. He looked like the result of an equation in which our creator (whoever that might be) had taken ten Mr McAmazings and ten Mr McAwfuls, multiplied them and divided them by twenty.

'Karen,' he'd said, 'go out into the yard with the other children. It's where you should be, anyway.'

He didn't even look around the classroom. My classroom was beautiful. I'd stay back for more than an hour on an evening working on my displays. There was the Timeline of Literature, stretching all along the top of the back wall, with small hand-drawn cartoons (I'm not an artist, but they were passable) depicting everything from Aeschylus to Martin Amis. I had a Sherlock Holmes corner, with a cardboard fireplace, on which I'd placed a pipe and a deerstalker. There was a small Shakespeare display near the whiteboard, with a plaster bust of the Bard and a poster of the Globe Theatre. I'd had to whittle down the displays quite a lot, as some of my students had destructive tendencies and it became exhausting to continually repair and replace them.

I sensed, however, that Mr McCommon was not there to discuss my efforts in creating a stimulating learning environment. He had a look on his face like I'd poisoned his cat. Once Karen had shuffled out and shut the door, he said to me, 'Does Karen Cholmondeley come to your classroom often, Maurice?'

'Most lunchtimes,' I answered honestly. 'I don't think the anti-bullying programme we have her in is working. She still can't walk down a corridor without an incident.'

He didn't sit down, so I remained standing as well.

'Some people have being saying things. We've received no official complaint, yet. But I thought it best to warn you. Two different students and a member of staff have raised concerns in the past month.'

'Concerns about what?'

'I couldn't possibly say.'

'Who's raised these concerns?'

'I couldn't possibly say.'

'Could you possibly say *anything* to shed light on what you're talking about?'

He raised his eyebrows, presumably at my slight impertinence.

'Maurice. Let's be honest. Your lifestyle is . . . unconventional. I know you don't rub it in people's faces, but people do *know* about it. And it makes people wonder. And Karen is in here so often. I've noticed that sometimes, when she's in here, the blind on your door is closed.'

'Yes. Sometimes I close it during afternoon break and forget to open it.'

During that fifteen-minute break I would occasionally lock myself in my classroom, pull down the blind and mark papers wearing one of Mum's angora jumpers. It helped me get through the day.

'There will be an investigation,' said Mr McCommon.

An investigation. I recall looking at the Christmas tree, the tips of its plastic branches pulsing with a cycle of light all colours of the spectrum. Laden with quotes about treasure and disguise and transformation. I think I knew then that I wouldn't be putting up a tree here next Christmas.

Now, in my icy bedroom, Karen's voice jolted me back from the brink of slumber.

'They thought you were fiddlin' with me. Back then. You never said. But I knar why they got rid of yer.'

I sighed.

'Yes. They did. I think they got it into their heads that I was some sort of pervert. Because I like to dress the way I do.'

'That's radged.'

'I know, Karen. People are radged about that sort of thing.'

We shivered ourselves to sleep.

24

Pompey Whore

The Pentagon opens at noon. As soon as the hour rolled around, we made haste there.

When we arrived, Neenie and Sheila were upon their usual perches before the Front of House fruit machines.

'What else has Nicolas Cage in it?' asked Neenie, rummaging in her enormous handbag.

'Erm . . .' Sheila looked up at the ceiling in deep thought. '*Face/Off.*'

Neenie let out a sound of unadulterated horror.

'No,' she said. 'No no no. That's the one in which 'e takes 'is face off.'

Sheila swung dejectedly on her stool.

'It's quite a good film, actually,' she said.

I was tempted to go over and share my extensive knowledge of Nicolas Cage films with the two of them, but I'd come to see Barnie.

'Hi there, Maurice,' he said, standing up quickly from his desk chair, a beam of hard sunlight catching the bald patch on the top of his head and glinting brightly enough to rival the blue neons on the ceiling.

'Barnacious-ness,' I said, striding over to him. 'Have you found the troll yet?'

He grimaced and turned a little red of cheek.

'No,' he said. 'But I'm confident I'll find it. Some fool has obviously moved it. You can't put anything down in this place. Really, if everyone just left everything *alone* . . .'

'Barnie,' I said, 'I don't want to sound impatient, but this really is quite important . . .'

'I know,' he said. 'I know. I'm on it.'

I could sense waves of anxiety shimmering off the man. There were faint dark circles beneath his eyes and his green work shirt looked uncharacteristically crumpled.

'I say, Barnie,' I said. 'Are you all right?'

He straightened his spine.

'Fine,' he said. 'Just fine. Bit tired. Bit of a battle going on with these trolleys from Almart at the moment.' He closed his eyes for a few seconds and took in a great, exasperated breath.

'Oh dear,' I said. 'More of them left round the back of the building?'

'Yes,' he said, a look of desperation in his eye. 'Fourteen.'

'Oh my God. That's not on, my man. Simply not on.' I must admit that I felt a little guilty. Karen and I needed our regular Tijuana Taxi trolley jaunts like we needed air, and had let the trolleys accumulate out of an innocent sense of mischief. Perhaps we should move them. 'How many letters have you written now?'

'Fourteen,' he said.

'Why don't you take the trolleys back to Almart yourself?' I asked.

'It's the principle of it,' replied Barnie. 'Hold this door open for me, would you? I've got to fetch out a box of temporary membership cards.' I obligingly held open the door to the large cupboard behind the membership desk.

As I did so, something horrific caught my eye.

It was hanging from a row of coat hooks against the back wall, beside Barnie's high-visibility jacket. It was large, and hairy, and human-shaped, and it was wrapped in transparent plastic, like a corpse at a murder scene. Its shoulders were slumped, its head flopped to one side, as though its neck had been broken. One enormous black hand extended from the plastic, thick fingers limp and rubbery.

'What in the name of Herb Alpert is that?' I asked Barnie.

25

Duck and Dive

'Oh,' he said, blithely, 'that's the costume for Monkey Night.'

'Monkey Night?' I said, approaching it tentatively and picking up the hand, turning it over in my own to study the creases on the fingers. 'You mean that jackpot evening? When they're playing for the statue?'

'Yep. Just the sort of thing the management love. The statue is worth five hundred thousand pounds, you see, and "Monkey" is slang for five hundred, apparently. And of course, the Deerpool Monkey legend, you know.'

I nodded and dropped the limp monkey paw.

'Realistic. Who's going to wear it?'

Barnie beamed with pride.

'I am,' he said. 'I'm going to be in it all night, interacting with the customers.' He picked up the box of membership cards. 'Fun and Theatre,' he said, sagely. 'Make 'em laugh.' He looked at me rather intensely. 'Make 'em laugh,' he repeated, a little more quietly.

I didn't know what else to do but nod, and hold open the door for him.

Once he'd deposited the box of cards on the desk, he tugged open the desk drawer, opened the cover of a large black diary and pulled out a piece of paper.

'This is the latest letter,' he said. 'Would you cast an eye over it?'

He handed me the paper, and then bent to pick up a lint brush and headed back into the cupboard, presumably to de-lint the monkey suit. Rather than read the letter (Almart, trolleys, yada-yada) I placed it on the desk and read a few pages in the diary instead. It seemed to be for all the reception staff, to communicate, pass on memos and such, though most entries were from Barnie.

26

Pick and Mix

November 12th

A woman called JANET TROWSDALE rang today about LUNCHEONS FOR THE VULNERABLE. Vulnerable in what sense I am not sure. Can we please ask someone in management to please get back to her ASAP on 01927 846276.

Thank you. Barnie

November 13th

The picture of a man in a hat (see Lost Property) belongs to MRS DRAKE who comes in on Tuesday nights. It is her son DO NOT THROW IT OUT. He is dead.

Thank you. Barnie

I am going to get the earwax removed from my ears at the hospital on Friday. Therefore I will require a shift swap. I would not need one though it is getting to the point where I cannot hear even the loudest of requests.

Thank you. Barnie

November 14th

Re. Hallowe'en decorations:

Do not forget to offer the PLUSH POSEABLE SPIDERS for sale at £5.50 as of Sunday afternoon. They are left over from Hallowe'en stock and we have TWELVE of them to get rid of. <u>PUSH THIS</u>

LEONARD: I received a phone call today about the <u>TOMBSTONE DECORATION</u> we had up in reception. It was the polystyrene tombstone that read 'YOUR TIME WILL COME!' Apparently MRS GAVISCON has been irrevocably disturbed by it (she has terminal cancer). She may take legal action. Please get back to her on 01927 937508.

Thank you. Barnie.

MAINTENANCE (WHOEVER IS IN TOMORROW): The small men's toilets are out of action because a large amount of loo roll has been put down them.

Thank you. Barnie.

Barnie – I wasn't aware we had a toilet specifically for small men.

Leonard

Yes, thank you, Leonard, I clearly meant the men's toilets which are smaller, which I know you are aware of.

Thank you. Barnie.

Gateway to Heaven

Barnie emerged again from the cupboard, and I guiltily slammed closed the diary. I picked up the trolley letter and gave it back to him.

'It's beautifully worded,' I said, through my teeth.

'Thanks,' said Barnie. 'I'll send it off, then.' He slipped the letter back into the front of the diary and resumed his seat. 'Are you playing the bingo this afty, then?'

'We thought we might,' I replied. 'Are there free books on?'

'Oh yes,' said Barnie. 'Still free books every weekday.'

'Karen? Are you up for a game of bingo?' I turned around and found I was addressing empty air. Sure enough, a quick scan of the vicinity revealed that she was standing mesmerised beneath the large LCD screen mounted high on the wall beside the CCTV camera. This set-up supposedly reminded the slot-machine gamers that they were being constantly watched – the screen displayed everything the camera captured, so the arcade's occupants could see themselves in real time. Karen seemed fascinated by the fact that when you looked at your own image on the screen, you saw yourself looking slightly off to the left. It was impossible to look straight into the eyes of your own image. Karen's head swivelled back and forth, directing her gaze first to the screen, and then the camera, and then back to the screen, her jaw hanging loose enough to give a clear view of the yellow fuzz on the back of her tongue. She looked haunted by that disorienting sense of being unable to catch herself. The inability to see herself as she truly was.

'We'll stay and play,' I said to Barnie, assuming Karen's assent.

'Excellent!' he said. 'You'll see my presentation. Today's the anniversary of my twenty-fifth year with the company.'

'Really?' I said. 'Congratulations. And how do they mark this great occasion?'

'Well . . .' he said, 'again, I'm not really meant to diverge this information . . .'

'Divulge,' I said, softly.

'Divulge,' he repeated. 'Yes. Divulge. Anyway, I have it on good authority – well, that is, Sheila told me that Chelsea, who used to work here, told her – that they give you a cheque for a whole month's pay on top of your regular wage. That's nearly a thousand pounds. And a watch. And a certificate. The presentation's at the start of the early session, so get your seats saved. I'll get looking for that troll.'

The phone rang. He picked up the receiver.

'Good afternoon, Pentagon Bingo. Barnie speaking. [Pause, eyebrows.] How may I help?'

28

Overweight

We entered the hall to the controlled cacophony of cash bingo – fast-paced games played in the intervals between the mainstage bingo sessions. We're dealing here with a different species of bingo. An animal altogether more streamlined, swift and slightly venomous. Eighty numbers instead of ninety. The boards are built into the tables. There are sixteen numbers set out in a square, each in a coloured circle. There are four columns of circles – yellow, red, blue and white. Customers feed money into a coin mechanism at the side of the table and use little plastic counters to cover the numbers as they're called. Most games are fifty pence or a pound. Most often you will need to cover all sixteen numbers to win. Occasionally there will crop up a whimsically named Pattern Game, for which you will only need to cover some of the numbers in a particular pattern. For the XXX game, for example, your four corner numbers and four centre numbers are free. Forming a pretty little cross, when the free numbers are covered with counters. Thus:

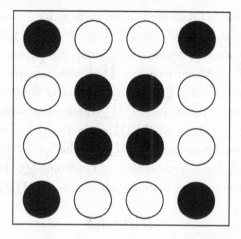

In between each game, the caller will announce the type of game and the amount of prize money and make known the availability of change-givers throughout the hall, all in their strange, hollow, seasick voice.

Every emphasis is unexpected. Insignificant words are stressed, and important words skipped over. Like this:*

Hello-ladies-and-gentlemen-and-welcome-to-this-afternoon's-bingo-for-the-next-half-hour-we'll-be-playing-back-to-back-cash-bingo-games-offering-prize-money-of-well-over-six-hundred-pounds . . . so-get-your-chips-at-the-ready . . . change-givers-are-walking-the-floor-so-if-you-do-need-any-change-raise-those-hands-in-the-air-and-a-member-of-the-team-will-be-over-to-you-as-<u>soon</u>-as-they-<u>can</u> . . . now-for-your-first-two-in-club-games . . . your-<u>kick</u>-out-the-corner-games . . . all-four-corners-of-your-'A'-board-are-<u>free</u> . . . that's-right-<u>free</u> . . . so-make-sure-you've-got-those-numbers-<u>covered</u>-before-

---

* Size indicates volume, and underlines indicate emphasis and an extra sort of manic urgency, such as one might use when shouting, 'Fire!' or 'Get this woman an ambulance!'

the-game-starts ['Kick the Corner' jingle music – something like the theme from *Knight Rider*] these-are-pound-games ... and-if-you-want-to-double-your-chances-just-pop-in-that-extra-pound-to-illuminate-your-'B'-board ... your-lucky-'B'-board ... and-for-this-game-I'll-be-setting-the-prize-money-at-fifty-three-pounds ... fifty-three-pounds-and-counting ... in-fact ... ladies-and-gentlemen-I'm-going-to-put-the-prize-money-up-to sixty-pounds-that's-sixty-pounds ... never-say-I-gave-you-nothing ... I'm-feeling-generous-today ... right-if-everyone's-in-and-ready ... your first number ...'

Blue 63

When the game begins, the numbers come out in a relentless deluge, fast as an auctioneer's rattle.

'Red 25, Blue 40, White 70, Red 13, Red 12, Blue 53, Blue 55, Red 17 . . .'

Since Divvy Karen and I are rarely flush enough in either money or luck to play cash bingo, we usually leave the proceedings and wander outside to the smoking shelter and smoke five or six cheapy tabs, pulling faces at the youths who tilt their bikes into wheelies in the car park.

'The payout on these games is wrong,' said Karen, glancing at the giant red LED board above the podium that displayed the game details.

'Wrong how?'

'Well, there are a hundred and twenty-nine people in, and fifty-two of 'em are playin' cash bingo.' How Karen had made a headcount of the hall observing which members were playing cash bingo in two or three seconds flat, I could not fathom but did not question. 'It's a buy-one-get-one-free, so they get two cards for a pound. That means there's one hundred and four cards in play and they're payin' out twenty pound and fifty pence prize

money. And when we were 'ere yesterday the club was takin'
fifty-one pence out of every pound 'cos the payout was thirty
pound and eighty-seven pence for sixty-three customers playin',
but today they're clearly takin' sixty-one pence out of every
pound so the payout's twenty per cent less. Which is shan as owt.'

[**Shan**
Pronunciation /shan/
Adj (slang)
1. Unfair, unnecessarily cruel or unjust
('The regime in Stalinist Russia was particularly shan.')]

I blinked.

'Shan as owt,' I agreed. (I hadn't followed her at all.)

As we talked, we cut a swathe through the bone-rattle of counters being swept off tables in a losing rage, the rustle of twenty-
pound notes clenched tightly in fists waved madly at change-
givers, the clank, rattle and rumble of pound coins toppling from
coin slots through mechanisms onto the conveyer belts that ferry
them into locked compartments at the end of rows (I know this
– I've seen staff open them to collect the takings).

The only empty table, it seemed, was next to Teddy Boy Bob.
This wasn't a disaster, but it wasn't a convenience. Bob was not a
follower of 1950s British subculture. No, Bob earned his nick-
name in quite another way.

29

Rise and Shine

As usual, Bob's teddy bears – there were three of them – were arranged carefully along the back of the table, in descending order of size from left to right. Bob was in his Triumph Rivton motorcycle jacket – a beautiful black leather number with thick red and white stripes down the arms, the Union Flag on the right bicep, the Triumph logo on the left. Big Ted wore a tiny matching jacket and a motorcycle helmet. Medium Ted wore a plain red jumper and no trousers. Little Ted was entirely naked (apart from his fur).

'Maurice!' he exclaimed, as we slid into our seats. His large face was rosy with windburn, the tight black curls of his hair damp and squashed-looking. 'I came on the motorbike! It's got new sprocket covers 'cos for some reason the old ones fell off. I'm waiting to hear back about whether I'm officially autistic. I was at the Teddy Workshop this morning. I thought I'd get Big Ted something special. His helmet cost fourteen ninety-nine, which was quite good really because it was reduced from twenty-nine ninety-nine. Are you playing the free books? I'm playing the free books. I know the prize money's not as good, but it's something for nothing, isn't it?'

'I suppose,' I replied. 'We can only really afford the frees.'

'Barnie's getting honoured today,' he went on.

'I know.'

'I've never been honoured for anything. It would be nice to be honoured for something. Have you ever been honoured for anything?'

'Once or twice.' This was true only in the loosest sense. I'd graduated with Honours from the University of Sunderland. And I was once selected as Teacher of the Year at school. 2007, I think it was. (The title has since been taken by Mr Blaine at Deerpool Grammar – but apparently his whole identity including all his qualifications was recently exposed as a fabric of cleverly woven lies.)

It was unnaturally hot in the hall. Stifling, in fact. Still, Bob hadn't removed his biker jacket.

'The Honda CB750,' he said, 'has an air-cooled straight four engine. It has a top speed of 125 miles per hour. It's Japanese. Honda also makes the Nighthawk. The Nighthawk has rear drum brakes. The CB750 is widely considered to be the first Superbike. Honda used Permanent Mold Casting to construct the engines.'

'I thought you liked the Triumph,' I said, eyeing his jacket meaningfully.

'Triumphs are my favourite. Hondas are my second-favourite. Oh, look – they're going up to honour Barnie.'

Sure enough, the clamour of cash bingo had sneakily abated, a little like a long-suffered headache fading into Nurofen numbness. The mainstage jingle had begun to play. I hadn't heard the jingle in a while. They must've fixed the sound system.

> *It's a Pentagon Bingo Day!*
> *A Pentagon Bingo day!*
> *You could be a winner,*
> *So come along and play*
> *At the Pentagon today!*

Someone somewhere will have been paid a couple of thousand quid for writing that.

Leonard made his way up on to the platform, beckoning Barnie to follow him. If at all possible, Barnie's trousers looked more than usually neatly pressed, his tie straighter, his slickened hair more immaculate. He mounted the platform and stood to Leonard's right as he took the microphone from its holder.

After the usual preliminaries, Leonard informed us that there was something special to be done before the session began.

'**In exchange for twenty-five years of unwavering service,**' he said, with great warmth and sincerity in his voice, '**it gives me great pleasure to present Barnaby Reynolds with this . . .**' he reached into a plain manila folder on the mainstage podium and withdrew a thick piece of pale-yellow A4 paper, '**. . . certificate of achievement and recognition.**'

30

Burlington Bertie

Barnie's face didn't so much fall as collapse. One moment his eyes were bright with life and hope, and his mouth was tucked up at the corners in a smart little smile. The next, all of his features seemed to droop and gather near his chin, his visage sagging like a water balloon held by the tied end.

Leonard seemed oblivious to the transformation – he was using half an eye to study the latest afternoon promotional leaflets in preparation for the session opening. He held out the certificate, and for a second or two Barnie simply stared at it, his sad, pale water-balloon face growing heavier and droopier. A little of the water seemed to leak from his eyes, making them glisten. Then he jerked into life, nodded curtly and took the certificate, shaking Leonard's small, fleshy hand with a surprisingly firm grip.

He beat a hasty path off the stage, and I watched as he wound his way efficiently through the tables towards Front of House.

'I'll see you after, Bob,' I whispered, beckoning Karen to follow me out front. Bob nodded distractedly – he was manipulating Medium Ted's paws, making him applaud along with the customers.

Out in Front of House, I spotted Barnie in his usual spot, behind the desk. He was pacing up and down, bouncing between the desk and the back wall haphazardly, like a Pong ball.

'Barnie,' I said, approaching him slowly. 'Barnacious-ness. Are you . . . all right?'

He stopped pacing. For several long moments, he didn't answer. Then, quietly, sombrely, he said, 'I think I'll spend some time in the cupboard.' And he opened the door to the cupboard behind his desk, walked in and closed himself inside.

I listened carefully outside the door for a minute or two, but could hear nothing.

I thought it best to leave him to it.

I pulled open the exit door and we stepped outside into the icy wind. Neenie and Sheila followed close behind us. Unusual for them to leave so early.

'Are you not staying?' I asked Neenie.

'Fuckin' goin',' she said, her face pinched. 'They're cowbags,' she said, gesturing towards the fruit machines. 'Cowbags. All of 'em. I've put eight hundred pound in that *Rocky* machine and 'aven't got a fuckin' penny out of it. They're fiddled, I tell you. They've all got chips in 'em.'

'Chips?' I asked.

'Microchips. To make us lose or win when they want us to.'

This sounded to me dangerously on the cusp of psychotic paranoia, but I chose not to comment. Instead, I said, 'Terrible wind this, isn't it?'

'Terrible,' agreed Sheila, drawing her cardigan across the swell of her boobs. 'It's a lazy wind.'

'Yes,' I agreed. 'Cuts right through you like an incompetent amateur magician.'

She nodded enthusiastically, and then took off across the car park after Neenie, who was already unlocking the door of her dark-blue G-Wiz. One of her Mobility Benefits.

'Yer remember yer gettin' those fish, right?'

'Oh yes. Oh yes. Certainly.'

'Get in, then,' she said. 'I'll give yer yers nails done for free and I'll throw in the fiver for the ticket to Sea Life 'n' all.'

All in all, Neenie isn't such a bad egg. I suppose she saw it as an investment in the boost to her business our sabotage would cause.

I opened the door of the G-Wiz and gave Karen's arse a gentle shove in the direction of the back seat.

31

Get Up and Run

'Two for French tips,' I said to the orange-faced, blonde-highlighted adolescent behind the counter. Her name tag said:

Destiny

'Have yers gorran appointment?' she asked, looking askance at me through long false eyelashes tipped with tiny pale-pink jewels.

'No,' I said, 'no, Destiny, we haven't.'

Nail Armstrong's salon was small, but striking in its decor. In keeping with the name, Neenie had plumped for the astronaut theme. The walls were painted a deep blue-black and speckled with glittering silver stars of all sizes ranging from the width of a fifty pence coin to that of a dinner plate. The swivelling, reclining treatment chairs, of which there were four, were upholstered in some sort of synthetic, futuristic-looking silver material, which gave them the appearance of console chairs from a spaceship in *Forbidden Planet*, and the long rectangular mirrors affixed to the walls in front of them were surrounded by plywood frames that transformed them into rocket ships, thrusters at the bottom, triangular wings at the sides and pointy noses reaching towards the velvet-black ceiling, which swirled with galaxies rendered in glow-in-the-dark paint. The large front window was covered by an opaque black blind, and the place was illuminated mainly by lava lamps, blue, red and green, all in the shape of rocket ships. There were black lights mounted high on the walls that set everything pale aglow. My Ivory Bow Boudoir Balconette bra from Ann Summers gleamed like an American movie star's teeth through my baby-blue H&M blouse. The waiting area – a small square of sleek black leather armchairs opposite the reception desk – looked almost out of place, particularly its table of magazines – ancient copies of *HELLO!*, *OK!*, *Not Bad, Then, How Are You?* and so forth.

'If yers 'ave not gorran appointment,' said Destiny, typing on a sleek black ergonomic keyboard with surprisingly unvarnished, bitten-down nails, 'yers will 'ave to come back . . .' – she hit the Enter key with unnecessary force and fixed me with a stare hard as nail lacquer – '. . . when yers 'ave gorran appointment.'

I bristled with impatience. We wouldn't be having this problem if Neenie wasn't still outside arguing with the fishmonger next door about her parking space.

'We're with Neenie,' I explained. 'We're doing her a favour. She'll be in in a minute – she'll explain.'

At that, she brightened suddenly, like an energy-saving light bulb. One of those that arses about for twenty minutes after you turn it on, giving off less illumination than an apathetic glow worm, before leaping all at once to life.

'Oh, well then,' she said. 'That's different. Would you like to take a seat over there?' She gestured to her left. 'On the seats?'

'Thank you,' I said, tugging Divvy Karen by the elbow over to the seating area. 'You've been most helpful.'

Not ten seconds later, the front door (painted to look like an airlock) sprang open, and Neenie barrelled through. Stopping off briefly to whisper a few terse words with Destiny, she turned in our direction. Just before she reached us, she made a sharp right turn and pointed to a silvery treatment chair in the back corner of the salon. We followed.

32

Buckle My Shoe

I took my seat before the mirror and Neenie settled on the low stool opposite me, like a proud, fat, ancient parrot, her arse cheeks spilling slightly over the sides of her perch. Her outfit never changed. Large-print blouse, slacks and blinding white trainers. 'French tips?' she said, looking from Karen to me and then back again.

'I don't want French tips,' whispered Karen, to me rather than Neenie. 'I want purple sparkly.'

Neenie eyed me and then Karen, and her eyes hardened as if she only just recalled their rift. She leaned over to the adjacent counter and pressed the button on the base of a small tannoy microphone.

'*This is a staff announcement,*' she proclaimed, with pronunciation so clipped it resembled an Edward Scissorhands topiary. '*I repeat, this is a staff announcement. Can Destiny please report to Cosmetic Dock 1? One for French Tips, one for Purple Sparkly.*' The microphone seemed slightly redundant, as the entire salon floor was not more than twenty feet square.

A brief pause, and then Destiny's voice boomed back over the tannoy.

'*I'm goin' on me dinner. I repeat, I am goin' on me dinner.*'

'*Fine then,*' Neenie announced back into her microphone, '*I'll*

*do them both meself, yer lazy meff. Bring us back a parmo. I repeat, bring
us back a parmo.'*

'Parmo', I should interject, is a peculiarly North Eastern name
for a pizza-style fast food often consumed after long and arduous
nights On the Lash. (On the Lash, I should interject into this
interjection, is slang for On the Piss.) It's short for 'Parmesan',
though the cheese in them is not even the most distant cousin of
Parmesan, and the 'pizza base' is constructed not from bread, but
from processed chicken. The topping consists of more chicken,
breadcrumbs, mayonnaise and a particularly foul brand of foot-
scented cheese. I've only consumed them in the most desperate
and inebriated of circumstances.

At that, Destiny tinkled out through the shop doorway.

'I'll do yer nails,' said Neenie, 'but I won't do hers.' Neenie still
regarded me with a measure of affection and respect, I could tell,
despite the fact I'd defiled her niece. I'd expected her to shun
both Karen and me equally in the wake of the unjust scandal, but
she seemed to blame Karen for the entire affair. She always had
looked at me with a rather fond eye during parents' evenings. A
little too fond, perhaps. And she laughed at my jokes – even the
terrible ones. There was something going on there.

Karen shrugged and settled down in a corner to sniff an
uncapped bottle of nail-polish remover.

I leaned close to Neenie.

'It's none of my business, really,' I said, 'but couldn't you
maybe . . . reach out to Karen? Make the first step towards
reconciliation?'

Neenie remained stony-faced.

'It's just that we have so few people close to us in this life,' I
said, more to myself. 'One day they'll be gone, and you'll realise
you failed them.'

33

Dirty Knees

Forty-five minutes later, Karen and I emerged from Nail Armstrong's. My nails were resplendent with tacky polish hardening quickly in the icy breeze, and Karen's were as short, ragged and unremarkable as ever. I led Karen in the direction of the Sea Life Museum, the fiver from Neenie tucked into the left cup of my bra. I carried with me an Almart bag containing the tools we'd need for our fishy theft – a large freezer bag, full of water and tied off at the top with a double knot.

We bore left down Eton Street, and took a sharp right by the Little Black Book strip club, walking past the College of Further Education, through the washed-out grey shadow of the enormous tarpaulined bi-plane in the car park. I assume it's something the engineering students are constructing. It's been there for months.

I took Karen's hand as we crossed the busy road in front of the museum, and she trotted along quite happily as we safely dodged the reckless cars and reached the other side. We passed beneath the shadow of the grimacing three-dimensional fibreglass shark hanging above the doorway, and made our way into the premises.

Even the reception area had an eye-stingingly briny scent about it. Under that, an odour of deceased sea creatures. Something like a fishmonger's ice display left out to fester for a week.

The walls were festooned with thick green fishing nets gathered into drapes. Here and there, an angry red buoy sprouted bulbously from a knot in the net like a bubo tucked in the gangrened armpit of a plague victim. The odd plastic crab dangled from the netting as well, spindly legs tangled in the spider's web of green. I'd seen similar décor schemes in low-end fish and chip restaurants. On a low ledge against the wall opposite the reception desk sat a small fish tank, glowing eerily from within with a blue aquarium light. There was something moving in there, but the water was too cloudy to make out exactly what.

I reached into my bra cup for the fiver, mildly alarming the adolescent boy on the reception desk. He seemed relieved when I simply produced the crumpled note, though he took it from me tentatively between finger and thumb, as if it might detonate at any moment.

I saw him eyeing the Almart bag.

'What's in that?' he asked. He probably felt he was justified in asking, in this age of heightened security vigilance. Though I don't think aquariums have been hit particularly hard by terrorism, to be honest.

'It's my colostomy bag,' I said. It worked. He made a disgusted face, and immediately looked away. He didn't even seem to notice that it lacked a tube connecting it to my person.

'It's a pound extra each if yers want the audio tour,' said the boy.

I didn't have a pound extra each, but asked anyway, out of curiosity, 'What does the audio tour involve?'

He gestured towards two sets of battered black headphones hanging on pegs behind the desk. They looked encrusted with the gunk of several hundred unwashed hairdos. Hanging pendulously at the end of their wires were bulky portable cassette players.

'I think we'll give it a miss, today,' I said. As though we'd ever be back.

'Suit yerselves,' said the youth. 'Put yer hands on the counter.'

A little warily, I laid my hand palm down beside the goldfish mouse mat on the desktop, and in a lightning-flash move, the boy snatched up a rubber stamp, pounded it down into a tiny tray of red ink to the left of the computer keyboard, and slammed it forcefully onto the back of my hand, hard enough to bruise the tendons.

'Ahh!' I said.

Upon inspection, I saw that he'd branded me with a little blue smiling octopus. The ink was bleeding slowly into the surrounding creases of my epidermis, spreading its smile into a frightening grimace.

Karen stepped forward for the same treatment, and we followed the lad's pointed finger in the direction of a door, fringed with long, translucent blue rubber strips like the entrance to an abattoir. It was guarded by a small metal turnstile, which seemed largely unnecessary, as we pushed through its rotating bars without impediment.

34

Dirty Whore

On the other side of the fringes, it was murky and dark as a seabed. A generous sprinkling of sand crunched underfoot as we walked, and when I groped for the wall to guide me, my fingers came away wet. I decided I'd find my way unaided. The corridor, in any case, was narrow, and seemed fairly straight. From somewhere unspecified came the rhythmic sound of dripping liquid.

After a minute or so of cautious shuffling, we came upon the first exhibit. A large-ish tank, perhaps four feet square, with surprisingly clear water. Well, I supposed they'd managed to comply with animal-care standards until now, or they wouldn't still exist. Inside bobbed half-a-dozen clownfish and one or two blue tang. There wasn't much else in the tank. A conspicuous lack of coral or greenery. I could see where they were going with this.

'Nemo!' shouted Karen, her sudden shriek startling the shit out of me.

'Indeed,' I said, when I'd caught my breath. 'Do you know that in reality clownfish are sequential hermaphrodites?'

'Seq-wha-wha her-wha-whas?'

'Sequential hermaphrodites,' I repeated patiently. 'It means that if the only female clownfish in a group dies, the dominant male changes sex to become the female. Then he mates with another male in the group to produce offspring, and thus the species is perpetuated.'

'Oh,' said Karen, absently, tracking the movement of the largest blue tang with her head and shoulders.

'So for the film to be accurate, when Nemo's mother died, Nemo's father should really have had a sex change and had inter-course with Nemo to produce incestuous children.' I contemplated this for a moment. 'Would've been quite a different film.'

Next, we came to a lobster tank. This aquarium was more lavishly furnished than the last, boasting a generous layer of gravel at the bottom, some large rocks and a piece of knotted wood. Resting on one of the rocks was a rather depressed-looking lobster.

'Do you know,' I began, 'that lobsters don't have red blood? Their blood is bl . . .' I trailed off in amazement.

A shadowy figure coalesced just to our left, emerging from the darkness into the halo of light surrounding the lobster tank.

A very familiar shadowy figure. Which became all the more familiar as it shrugged off the shadows.

'Well, shitballs,' it said. 'Maurice Turbuton. Of all the lobster tanks in all the Sea Life Museums in all the world.'

It was Duke McGee.

35

Jump and Jive

Duke McGee. The Man, The Myth, The Legend. Duke McGee, with whom I'd spent every lunch break at Deerpool Comprehensive, holed away in the back cupboard of his Maths classroom, eating piccalilli sandwiches and discoursing on the breasts of Mrs McGugan, head of Design Technology. Duke McGee, who'd tried his best to stand by me through the unpleasantness that precipitated my leaving, though in the end, like everyone, had been forced to cut ties to save his own skin. I could hardly blame him.

Duke McGee's sheer bulk has always awed me. Now, in the navy-blue dark of the aquarium, his great form dwarfed me like a gentle giant of a sea monster. I felt like an awestruck diver coming face-to-face with a sperm whale, treading water in the orbit of his barrel chest and rock-hard, protruding stomach. He was dressed more casually than I'd ever known him to – in simple jeans, a button-down grey shirt and a green rainmac. Though he had the same formidable buzz cut, squashed nose and tiny, glitteringly intelligent eyes as he'd had when we taught together.

Not only was Duke physically enormous, but his presence was truly epic. It had certainly struck me across the head quite forcefully when I first encountered him at the staff Christmas meal in 2006. Funnily, it wasn't anything he said or did that came flying at me through the air unexpectedly to smack me in the chops as he arrived through the restaurant door in his reindeer tie and light-up antlers. It was more the fact that I knew at once that he was wearing the tie and antlers ironically, and that we were going to get along famously. I sneakily moved Marge McGugan's place setting so that Duke and I would be sitting next to each other, and as we talked, at first politely and then with increasing candour and intimacy, I discovered that he was frighteningly good with computers, as well as brilliant at maths. Also that he said the words 'basically' and 'actually' a hell of a lot, and had a laugh like he was plotting to take over the world.

Five years since I'd seen him last.

I'd called him 'the Grand Old Duke of York' in those days. Because he came from York.

'I've been fine thanks,' I lied, meekly accepting his semi-violent thump of a greeting between the shoulder blades. Duke had studied karate in his youth, and liked to incorporate Eastern self-defence techniques into casual conversation. 'It's great to see you.' There, I was genuine. 'How've *you* been?'

'I'm actually at a loose end,' he admitted through his teeth. 'Gave up teaching year before last. Basically, too much paperwork. Too much *politics*. Too much actual . . . *scapegoating*. I mean – I never really got over what they did to you. That was . . . *bang* out of order. I still say it was that Christine Spollen who stirred up the shit. Thought she was the guardian of morals or something 'cos she was head of Religious Studies. She hated transvestites – she told me, you know. Horrible place, that school. Only perk was basically Marge McGugan's breasts.'

I nodded in agreement. 'Busty McGugan,' Duke had christened her, some time in late 2007. Duke had even composed a long set of lyrics to the tune of 'Camptown Races' entitled 'The Ballad of Busty McGugan', which mainly consisted of lewd references to Marge's breasts, cleavage and the prominence of her nipples. He licked his lips, sinking into memory for a moment. Though he resurfaced quickly.

'Actually took up hacking full time, for a while,' he went on. 'But it was basically too easy. No actual challenge about it. The actual assignments I was given . . . basically, they weren't actually very *sexy*.'

Hacking was something of a sideline of his, back in the day. In any case, I know that he had unfettered access to the head teacher's private computer files, all of the head of year Department meeting minutes and the school's budget planning, without the knowledge of any of the higher-ups.

'Was it ever sexy? Hacking, I mean.'

Duke looked at me as though I were crazy. 'Basically,' he said, 'hacking actually *is* sex. Penetration. Actually.' He sucked air through his teeth and tapped his thick index finger against his cleft chin. 'It's basically actually penetration. It's basically just illegal penetration without consent.'

I thought about this for a moment.

'Wouldn't that make hacking rape?'

He looked briefly horrified, then seemed to recover.

'Well, basically,' he said. 'But not *actually*.' He took a deep breath.

Everything was still 'basic' and 'actual' with Duke, I saw. It was as though he'd glimpsed the infinite complexity of the universe and decided to remedy it by reducing everything to the simple and empirical.

'But moving swiftly on. How's your mam?'

He wasn't to know. Still, I felt the back of my throat constricting and my eyes pricking with tears.

'She passed away. Just six months after I left the school.'

'Oh, *marrah*.' His tone was stricken. 'I'm so sorry.'

'It's okay. It's okay.'

It wasn't quite okay, and I think he knew that. I'd felt

dreadfully alone during those weeks. Holding Mum's hand in her stuffy little bedroom, in that heartbreakingly familiar little detached house in the Fens. I never even told her I was fired. They found the leukaemia just around the time of my disgrace, and she never really bothered to read the paper from that point on. So she never saw the headlines in the local news. And she didn't really talk to the neighbours, so . . . They'd found the disease late, and it was a quick decline. For the final week, I slept in my old bedroom, listening breathlessly for a break in her snoring from the other room. My old room made me want to cry. My poster of Tim Curry was still on the wall. My bed was too short for me. My stash of half-used lipsticks was still hidden behind the wardrobe.

Mum's snoring was very distinctive. She'd give a little gargle, and then after three seconds of silence, she would exhale in a very distinctive syllable, 'Boooooo'. It sounded like she was half-heartedly jumping out to surprise someone, over and over again. I was looking at the Tim Curry poster – at the redness and fullness of Dr Frank N Furter's lips – when I heard the last 'Booooo'. And as I stood moments later beside Mum's bed, looking at the translucent, ossified earthworms of her lips, I remember thinking that I'd failed her. The house where I stood was still rented. She owned nothing. I owned nothing. Neither she nor I were living well. She'd died adrift, and so would I.

For a while after this, I simply stood and looked at her, though eventually I roused myself and got the tape player from the kitchen (earlier I'd been heating ravioli to 'Making Love in the Rain'). I fetched the ancient toy car horn from the box under my bed – I hadn't touched it since childhood, and it looked a little battered and deflated. Then I sat on the end of Mum's bed and pressed 'Play' on 'Tijuana Taxi'. When the horn part came, I squeezed the bulb, but no sound came out.

I could have told Duke all of this. But we skipped past the

awkward part of the conversation like you might deliberately skip a brutal murder or a naughty bedroom scene in a book.

'All right, Karen?' he said brightly to change the subject.

Karen gave a non-committal grunt. He looked back and forth between us for a time, as though he was watching a very small tennis match. 'So . . . You two are . . . actually . . .'

I shrugged and smiled.

'There's no reason we shouldn't do whatever we want, now,' I said.

'Hey, hey,' he held up his hands. 'I never actually said there was owt wrong with it. You basically go for it, marrah. Whatever makes you basically happy.'

I always did like Duke.

Three Dozen

It turned out that there was a café in the Sea Life Museum. Or rather, a table, four chairs, a plate of raisin flapjacks and a coffee machine that called itself a café. It was manned by the self-same adolescent who'd served us at reception. He seemed able to juggle both jobs effortlessly, as the café was in the corner of reception. And there were no other customers.

I could scarcely believe I was here, sharing an awful coffee and a decent flapjack with old Duke. (I say 'old' – he was only a year my senior. Somehow, though, he'd always seemed far more sensible and resourceful than me.)

He took a mouthful of flapjack and grinned at me to reveal a raisin stuck in his teeth.

'I actually lost your actual number when my phone got stolen,' he said, spraying a couple of moist oats in my direction. 'Or I would've actually tried to call you by now.'

At the time of my disgrace we'd deemed it safest to part ways. When the accusations began at the end of the autumn term, 2008, Duke was, of course, implicated. No one believed that he could've been ignorant of the supposed 'situation' with me and Karen – not with our friendship as strong as it was. It broke my heart to split ties with him. We'd faked a rift – in a charming book-endy sort of way, we staged a fight at my final staff

Christmas meal. Cranberry sauce was thrown, and Duke managed to keep his job.

'Your phone was stolen? Ah. That explains why a Turkish restaurant answered when I tried to call you three months ago.' I'd been drunk and unhappy, and missing him terribly. I'd thought it was safe to rekindle our friendship after so much time had passed, and was so intensely disappointed at my failure to telephonically connect I'd been rather hard on the young waiter who'd answered. After absorbing a string of Turkish insults into my right ear, I'd considered it a sign that Duke and I weren't meant to reunite.

He turned his attention to Karen. She'd been his prodigy, after all. Before the overdose, he'd wanted her to apply to work at NASA, or crack codes for MI5. Now it transpired that had all been a pipe dream.

'How are you doing, Karen?' He craned his neck to try to catch her eye. She seemed zoned-out – on a different wavelength. She was emptying packets of Demerara sugar onto the table and spreading them out to coat its surface. He turned back to me. 'What's actually up with her?'

I sighed. 'She had a little bit of an accident. The doctors say her brain has permanent deep white-matter abnormalities.'

'Jesus. I'm sorry.' He said this to me, rather than Karen. 'Can she still actually do sums?'

'Oh, yes, her facility with numbers is unaffected – she's possibly even better than before.' It was true. Now that the clutter of social awareness, communication skills and grasp of reality had been burnt away, Karen's genius gleamed even more brightly.

'Karen,' he said, excitedly, 'can you tell me the square root of twelve hundred to the power of two times twelve divided by eight hundred and ninety-one, plus pi to seven integers and then divided by 3.5?'

Karen shrugged, and drew '40.687' in the sugar on the tabletop.

I shook my head in wonder.

'How does she do it?' I asked, half-rhetorically, because I knew that Duke had some insight into how she did it.

'It's as easy as breathing to her,' he said, his tone awed. 'She basically sees numbers differently from us. God knows what she actually sees. But whatever it is, it's beautiful.'

I tried to imagine what she might see. It was hopeless.

'I can see a bit of it,' said Duke. His eyes glazed over slightly, and his voice took on a breathy quality, as though he were watching soft-core erotica. Which, admittedly, we had done together once or twice. 'There is beauty in numbers. A purity.'

'There is?'

'Yeah. Yeah. Take the number five, for instance. Not only is it a prime number, but it's actually a *safe* prime. Which basically means that it has a special relationship – a *very* special relationship – with *strong* primes.' He said 'strong' almost obscenely. As though describing the thigh of a female Scandinavian bodybuilder.

'What kind of relationship?' I asked.

'It's basically too complicated to explain. You wouldn't understand.'

I wasn't at all insulted. This was undoubtedly true. You might as well expect me to follow the plot of an un-subtitled Mexican tele-novella.

Karen was quietly reciting prime numbers in the background, rearranging the sugar granules into what looked like an intricate fractal diagram.

'Two, three, five,' she whispered. 'Seven, eleven, thirteen.'

'A five-sided shape is called a pentagon,' Duke continued. Well, I knew that. 'So all figurate numbers representing pentagons are basically *pentagonal* numbers.' He'd lost me again.

'Twenty-nine,' said Karen. 'Thirty-one, thirty-seven, forty-one.'

'Anyway.' Duke shook himself, as though awakening from some strange slumber. 'Moving swiftly on . . .' He chewed for a minute on his bottom lip. He seemed to be contemplating something. 'I actually have to get going. I'm . . .' The pocket of his polo shirt began to shiver quite madly. He looked down at it excitedly, and then fished out a sleek black rectangle the size of a small chocolate bar. I recognised it as one of those phones without buttons. The ones you prod and stroke to operate. I'd seen people using them, but never up close.

I watched with fascination as he tickled the shiny black surface of the phone in a deliberate pattern. This brought the screen to life with light. He pressed his thumb against it once, and then again, and then grinned widely.

'It's Bronya,' he said, still gazing at the phone. 'She's texting me. We've basically been seeing each other for about six months now.'

That was a record, as far as Duke's relationships were concerned.

'Well done,' I said. 'How did you meet?'

'On Plenty of Fish.'

'Plenty of Fish?'

'It's an Internet dating site.'

As he spoke, he tapped the screen with his thumbs at incredible speed – replying, I assumed, to this 'Bronya' woman. I simply couldn't figure out how he could type letters without the use of keys.

'You see, marrah, the chances of meeting someone in real life that you actually get on with are basically nil. If you want to find your soulmate, you've got to use specialist equipment. On sites like these, you've got a powerful search engine that matches you up with someone with exactly the same traits and desires as yourself. Why stand your whole life waving a little fishing rod made of string, with no bait, into the deep dark water, hoping you'll catch something? I say, spear the perfect fish with an intelligent, targeted harpoon.'

I could see the sense behind it, I supposed.

'Bronya's a marine biologist,' he said, proudly. 'Studying the eating habits of rare sharks. I'm actually here on a bit of a mission.'

I almost exclaimed, 'Me too!' but thought I'd let him speak first. He seemed on a roll.

'She wants me . . .' – he leaned in close to my ear, apparently far more concerned with concealing this from the spotty Sea Life employee than his hacking habits – '. . . she basically wants me to *steal a shark.*'

'That's an odd request so soon in a relationship,' I said.

'Not really. She basically needs one, you see, to study to complete her thesis. A zebra shark. She can't actually afford the plane ticket to wherever these zebra sharks live, so I said I'd get her one.'

Duke had a habit of making his paramours near-impossible promises. During his brief fling with Marge McGugan, he'd promised her he'd avenge her of her ex-husband's betrayal by framing him for murder, though thankfully the affair had ended before she'd had time to hold him to it.

'So they have zebra sharks here, do they?' I asked.

'Not *exactly*. Come with me.' He stuffed the remainder of his flapjack into his mouth and launched himself back towards the dark portal of the museum entrance. Karen followed, still mumbling primes under her breath.

We passed quickly by several exhibits – some sea snails, an eel and, for some reason, a grass snake, looking quite embarrassed to be there, as if it had crashed a party. Duke eventually came to a halt before a tall, thin tank, the water slightly green-tinged with algae. Inside were suspended four small, anaemic pouches, buffeted gently by the bubbles from the electric oxygenator. They looked like oversized ravioli just coming to the boil on a hob.

'Mermaid's purses,' said Duke, reverently.

37

A Flea in Heaven

'Shark eggs,' I said, to demonstrate my acquaintanceship with sea-life trivia.

Sure enough, a close look at the little plaque beside the tank revealed that they were:

ZEBRA SHARK EGGS

Perhaps aquariums weren't terrorist targets, but it certainly seemed this one was going to be the focus of a sudden wave of burglary.

'What are you going to do with them after you steal them?' I whispered.

'Thought I'd basically prevail upon a friend with a bathtub. I've only got a shower myself. Course we'll have to find somewhere bigger for them once they basically hatch. But we can cross that actual bridge when we come to it.'

Perhaps I enjoyed courting trouble. Perhaps I was simply so happy to see Duke again that I wanted to manufacture any opportunity for interaction. But whatever the why, I found myself saying, 'You can keep them in my bathtub, if you want.'

He seemed over the moon with this arrangement.

'Cheers, marrah!' he said, slapping me so hard on the back I brought up a raisin from my flapjack.

It wasn't too much of a hardship. I never really bathed anyway – the water heating in my flat had gone the same way as my electricity. I tended to shiver through a sponge bath at the sink, or use the shower head to blast myself with freezing spray until I was clean.

'You're an actual ledge.'

'A what?'

'It's short for "legend".'

'Oh.'

'So. Right. We basically need to get two or three of those purses into these freezer bags.' He produced a wad of freezer bags from his jeans pocket (what an incredible coincidence that we'd both chosen freezer bags as our instruments of crime). 'Seriously, marrah,' he said. 'I appreciate your help on this. Is there anything I can actually do for you in exchange?'

And that was it. As I stared at the jelly-like, embryonic form of the shark in its mermaid's purse, an idea began to twitch and wriggle in my brain, slowly shifting its rubbery shape as it grew larger, more defined, and strained the elastic bonds of its casing.

There *was* a favour Duke could do for me.

A very big favour.

38

Christmas Cake

'Seven Jäger Bombs and a Toxic Avenger,' I requested of the barman. I didn't recognise him. He must have been new. It was highly probable that he didn't even know how to mix a Toxic Avenger. This is the Presley's signature drink, and every bit as noxious as its name implies. I'd probably have to show the young tyro how to do it myself. Surprisingly, though, he pottered about competently enough, snagging a pint glass and pouring from the requisite bottles of Blue WKD, Green WKD and Yellow WKD, followed by two shots of Apple Sour and one of Blue Aftershock.

'Tell your mate she can't keep her fish in 'ere,' said the barman as he plonked the highball glasses of Red Bull on the counter, dropping a little plastic shot glass of Jägermeister liqueur quite delicately into the centre of each, where they floated like tiny islands of molten orange lava.

I looked over at Karen, who was sitting at our usual small circular table underneath the large LCD television, clutching the bag of ten bristlenose plecos we'd snaffled from the Sea Life Museum. It hadn't taken long to find them, after we'd parted ways with Duke – in fact, they'd been the next exhibit after the lobster. It had been an unpleasant and slippery task, reaching in with my bare hands to snatch them (how could I forget gloves?), and had made me curse the fact we hadn't thought to bring a long-handled net. But we had them, and they were in Karen's care, all ready to destroy the foot fish at the salon. They were ugly little suckers. About the size of small goldfish, and almost the same colour, although slightly more vividly orange. Their faces were like those of mini Creatures from the Black Lagoon. Tiny red eyes, warty flat faces with fringes of whiskers along the sides of their snouts, and striking little Mohicans of dorsal fins not far back on their slender bodies. Right now, Karen was gazing down at them affectionately, almost maternally.

Tomorrow, we'd run Neenie's fish errand. Tonight, we were here for a meeting. A serious meeting. Overnight, clutching onto Karen for warmth in the confines of my tiny bed, the idea born in the aquarium had become a fully fledged infant shark. And I was taking steps towards rearing it into a monster.

Within the half-hour, Barnie and Duke McGee would meet us here, and I'd lay out the bare bones of my plan. I'd asked Leonard Overall, mainstage caller at the Pentagon, to meet us here too. I didn't know Leonard as well as the others, of course, but as far as I could see, there was no way that my master plan would work without him. Five of us. The Pres-lash was perhaps not the most appropriate venue, but it was karaoke night, and Karen and I never missed one of those. Something of an agreement with Neenie, who happened to be the landlord of this place. She seemed to think we were decent singers, and liked us to warm up the crowd. And of course, a cordial relationship with Neenie had myriad benefits. Free drinks, for one. Free nails, for another.

'Where's Neenie?' I demanded. 'She'll let us bring fish in here. She knows us.'

The barman screwed up his face in distaste and impatience.

'Fine,' he said, 'but I'm checkin' about this. That'll be fifteen pounds seventy-nine, mate.'

'Put it on my tab.'

'We don't have tabs.'

'I have a tab.'

'You can't have a tab. We don't have tabs.'

'But *I* have a tab.'

'Listen, mate—'

'That reminds me. Can I have a packet of tabs?' I gestured towards the row of Marlboro Light packs propped on the shelf next to the Famous Grouse.

'A packet of tabs? I suppose you want me to put that on your tab, as well, then?'

'You're getting the idea.'

'We don't *have* tabs.'

It was perhaps fortuitous that Neenie entered at that moment, as this might have gone on for hours. I was greatly relieved to see her large rectangular form emerge from the employees' door just to the right of the bar.

'Darren,' she said, leaning towards her green employee, 'Maurice 'as a tab. Put the drinks on it. And the tabs.'

And with a dumbstruck look on his face, Darren was forced to do just that.

Hah.

I gathered up three of the Jäger Bombs and the Toxic Avenger by pinching the rims of the glasses cleverly between my fingers and letting them dangle down together in a bunch. True to form, Karen appeared at my side, snatching up the remaining Jäger Bombs. We proceeded to the table and deposited our spoils.

I was trembling with excitement.

Duke, Barnie and Leonard would be here any minute. Perhaps I was insane. Perhaps I'd finally lost it – or at least, the last of whatever I had left to lose. Perhaps, though, the insanity I had planned would set the five of us, finally, for the first time in our lives, on the road to winning.

39

Those Famous Steps

I'd had time to change before coming to the Pres-lash. I was wearing my Minuet Petite revere-collar ladies' suit jacket in graphite, accompanied by my Bolongaro Trevor ruche-neck raspberry top and my tweed eyelet knee-length skirt. I had also applied a fresh coat of sea-green eyeshadow and butterscotch wet-look lipstick.

I set the Toxic Avenger aside for the moment and lined up the seven Jäger Bombs. Beside me on the long, cushioned seat, I could sense Karen psyching herself up for the event. I lowered myself into the seat beside her.

'You ready?' I asked.

'Yeah,' she said, 'mint.'

With lightning speed and incredible dexterity, we worked from the outside of the line of drinks to the centre, first using our index fingers to press the small shot glasses of Jägermeister down into the energy drink, submerging the treacly liqueur in the busy fizz of caffeinated soft drink. Then we picked up each larger glass in turn, downing the frothing contents in one. Our game: whoever reached the centre first got to drink the middle glass.

Today, I was triumphant.

I emerged, gulping desperate breaths, head spinning and fingertips buzzing with warmth. I looked into Divvy Karen's flushed face and saw the same exhilaration.

We came together, snogging like our lives depended upon it.

We thrust violently into each other's mouths, without waiting for tongues to knock politely on doors. I dragged the tip of my tongue along the sharp line of her lower incisors, pressing down hard enough to part the rough bobbles of my taste buds and slice slightly into the vulnerable surface of the muscle, adding a taste of copper to our exploits. I tongued her lower molars and premolars with the raw aching end of my bleeding tongue, and then tickled the ends of her upper canines, sliding back smoothly to lick along the protrusive ridge of her hard palate and back to the fleshy pliancy of her soft palate, following its path right down to the end of her epiglottis, which I batted repeatedly with the tip of my tongue as though it were a tiny punching bag. The whole, hollow cavity of her mouth tasted of sweet hot carbonated juniper-scented copper-edged saliva-diluted glory, and we kept snogging deeper and deeper until I felt my nose touch the soft place just beneath her earlobe. The butterscotch lipstick added an extra layer of flavour to the whole experience.

I was vaguely aware that we'd abandoned the fish, but for the moment, I didn't really care.

Then someone tapped me on the shoulder, and we wrenched apart with a reluctant squelch.

40

Life Begins At

Barnie had arrived. Right on time, too – I checked my watch. Eight-thirty precisely. His punctuality was testament to his ingrained work ethic.

I pointed for him to sit, and he did.

Despite his excellent timekeeping, there was something a little less pressed and immaculate about him than I'd come to expect. His civvies looked to be of high-quality fabric – a pair of smart khaki slacks, a pale-blue shirt and a deep-blue cashmere cardigan (grandad-ish, but nice), though his collar hadn't been ironed correctly. His expression was downcast, and when he folded his hands on the table in front of him, I saw that his thumbnails were chewed almost to the quick.

'Barnie,' I said, 'thanks for coming. I'm sure you're wondering why I asked you here this evening.'

'I suppose,' he replied. It seemed that all of the sparkle had gone from him.

'Yes. Karen . . .' I looked around. Karen was nowhere to be seen. Then I felt a set of teeth close gently around my left ankle, and realised she was underneath the table. I knocked smartly on the tabletop. 'Karen,' I said, 'stop horsing around. Barnie's here. You'll need to listen to this as well. It involves you.'

'Sorry,' came her muffled reply. She popped up like a meerkat from a burrow and shuffled backwards into her seat, her hair slightly disarrayed.

'Right.' I laid my hands flat on the table, and then realised it was minging and sticky with spilled drink. I removed them, wiped them on my knees and folded them in my lap. 'In short,' I said, 'I have a plan.'

'A plan to do what?' asked Barnie, looking downwards forlornly as the cuff of his right shirtsleeve absorbed spilled lager from a puddle on the tabletop. He looked worried by this, but didn't seem to have the heart to move his arm away.

'Barnie.' I'd need to pitch this carefully if I was to enlist Barnie's help. 'I'm so sorry about the ... certificate situation. It's unforgivable that you're not getting the reward you deserve. What on earth went on there? Why didn't you get the thousand pounds and the watch?'

'I ... Apparently they *used* to give a thousand pounds and a watch. Until last year, when they changed it to a certificate.'

'So, let me get this straight. Twenty-four years into your term of service, they changed the reward for twenty-five years of service?'

He sniffled, and said quietly, 'Cutting costs.'

'Do you not feel badly done by?'

'I do feel ...' – he screwed up his face, apparently looking inwardly with some ferocity – '... a sense of injustice.'

I nodded.

'I think we have the remedy for that, Barnie. I'll go into more detail, but not until Duke and Leonard get here.' I wasn't about to go through the whole thing more than once.

41

Life's Begun

'Maurice!' came an insistent, feminine voice from above me. I looked up. It was Neenie.

'What?' I asked her, somewhat impatiently.

Her face looked more like a latex mask than ever under an extra layer of liberally applied makeup. She offered me the list for the karaoke. If I'd known it was that important, I would've been more immediately receptive. I snatched the list from her hands and began to peruse it in detail.

'What can I put yers down for?' she asked, sliding onto the seat beside me and clicking her Pilot Rexgrip retractable ballpoint into a state of readiness.

The sheets of song titles were laminated to protect against spilled booze. I wiped away a smear of vodka and Coke from the plastic surface and sucked it off my finger.

Hmmm.

'I might do "Build Me Up, Buttercup",' I said. 'Though "Eye of the Tiger" is tempting.'

'What about "They Tried to Make Me Go to Rehab"?' said Neenie to Karen, a little unfairly, I thought. Still, Karen had the grace to laugh.

'No,' I said, 'I think it'll have to be "This Guy's in Love with You".'

'You sure?' she asked, the pen nib hovering over the page, offering me one last window of opportunity to reconsider. 'You always do Herb Alpert.'

I stood my ground.

'Absolutely,' I said. '"This Guy's in Love with You". Me and Karen. Put both of our names down.'

'But it's not a duet!' she protested.

'We'll make it one,' I said, with conviction.

Another voice boomed from the direction of the bar.

'Still singin' karaoke, then, mos-mosh?'

Duke McGee. All of a sudden, it felt like a party.

'Always!' I shouted back, flipping him the middle finger with a grin.

I saw that Duke was getting in a full round – three more Jäger Bombs and four cans of Strongbow. I could always count on that man.

He came over with the drinks on a bar tray. Neenie stood up and waddled to the next table with the song list, and Duke slid into the space she'd vacated. He nodded towards Barnie, looking a little puzzled by the presence of the stranger, and then looked guiltily at the selection of drinks he'd deposited in front of us. Clearly they were all intended for us three – he hadn't factored in an additional party member.

'Oh,' said Barnie, quickly reassuring him, 'I don't drink.'

Duke looked immensely relieved. He snatched up a Jäger Bomb and tossed it back, catching the little plastic shot glass between his uneven teeth. He slammed the larger highball glass down onto the table, and triumphantly spat the shot glass into it. Bull's eye. It hit its mark with a gunshot crack, followed by an anti-climactic tinkle.

'So,' he said, licking the Red Bull off his glistening lips. 'What're we here for? Sounded . . . intriguing, on the phone.'

As if on cue, the pub door swung open and in walked Leonard

127

Overall. He looked a little out of place in the Pres-lash, and rather odd without his caller's uniform. He was wearing a pair of brown corduroys and a blue button-down shirt beneath an open thick black winter coat. His face was shiny with the sort of sweat that gathers when one exerts oneself beneath heavy clothes in freezing temperatures.

He looked around for a moment, warily it seemed, though not nervously. When he spotted us at our corner table, he raised his fingertips to his damp forehead and flicked them forward in a slick little salute. He came over and slid into the empty seat beside Barnie, crossing his legs. He didn't remove his coat.

It was a risk, bringing in Leonard on this. He was the only unknown factor. I knew I could trust Duke, Barnie and Karen. Leonard, I didn't know so well. But I absolutely couldn't see a way that my scheme would work without him. It was a gamble, and for someone who spent so much of his time in a bingo hall, I really didn't like to gamble. But if we don't take chances, nothing ever changes.

I decided to get straight down to business.

'Duke,' I said. 'Barnie. Karen. Leonard.' I looked at each of them in turn for a long beat. 'Thank you for coming here tonight. In a little while, Karen and I are going to sing karaoke, and I'd like you all to stay for the show. First, though, I should let you know the purpose of our meeting. I have a plan. It's a plan that will be complex in its execution, but extremely beneficial – life-changing, even – for all five of us. What we have here, and what we will need to make this work, is a circle of trust. So before I say anything, I'd like us all to make a pact.'

'Come on,' said Duke. 'Basically you need to tell us what the hell you're on about.'

'Okay,' I said. I took a deep breath. This was 'make or break'. But, at this point in my life, I had nothing left to lose. So I just said it. 'I think we should rig a game of bingo.'

42

Winnie the Pooh

A spark of interest ignited behind Barnie's eyes. Or perhaps it was panic.

'*Fiddle* the bingo?' he asked. 'Why? Why would we do that?'

'Yes,' I said. 'Fiddle the bingo. And win a solid gold monkey worth five hundred thousand pounds.'

I let it sink in.

'The Monkey Night game?' said Leonard. His expression was impassive. He blinked very deliberately, as though clearing a speck of dust from his eye.

I nodded.

'Is it possible?' asked Barnie, finally shifting his arm away from the spilled beer.

'It has to be,' I said. 'Everything's possible. And between the five of us, I believe we have the skills and the resources to make it happen.'

Duke cut in. 'Hang on, mos-mosh. Hang on a second.' He looked dubious, but not entirely dismissive of my idea. 'How long has this idea of yours basically been stewing?'

'I'm not sure. I only saw it clearly when I met you in the aquarium the other day.'

Duke *knew* bingo. He'd been pretty much addicted to it when we worked together at the school. His tremendous, inquisitive mind was fixated on the mechanisms of bingo. A couple of times in the staffroom he'd tried to segue into lectures about Random Number Generators. I myself only got into it after I found my days empty of responsibility or routine. It began as a hotline to reality – something to get me out of the flat and amongst people. Eventually, it had become a hobby and a pleasure. For Duke, however, bingo was a way of life. Our only major 'fight' had occurred one night when we were due to see Caryl Churchill's *Vinegar Tom* in Billingham and he'd ditched me for the bingo at the last minute.

The table fell silent. Duke whistled the tune to Laurel and Hardy. After the first three bars, he trailed off thoughtfully.

'It's a bit out of the blue,' he said.

I scanned the others to take a quick poll of reactions. Leonard was still unreadable. Karen was poking at the bag of fish. Barnie looked a little like Meryl Streep in *Sophie's Choice*.

'I've thought it through,' I said. 'The scheme is far from hair-brained, I assure you.' Outwardly, I was Confidence itself. Privately, I was quite panicked. I had a rough sense of the plan I intended, but I by no means possessed the technical knowledge to work out its intricacies on my own. I needed these four people to pull it off. But I needed to present my case eloquently, and make it sound like a sure thing, or I'd lose them.

Duke leaned towards me. 'You always were an optimist. Let me tell you, marrah. It's basically impossible to fiddle a game of bingo nowadays. What with all of the computers and . . . what-not.' He looked to Leonard to back up his point.

'It's true,' said Leonard, coming to life suddenly. 'I mean, from what I know. The computers we use now – the Random Number Generators – they're state-of-the-art. The whole setup is designed to prevent fiddling. We've got the Gambling Commission breathing down our necks twenty-four-seven. Don't think anyone's attempted to tamper with a game in decades.' He paused.

'I mean – it's not that I don't *want* to do it. I could use the cash. We used to fiddle the odd game when I worked at the old place in Peterlee, before they brought in all this newfangled technology. It was a good little sideline. If I thought for a moment that it would work . . .'

'It will work,' I said.

'Shit,' said Leonard. 'But . . . five hundred thousand pounds. That's . . .' He turned and focused his gaze on me fiercely. 'I'm listening.'

Duke looked at Leonard in disbelief.

'It's basically impossible!'

'It's *basically* impossible,' I interrupted. 'But with a master hacker, a maths genius, two inside men and a creative mastermind,' I gestured to myself, 'it might just be *complicatedly* possible.'

Five of us. A pentagon to bring down the Pentagon. How . . . perfect.

I fished around in my bra and pulled out the folded-up scrap of newspaper I'd concealed there earlier. I tended to keep newspapers, and I'd sifted through my old copies to find this story in preparation for this meeting. The article was from 2003. It had stuck in my mind, partly because I was a bingo fan and partly because, even then, I'd had an idea that it might one day be useful.

Barnie picked it up and perused the newsprint.

'BINGO CALLER SACKED FOR ALLEGED £2,000 GAME-RIGGING PLOT,' he read. It was a story about a fiddled game at Lucky Sevens' bingo hall in Sunderland. It had been quite the hot topic at the time – everyone at the Pentagon had been abuzz with it. Enough time had passed, though, that it was more or less forgotten – it lingered in the atmosphere only as a sense of caution about ever attempting to replicate such a scheme.

'Well,' said Duke, 'that just proves it. They were caught.'

I snatched back the article from Barnie.

'They *almost* got away with it,' I said, pointing to a passage in

131

the clipping. 'Look. Here, it says, "It is thought the caller used an item called a link key to manipulate the system and control which numbers were generated for the game. The win was investigated after a customer reported that the caller was acting suspiciously and pausing for a long time in between bringing out numbers." Well. That's just sloppy. We could do better than that.'

'I don't know,' said Leonard. 'It'd be fairly difficult to call a game like that *without* arousing suspicion. I know about these link keys. I've only had to use one once. Sometimes, when a big game is linked up with lots of different clubs, you lose the connection with the club that's generating the numbers. At that point you'll get in touch with the calling club and they'll give you the numbers over the phone, and you'll turn this key to put the system into a sort of manual mode so you can type in the numbers yourself. But the average pause between one number and the next in an ordinary game of bingo is one and a half seconds. It takes at least three seconds to turn this key and type in a number. Someone would notice.'

'What if we only had to generate one number?' I asked. 'Isn't the Monkey Game one of those flyers with a Super Number?'

A Super Number adds another level of tension and complexity to an ordinary game of bingo. In addition to the six standard bingo tickets, each customer's flyer will have one number (in the case of the Pentagon the Super Number is displayed prominently in a star at the top of the ticket), akin to the Bonus Ball in the National Lottery. The winner of the full house will take a modest cash prize, and then one more number will be drawn from the Random Number Generator. If this matches the full house winner's Super Number, they take the jackpot – in this case, the golden monkey. The chances, however, of winning the full house *and* your Super Number being drawn are infinitesimal.

'Yeah – I've played one of those games before,' said Duke. 'They actually had them on Saturday nights at the Octagon. Used to basically give away a microwave oven or summat on the Super Number. But you'd need to know all the other actual numbers on the winning ticket in order to *just* have to type in that one number at the very end to basically complete the win.'

'What if we *did* know all the other numbers?' I said. 'What if Barnie could find a way to divert the delivery of books for Monkey Night to somewhere we could study them, choose a winning ticket and make sure the computer generated those numbers?'

'But we'd have to know the actual algorithm for generating the numbers,' said Duke. 'We'd basically have to be able to predict what numbers would actually come out during that game on that evening. And in order to do that, we'd have to be able to actually work out the formula. Basically we'd need to extrapolate it from the numbers that have come out of that Random Number Generator for the past . . . say . . . five years or so?'

I looked at Karen pointedly.

Leonard looked astonished.

'She could do that?' he asked.

'She could,' I said. Duke nodded – he'd seen examples of Karen's prowess far more startling. 'And Duke – you could hack into the computer system to make it disconnect during the link game? After the full house is won, and just before the Super Number was called? So that Leonard could type in our winning Super Number manually, and it would look like the calling club generated it?'

'I . . . basically could, I suppose.'

'Could you make it look as though the link game is still live? So that no one else would know that the game is now in Leonard's control as he calls the final number?'

'I suppose I basically . . . could. Yes.'

'Like I said. It's *possible*. We have all the best resources at our disposal. Karen's almost supernatural ability with numbers. Duke could hack his way into the Pentagon Department of Defense in

Virginia if he wanted to – the Pentagon Bingo Hall Deerpool should be a breeze for him. Barnie can manipulate bingo book orders and gather information. And Leonard – you know everything there is to know about bingo calling. We have got this. It can *work*.'

I looked at Leonard. Was he about to turn us in? I looked for signs – a twitch of the eyebrow, a shake of the head. At the first indication he was an enemy, I would launch into my 'Ho, ho, ho! You thought we were *serious*?' bit and hope like hell I hadn't taken a gamble too far. We needed Leonard to turn that link key. We needed him to type in the number. But I had no idea whether he had the motivation to take part in a plot like this. He had a steady income. A job he seemed to enjoy. My hopes all hinged on my instinct about him. He seemed ambitious. Borderline-greedy. Would the thought of a fifth-share in a golden monkey worth five hundred thousand pounds be enough to tempt him?

'Do you know,' said Leonard, 'that the average bingo caller gets insulted roughly twenty times a day?'

I don't know what I'd expected him to say, but it wasn't that.

'Yes,' he went on. 'Twenty times a day. That's more often than a call-centre adviser.'

An impressive statistic.

'And the reason we get insulted?' said Leonard. 'People think we're responsible for fate. People think that, in the moment between calling one number and pressing the button to bring out another, we're thinking of them and them only, and the numbers on their ticket. That we decide in that moment whether they win or lose.'

I'd never thought about it quite like this before. From the bingo caller's point of view, I mean. Of course, I'd heard some of the more dedicated customers banter with Leonard, threatening him with mild forms of violence if he didn't bring out their numbers. I'd even heard the tone of those customers slip a little into serious bitterness. I'd never stopped to think what it might be like, though, to have these things said to one day after day after day.

'When I first started calling bingo,' said Leonard, 'eleven years ago now, I was amused, even charmed, by the old ladies that came up to me and teased me after their losses. When they said, "You're rubbish", "You're shite", "You're hopeless", I laughed it off as playful banter. A lot of it was, but I soon began to notice an edge of genuine resentment beneath the jokes. As the customers became more familiar with me, they got braver with their taunts – as if I'd become established in their mind as a controller of fortunes. Someone once threatened to run me over. "I'm going to string you up and watch you burn" is another one that stuck in my mind. And this from an eighty-nine-year-old retired librarian.' He paused for a moment, as though assessing whether his next anecdote was appropriate to share. 'Once,' he went on, 'I was calling a massive jackpot game. A bit like Monkey Night – a little less spectacular, maybe. The jackpot was fifty thousand pounds. A regular customer called Judith, who'd always been fairly nice with me in the past (now and again she used to give me fairy cakes she'd baked), won the two-line prize. I pressed my button to reveal which numbers she needed for the full house. She only needed the number 37. You needed to call in forty-five numbers or less for the big jackpot. There were forty-four numbers out. I called the next number. It was 38. As I got down off the stage that evening, Judith was waiting for me. She punched me square in the face, harder than I'd ever been hit before, even in a bar fight. Got me right in the nose. Her signet ring split my left nostril – I needed three stitches.'

Leonard surveyed his audience – we were rapt.

'What I'm saying is,' he continued, 'bingo callers get blamed for a lot of shit that they can't control.'

'*O Fortune,*' I quoted in a whisper. '*Never have sceptres obtained calm peace or certain tenure; care on care wears them down, and ever do fresh storms vex their souls.*'

Leonard looked at be doubtfully.

'Seneca,' I whispered. 'Sorry.'

'What I'm *saying* is,' he said, clearly irked at the interruption, 'that it would be nice to *actually* control something for once. And to control it in my favour.' He spoke decisively now. 'I'm sick of being blamed for the misfortunes of others.' He slapped the table. 'I'm in.'

Immense relief. And a little surprise – I had no idea Leonard possessed such uncharted depths. I almost felt guilty for thinking him shallow.

I had Duke and Leonard on side now, I knew it. There was only Barnie to win over.

Barnie was chewing on his lip.

'But . . .' he began to say something, and then stopped himself. Then tried again. 'I'm not sure I could . . . It wouldn't be . . .' He lost it again. Finally, he looked me straight in the eye and went with, 'Wouldn't we get into terrible trouble?'

'Not if we don't get caught. And we won't. Because we have the perfect team.'

'It's not right, though!' he said.

'Isn't it? Think about it. How many years' service did you give to that place? A quarter of your life that you'll never get back. And what did you get in return? A beige piece of paper with your name printed on it.' I knew what it was like to give your best years of service to a place, and then find you meant nothing to them.

His eyes began to glisten, much like they had on mainstage during the presentation.

'You deserve what you were promised. You deserve *more* than you were promised.' I could tell that, in his heart, he agreed. 'Help us rig the bingo, Barnie.'

43

Down on Your Knees

Barnie breathed deeply and quietly for a moment. He looked as though he was considering it.

'Listen,' I said. I reached for one of the pints of Strongbow on the tray, drawing strength and comfort from its cool, solid form. 'I've thought about it. Long and hard.' I could see Duke stifling a laugh at the words 'long and hard', but refused to rise to it. I forged onwards. 'And by jingo, we *deserve* that money.'

'How do you reckon that?' asked Duke, now openly tickled. He never felt the need to rationalise his misdemeanours.

'Because we've been shat on, my friends,' I said. I let that digest for a moment. 'We've been absolutely shat on, in copious amounts, and from a great height. Barnie here was meant to get a year's extra wages and a gold watch for a quarter-century's service at the bingo, and they gave him a *certificate* instead. Karen and I lost everything – our careers (or career prospects, in Karen's case), our livelihoods, our families, our ... our very dignity, and all because we found kindred spirits in each other.'

'That's a fancy way of describing cradle snatching,' muttered Duke. I arranged fingers around the Strongbow glass so that only my middle finger was pressed to the front, pointing in Duke's direction.

'Hey,' I said, taking genuine offence. 'Listen to me, Grand Old

Duke. This isn't going to work if you're not on my side. We *all* need to be on each other's sides. I never, *ever* took advantage of Karen, and you know that. The school administration imagined all sorts of sordid activities, but the truth of it was that we never even kissed, Karen and I, until eight months after I was fired. Just, as it happens, after Karen's seventeenth birthday. At that point, we figured we might as well – there was nothing to lose any more anyway. We were *friends*. We were soulmates. I need you to believe me.'

Duke looked chastened.

'We might be strange,' I went on, 'but we're good people. We care for each other. And I want to take Karen away from this place. I want us to go far away, before something terrible happens to us. Barnie – that troll doll we lost, and you found, and you lost again – it's Chunky's. That horrible man Chunky's. It's his lucky charm, and he's furious that we've lost it. And if we don't find it, he's going to knack us and kill us.'

'Oh my God,' said Barnie, looking as though he'd inadvertently murdered someone with a breadknife while trying to make a sandwich. 'I'm so sorry. I thought it was in Lost Property. I was *sure* it was in Lost Property.'

'And what are we stealing, anyway?' I hefted the Strongbow towards my mouth and took a long draught. 'They're *giving* away that golden monkey *anyway*. Someone's got to win it. Why shouldn't it be us? We're not stealing it, so much as . . . tilting it in our direction.'

'And then stealing it,' said Duke.

'Technically,' I said, 'yes.' I glanced then at the fish, which had been left largely forgotten on the plush bench to my right. Thank God Duke hadn't sat on them. They glittered golden orange in the warm lights of the pub. 'Everyone's due a bit of luck in this life. Some of us have had less of it than others. Therefore we need to make our *own* luck.'

I grabbed Karen's hand. Then I clasped Barnie's with my other. Barnie seemed to get the idea, and tentatively took hold of Duke's hand, who at first looked mildly stricken by internal homophobia, but seemed quickly to overcome it and took hold of Leonard's nearest hand. Leonard took Karen's, and completed the circle. Well, not so much a circle, really. Evenly spaced around the table as we were, and with our arms straight, we formed something close to a perfect pentagon.

44

Droopy Drawers

Neenie was hovering again. I didn't think she'd overheard – she'd appeared quite suddenly, and looked preoccupied. 'Oy,' she said, her voice low and conspiratorial, 'Chunky's lookin' for yers.'

Karen, thankfully, didn't hear this. Her attention span being even shorter than a bristlenose pleco, she'd wandered over to the fruit machines in the raised area and started to bash at the buttons.

A creeping, flesh-prickling sensation wound its way from the nape of my neck to my coccyx.

'Chunky?' I asked, attempting nonchalance. It wouldn't do for my dread of Chunky somehow to be broadcast back to him. It would just make him thirstier than ever for blood. 'How is the old chap?'

'Said 'e was going to come and sing "Under the Moon of Love" and then knack yers to buggery,' said Neenie.

'Shit,' I said, hissing through my teeth. 'That's a terrible song.' I nodded towards the bag on the table. 'As evidenced thusly, we've got your fish. Tomorrow, Operation Garra Rufa Terminatia will be put into action.'

'Mint,' said Neenie.

I glanced at the raised area to make sure Karen wasn't spending all our food money on the fruities. It seemed there was no danger. She was hammering away at the buttons quite frantically, with the

140

superficial appearance of expertise, though I knew she had no clue how to play the thing. Fruit machines in pubs have always baffled and angered me. They are deliberately and needlessly complex, confusing you into thinking you're getting your money's worth when in fact you're simply thrashing about in the dark like an adolescent who's paid for a prostitute before his testicles have even descended.

As I waited for the karaoke to start I worked my way slowly through another Toxic Avenger, hoping to quell my rising anxiety. Leonard and Duke stuck around, drinking quietly, probably mulling over everything we'd discussed.

By the time it came for Karen and me to sing, I was, if I was honest, approaching comatose. I knew that I should be worried about something, but couldn't quite put my finger on what.

'We should all exchange numbers,' said Duke. It seemed I'd won him over. Both him and Barnie. It was almost unreal. We were going to *do* this. 'Do you know how to text?'

'Karen will show me,' I slurred, fishing my ancient Nokia from my handbag and fumbling to add Duke's number to the Contacts list. 'I only really have it for emergencies. There's only . . . like . . . fifty pence credit on it. Is that right?' I looked to Karen for help. 'Credit?'

Duke handed me a fiver.

'Put that on it,' he said. I laid the fiver on top of the phone. 'You meff,' he said. 'Go to Almart, go to the small cash desk where you buy tabs. Ask for a fiver on your pay and go phone. They'll give you a little ticket. Follow the instructions on that.' I was vaguely aware of him taking the phone from me and inputting his number. He and Barnie muttered numbers at each other, and typed them into their own phones. 'Okay,' said Duke, slapping me lightly over the face. 'You had this idea. Now you need to execute it. We need to meet and assign specific tasks. Tomorrow morning at eight? Your place?'

I nodded blearily.

'Ladies and Gentlemen,' announced Neenie, 'to start off yer karaoke, we'd like yers to welcome to the stage Maurice and . . . accompaniment. Tonight, they'll be singin' Herb Alpert's "This Guy's in Love with You".'

Karen scurried to my side. She took my hand and hauled me up on to the raised area.

I squinted at the blue LCD screen until the words

INTRO

(9 MEASURES)

came into focus.

Neenie furnished me with a large radio microphone, which I brought to my mouth. It smelled slightly of other people's spit.

45

Halfway There

Karen took up her position stage right, kicking off her shoes and leaning coquettishly on the brass barrier that separated the raised area from the lower.

The strains of Herb's organ lulled me into a somewhat mellow frame of mind, and I was almost calm and nearly on-key as I sang the first line.

It wasn't the worst performance we'd ever given. We told the story of the song with our gestures and expressions as well as our voices, and the audience seemed vaguely interested, which was an achievement for the Presley. Karen turned some of the lyrics into spoken asides, which I thought worked quite well.

When we reached the chorus, Karen took centre stage, belting it out with a force that made my throat clamp shut in surprise and my testicles shrink back into my scrotum. To be truthful, the sounds emanating from Karen's mouth sounded more like howls of pain than musical avowals of devotion, but the sentiment behind them was the same.

As we neared the final verse I fell quite dramatically to my knees at Karen's feet and gazed up moonily into her eyes.

At that moment, I heard the front door open and felt a draft skitter up my skirt and ruffle my knickers. Instinctively, I turned to see who had just walked in.

Chunky.

I continued singing, jerking my head subtly in the direction of the threat, hoping to alert Karen to its presence. I knew the second that her eyes widened in terror that she'd seen him, worming his way through the restless crowd to the bar.

We understood each other instantly, no words required.

We've got to bugger off. NOW.

I saw Chunky exchange a fiver for a neat double Jack Daniels. He was not looking at his drink, the money or the bartender, though. He was looking at me. The second our eyes met, his gaze felt like a high-speed wood drill, boring holes of pure hatred straight through my irises.

I began to sing the last line, my voice strained, trembling.

Chunky downed his drink in one swallow.

I looked at Karen meaningfully, then at my chest, then towards the door. I hoped to goodness that she understood what I was attempting to communicate.

And then it all kicked off.

46

Up to Tricks

It happened so quickly and I'm surprised to find that I remember now, with startling clarity, that events happened in the following exact order:

Karen lunged towards me and thrust her hands down the front of my bra. At the very same moment, Chunky launched himself at the stage with all the enthusiasm of an enraged bull rhino, and accompanying sound effects.

Meanwhile, Karen – God bless her cotton socks – had retrieved the chicken fillets from my C-cups and, hefting them like shot-puts, executed two swift and powerful overarm throws, launching them towards Chunky's misshapen, stubble-dusted head. (Despite her brain damage, Karen's ability to hit a moving target at mid-range remains remarkable to this day.)

My fillets are substantial beasts – I like a bit of zest in my chest – and they landed, one after the other, with impressive, moist-sounding slaps, against Chunky's forehead, dazing him enough to stall him in his tracks for the three seconds it took us to leap from the stage and barrel through the door out onto the street.

Somehow I maintained enough presence of mind to grab the bag of bristlenose plecos from our table on the way out.

I knew without looking that Chunky was following.

'What about yer fillets?' asked Karen.

I looked down with regret at my chest.

'Never mind that now,' I said. 'Just move.' I broke into a run, forcing Karen to do the same. I glanced over my shoulder. Sure enough, Chunky was emerging from the Pres-lash doors, scanning the street for us with murder in his eyes. I ducked down the alleyway between Loonies Club and Yatesy's Wine Bar, ignoring Karen's whines of, 'Yer pullin' me fuckin' arm off, yer fuckin' Ding!'

We collapsed against the damp wall of the alleyway, gulping excruciating breaths and clutching each other for comfort. I looked briefly at the fish, to check I hadn't stunned or killed them. They seemed perky enough. Lucky, oblivious bastards.

'I think we've lost him,' I said, peering cautiously towards the watery spot of gloaming at the entrance to the alley, but before optimism could find a foothold in my chest, it slipped and plummeted into a black pit of despair in my stomach: Chunky's wiry, sharp-edged silhouette coalesced, charcoal black against the setting sun in the alleyway entry.

'Oh God,' said Karen, 'Oh fuck. Oh fuck.'

Chunky advanced upon us, his silhouette looming larger and larger.

I looked over my shoulder. There was no other way out – just a concrete wall, featureless apart from a high, fresh, pungent arc of still-glistening urine, no doubt left by a reveller too impatient to seek a public toilet.

'Karen,' I said, taking her shoulders quite forcefully. 'Karen, look at me.'

She had passed trembling several seconds ago, and had now progressed to uncontrollable shuddering. I feared she might actually be suffering the early symptoms of a seizure.

'Karen,' I shouted at her, as she regressed further into her fear, her eyes beginning to glass over and a low, disconcerting humming leaking from the back of her throat.

There was nothing for it. I slapped her, hard, across the right cheek.

'Listen to me,' I said, loudly and urgently. 'It's okay.'

Some of the glassiness dissipated from her eyeballs, and she made a species of eye contact with me.

'It'll be okay,' I repeated, more softly now. 'We'll go to Tijuana.'

She hiccupped in fear.

'Yes,' I said. 'We will. We'll get a Tijuana taxi there.'

'Will we?' she said, in a small, hopeful voice.

I looked past her shoulder to Chunky's form, moving at a tortuously languid, threatening pace, so close now that he nearly blocked out the light at the end of the alleyway entirely.

'Why aye,' I said. 'We'll ride through Tijuana, by the Plaza Río, the Plaza Monarca and the Cinépoli, on a warm evening, with the smell of fajitas rich in the air.' I cuddled her close. 'We'll stick our heads out of the window,' I went on, 'and watch the dancers coming out of the clubs in La Coahuila. I'll wear a Vivienne Westwood scarf, and you'll be decked from tip to toe in Swarovski jewels. We'll pay the driver enough to ride us around until we're bored, or dizzy, or so tired we fall asleep, right there in the back of the taxi. And when we wake up, we'll pay him more, and get him to drive around the same route again.'

I could feel the fish wriggle in the bag squashed between our stomachs. It was disarmingly like what I imagine a shifting foetus must feel like to a pregnant woman.

Karen laid her head on my shoulder, and I hummed the tune to 'Tijuana Taxi' in her ear. All the while, walking us both backwards, slowly. The rough brick walls of the alleyway seemed to be closing in on us like a booby trap in an Indiana Jones film.

47

Four and Seven

Chunky was so close now I could smell him. Sickly and minty. Lynx Chocolate and Extra chewing gum.

'Ave yers got me troll doll?' he said, breathing the words into my face sibilantly, like poisonous fumes leaking from a gas fire.

'Chunky,' I said, insanely convinced that I could talk my way out of this. 'We're looking for it. It's almost certainly somewhere we can . . . almost certainly get our hands on it. It'll be with you within the . . . next two days.'

The glint of his flick-knife told me it was futile.

'DAY!' I quickly amended. 'The next day. In the next day, it will be with you.'

'Right,' he said, his voice as sharp-edged as his silhouette. 'I am gonna knack yers . . .' – he raised the knife – 'like yers 'ave never been knacked before.'

With that, he sprang forward and sliced a clean, short cut in the bag of bristlenose plecos. It began to haemorrhage like a ruptured artery. Two of the fish were sucked out with the spray, one of which – and for this I shall always be grateful – landed squarely in Chunky's suprasternal notch and slithered down immediately into the neck of his shirt.

It took him perhaps a second to realise what had occurred, and to register the small, cold organism wriggling its way from his sternum to his crotch. Then he quickly began a strange sort of gyrating dance, tearing at his shirt in an attempt to release his tormentor.

I wasted no time, darting after Karen, past Chunky and out of the alleyway towards freedom, my left index finger plugged in the bag's puncture to preserve the remaining fish.

No sooner had we spilled out on to the street than I heard a car screech up beside us. Galvanised by fear, I grabbed Karen and made for the vehicle, bending to get a glimpse of the driver – Duke McGee, though, to be honest, I didn't really care who it was. In the car with him – the same battered brown Ford Anglia that had occupied my neighbouring parking space at Deerpool Comprehensive – were Barnie in the front (looking determined and chewing anxiously on his thumb) and Leonard (perched primly in the back behind the driver's seat, his knees pressed close together). I threw open the back door, and Karen and I scrambled inside.

48

Four Dozen

The five of us huddled around the table in my freezing kitchen. I was wearing my caving headlight to provide illumination. Karen seemed still to be trembling slightly from the trauma of the chase, though she may simply have been shivering in the arctic cold. I'd made us cups of tea on my little Calor Gas camping stove, but since I had no milk we were drinking it black, clutching the mugs close to warm our hands and faces.

The scheduled meeting had been moved up. After all, we were all here, weren't we?

I was using a green permanent marker to map out my plan on the tabletop, as I had no paper. It struck me that I didn't have much of anything, really. I'm not sure where the permanent marker came from. Probably a relic from my essay-marking days.

'Leonard,' I said, 'first thing's first. Where do they keep this link key? The one you need to turn to manipulate the numbers.' Leonard opened his mouth to speak.

'Do you have any sugar?' asked Barnie.

'I'm sorry, no,' I said. I hadn't told the others but the teabags I'd unearthed were at least three years old. The tea did taste a bit musty.

Leonard gave Barnie a pointed look that said, 'Can I speak now? Thanks so much.' Then he said to me, 'It was at least two years ago when I used it for a game. I think it was brought out from the Admin office.'

'Can you get to it?'

'There's a fingerprint lock. They had it installed last month. Only the managers and the Admin staff have access.'

'Duke,' I said, 'do you know anything about overriding fingerprint locks?'

'I did actually manage to get into my hairdresser's iPhone 5S.'

'What's one of those?' I asked.

'It's a . . .' I could see him mentally translating his definition into 'Maurice Friendly' terms. 'It's basically a really, really, really fantastic phone that has a fingerprint lock.'

'And you "picked" this fingerprint lock, so to speak?'

He nodded. 'Did it for fun, more than anything. Basically, while she was going for the hairdryer I nicked the bottle of TRESemmé she'd been using on my bonce and when I got home I dusted it for fingerprints. When I found one I photographed it with a high-resolution camera and printed it out with my laser printer. Then I got an actual condom, ripped it open, stretched it out, actually laid it over the picture and carefully etched the lines of the fingerprint into the latex with a dried-out ballpoint pen and then let the latex contract again to its normal size. Next time I was at the hairdresser's I basically slipped her iPhone out of her pocket while she was doing the hot rinse and conditioner massage and when she went to get the clippers I took the doctored condom out of my own pocket, wrapped it around my finger and pressed the print to the iPhone lock. It actually worked.' He'd said most of this in one breath, and paused for oxygen. 'It has to be a lubricated condom. The lock expects the finger to be slightly moist.'

So many astonishing particulars in that small speech, not least that Duke goes to a ladies' hairdresser's.

'So if we had the fingerprint of a member of the Pentagon's Admin staff,' I asked, 'we could get this key out of the office?'

'Don't see why not,' said Duke. 'I have a couple of condoms left over from the Busty McGugan Days. Might actually be expired. Though I can't see that being a problem.'

'Barnie,' I said, 'do you have your own personal mugs in the staffroom?'

'Er . . . yes.'

'Could you steal the mug of one of the Admin staff and replace it with an identical one?'

'I . . . don't know,' said Barnie. 'They're all a bit quirky. I think a lot of them are bought off eBay. April's from Booksales is one of those ones where a naked man appears when you fill it with a hot drink. No – wait. Tracey's from Admin is fairly ordinary. I could probably find a fatsimine.'

'Facsimile. Excellent. So we know how to get the key. Now we need to get the Random Number Generator to produce the numbers on the winning book – all of them apart from the Super Number. For this, we need the books themselves. Bingo books are printed with tickets in a recurring, predictable pattern. We need to look at the serial numbers, and from that we can work out which book will win, and in how many numbers.'

'This tea basically tastes a bit musty-fusty,' said Duke, smacking his lips in disapprobation.

'Really? It tastes fine to me.'

The word 'musty' must have reminded Duke of his old song about Busty McGugan, because he began to hum it quietly beneath his breath. I recalled that he'd worked another character into the story of the ballad – a stale-smelling young lady called Musty BcGugan, whose bust was only slightly less impressive than Busty's.

'So,' I said, 'we divert the shipment of books to somewhere secret, and find the right ticket.'

'How do we divert the books?' asked Duke.

'Barnie,' I said, 'you're responsible for ordering the shipments at work, no?'

'Er . . . yes.'

'Could you divert a shipment and cover it up well enough that they wouldn't realise it wasn't missing?'

Barnie looked mildly panicked that so much of the plan hinged on him.

'Ah . . . oh dear.' He slurped his tea, and spilled a little of it. 'Yes,' he said, wiping at his chin, 'Possibly. I'd have to . . . Let me think. I'd have to order a double shipment of another set of books, and have both of them delivered early in the morning, before there were any other staff about. Then I could switch the labels on one of the sets, so that they looked like the books for Monkey Night.' A little of his anxiety seemed to fall away as his idea came together. He began to talk more confidently. Almost, dare I say it, approaching excitement. 'I could order the real Monkey Night books to be delivered to another address, and I could . . . yes. You know – I could. I could easily cover it up in the paperwork. Tracey doesn't look too closely at the figures during the audits. And if she did notice a discrepancy, she'd ignore it or cover it up rather than go through the hassle of dealing with it.'

'Are you *certain* of this?' I asked. It wouldn't do to be discovered after the fact.

'*Certain*,' said Barnie. 'Tracey once disguised the loss of a massive shipment of books rather than have to account for it during an audit. She told me when she was drunk at last year's Christmas party.'

'Fabulous,' I said. Poor Tracey. Her fingerprints stolen *and* her paperwork fiddled. Little would she know her integral part in The Monkey Night Plot.

Barnie looked down into his tea as though it could offer him absolution.

'It's not really . . . I mean, it's not going to harm the bingo hall at all, really, is it? Someone would have won the monkey anyway.'

I should have been surprised at Barnie's concern for the

organisation that had failed him so spectacularly, but I wasn't. Pentagon employees like him didn't come along very often, I was sure. It was rotten of them to treat him so shabbily.

'No, Barnie,' I said, emphatically. 'The Pentagon won't be hurt financially in the slightest by our gain.' I was curious. 'What will you do, Barnie? With your share of the money, I mean. Where will you go?'

He didn't answer right away. First, he flushed from his nose outward, a livid stain spreading over his face like a blot of pink ink on pale paper. 'I've been thinking,' he said, 'that I could go to Bristol. There's a woman there I knew once. When I used to fly a light aircraft for a living. Doreen.'

I was a little taken aback.

'You used to fly a light aircraft?'

'Oh yes. I've done lots of things.'

I raised my eyebrows.

'But yes, I've been meaning to go back to Bristol and visit – I found her again recently on Plenty of Fish.' Again, that website. Lots of people seemed to be dangling their rods into that particular online reservoir. 'Last week we talked over the phone for the first time. If this works out . . .'

I patted Barnie on the hand.

'Don't worry. It'll work.' He beamed.

49

PC

Next, I turned my attention to Duke.

'What do you need to hack into the Random Number Generator?' I asked him.

'You should see these RNG rigs,' said Duke. 'They're flabbergasting. Not much to look at from the outside − if you actually watch the bingo callers, the interface on the screen looks like an old DOS operating system. All blocky and pixelated. But behind that is massive, massive power.'

I must've looked a little lost, as he paused to elaborate.

'There's basically no such thing as a random number, marrah,' he said. 'You have to understand, you see, that what would appear to be a random number is in fact *generated*. The clue's in the name. *Random Number Generator*. If something's generated, it can't be random now, can it?'

'I see what you mean,' I said. 'A bit of an oxymoron. So . . . how are the numbers generated, then?' I was 99.99 per cent sure I wouldn't understand, but I wanted to have a shot at it anyway.

'Algorithms are basically sums,' he offered. He took my drywipe pen. On the tabletop, he scribbled:

$$X_n + 1 = (aX_n + b) \bmod m$$

'That's your basic formula,' he said, as though it might mean anything to me. I was thankful in a way that he wasn't patronising me, but finding it increasingly difficult to pretend that I understood anything he was saying. 'There's a seed, from which each "random" number is actually generated. Sometimes the bingo RNGs use a clock as their "seed", 'cos it's always changing. Others use each number generated as the seed for the next number. So, basically, what they actually have in the computer is this actual algorithm—' Here Duke scrawled across the table a bewildering gallimaufry of numbers, letters, asterisks and ampersands, interrupted here and there with the odd recognisably English word, such as 'random,' 'initialiser' or 'result'. It spread across the table in a burst of chartreuse bright as a firework, though far less temporary – that marker was permanent.

```
z_m = <choose-initializer>; /* must not be zero, nor 7x98936pfffffffft
z_m = <choose-initializer>; /* must not be zero, nor 7x98936pfffffffft

get_random ( )

b_r << 8739 *** >> <choose-initializer> (g_h & m_b) +
(m_z >> d_r) 9823945 ;

* /64 bit result/ *
```

Which produces a series of numbers that are "random" until they repeat. But the sequence is so long that no one could possibly notice it's repeated. *Unless . . .'* – here he paused for effect – 'you're using a slightly outdated piece of software called Blind20. Now. Most of the enormous chain bingo halls updated their systems to Blind60 three or four years ago. But I happen to know that our particular chain, which includes the Pentagon and Octagon, are still on the old system. Blind60 has beasts of algorithms that produce sequences of numbers so long they'd take thousands of years to repeat. Blind20, on the other hand – well. The pattern would only take about six years to repeat. Still far too long for your average bingo customer to notice and exploit. But if . . . *if* you actually knew where the sequence started and where you are in the sequence, then you'd be able to know what numbers would be called out next.'

I was hopelessly lost.

'Look at it this way,' he said, sensing my confusion. 'It's like sex.'

'Oh?' I said.

'Yes,' he said. 'Sex. Say the number ten is a bloke . . .'

'. . . Aha . . .'

'. . . and the algorithm is a lass . . .'

'. . . Right . . .'

'. . . and we put the lass in front of the bloke – we know she's so fit he just can't resist her . . .'

'. . . Okay . . .'

'. . . so he gets it on with the algorithm and she gives birth to the number sixty-five.'

'Why sixty-five?'

'I don't know, marrah. I'm just choosing random numbers. Well, you know what I mean.'

Now that he'd used the sex analogy, it was beginning to make a certain sort of sense to me.

'Is there any way to produce a completely and utterly random number, then?' I asked, my curiosity completely and utterly piqued.

'Ah, now . . .' said Duke, quite sagely. 'For that, we would basically have to delve into the realm of quantum physics.'

'Delve how?'

'There's randomness, as we understand it, on an atomic level. There again, there's patterns and intelligence, too.'

'But there's randomness in nature, surely?' I asked, unable to believe that absolutely *everything* in existence was pre-determined.

'You tell me,' said Duke. 'Is natural selection random? Is the way one actual tree bears a fruit that feeds an animal that feeds another actual animal random? Is human civilisation basically the result of a series of random, unconnected events?'

'What do you believe?' I asked, almost afraid of the answer.

'I believe,' he said, 'that there's always some connection between one thing and the next. Always. But moving swiftly on from that. With Karen's help, I believe we could find out where the sequence started and where we are in the sequence. I'd need the manager's username and password to hack into the system and discover the algorithm. From the club where the game's called.'

'That's the Stockton Octagon,' said Leonard. 'They call all of the linked games. One of their callers will control the game on Monkey Night, do all the speaking and bring out the numbers. I'll just really be standing there like a bit of a lemon on the podium in the Pentagon, making sure everything goes smoothly.'

'Can you find out the username and password to their system?' Duke asked Leonard.

'I never really go there. We're not allowed to play bingo in our "sister clubs", in case of rigging accusations.'

'Could it be the same as the password for your system?' I asked.

'Nah,' said Leonard. 'Every club has a unique username and password.'

Something occurred to me.

'We're going to the Octagon on a coach trip,' I said, 'the day after tomorrow. We could find out the username and password then. What else would you need?'

Duke thought for a moment.

'I'd need lists of numbers from Octagon-called link games going back years.'

'How many games would you need the numbers from?' I asked.

'One a week, at least.'

I turned to Karen.

'I can remember those,' she said, dispassionately.

'I still don't get how . . .' Leonard floundered.

'Karen can remember strings of numbers,' I explained, 'and she's been a regular at the Pentagon since she was fifteen. That's at least three link games a week, for the last seven years. Will that do?'

'Should do,' said Duke. 'It may just be possible for Karen to extrapolate from all that information what numbers will be called during the Monkey Night game. I reckon that she could actually do it. Her brain's a strange and wonderful thing.'

'Right,' I said.

'Karen?' asked Duke, looking around for her. It seemed she'd left the table. I swung the beam of my caving light around until it discovered her crouched down next to the kitchen unit, wedging one of her flat shoes into the space between the fridge and the sink unit.

'Wha?' she said, defensively. 'There was an 'ole there.'

'Have you been listening, Karen?' asked Duke. 'Do you think you could do what we've been talking about?'

'Algorithm,' she muttered. 'Numbers, winning ticket. Why aye.'

Duke looked at her in fear and awe. I wasn't sure whether he wanted to kill her, study her or marry her.

He shook himself.

'Right,' he said. 'Moving swiftly on from that. Basically you can come and help me get the baby sharks from the boot of my car and into your actual bath.'

50

Hawaii Five-0

I was amazed that the shark eggs had survived a night in the hot, smelly interior of Duke's car boot. But sure enough, I could see them wriggling in their little silky sacs as I held the water-filled plastic bag up to the street light.

In my tiny bathroom, Duke filled the tub with cold water, and I added a generous amount of salt at Duke's insistence. It was tough-going, as my bathroom had no window, and one of my caving lights broke, ironically, when I stood on it in the dark. Though I tried to direct the beam of my remaining headlight to assist him as much as I could, Duke was working more or less blind. As well as the salt, Duke had brought along a small bottle labelled 'Aquasure Water Conditioner'. He added a generous dash of this to the mix.

'Makes tap water safe for fish,' he explained, when he saw me looking at the bottle.

I emptied the bag of eggs into the bath. The sacs floated for a second like tiny life preservers thrown to save the lives of drowning insects, and then sank beneath the surface.

Duke looked down at them fondly, like a proud new father contemplating his children's college fund. 'We'll need somewhere to move them once they get too big for the bath,' he said. 'Got any ideas?'

'Let me think on it,' I said.

All at once, Barnie barrelled through the bathroom door.

'Sorry. Can I come in here with you? Karen bit me.'

'Of course,' I said. 'Sorry. She gets bitey when she gets bored.'

Barnie blinked in the thin, intense stream of light emanating from my head. 'We should really arrange our next meet-up, anyway. Barnie, tomorrow you will order the bingo books and cover up your tracks just as we discussed. At break time, steal Tracey's mug from the staffroom. Karen and I will come to the Pentagon at eleven-hundred hours to get an update and collect the mug to bring to Duke.' It seemed important that I use the twenty-four-hour clock to express time. 'Duke. You meet Karen and me at the fish-foot salon in town at twelve-hundred hours.'

'Why there?'

'We have some business to attend to. When we meet, we'll pass the mug into your possession to dust for fingerprints and do your . . . condom trick . . . and we'll bring you up to speed. I'll find a base of operations. We can't divert the books to my address – a home address will look too suspicious.'

Duke nodded curtly.

'Hey,' he said, as an afterthought. 'How much of a cut are we actually getting each?'

'Oh,' I said. 'We'll just split it five ways, of course.'

'Hundred thousand each.' He shrugged. 'Seems reasonable.'

51

Tweak of the Thumb

'What in the name of Busty McGugan were you trying to say in that text?' asked Duke, bursting through the door of the fish-foot salon.

'Couldn't you understand it?' I asked, slightly offended.

'No,' said Duke. He took out his phone and read out the message.

> Krypton and I are
> scorching for a
> loves trig for book
> dovetails. Barbour
> has detonated the
> office and tomahawk
> he will divulge it.
>
> xxx

'Oh. It was meant to read: "Karen and I are searching for a location for book diversion. Barnie has detained the order and tomorrow he will divert it—"' I paused. '"—kiss kiss kiss." I pressed the right buttons. I don't know why the words didn't come out right.'

'Predictive text,' mumbled Karen.

'What?'

'The phone predicts what you want to say.'

'That's ridiculous. How could it possibly know what I want to say? Can it read fortunes? Tell the future?'

'It's clever.'

'Well, it's not, is it? Because it got it wrong.'

'It uses the first letter to guess what you'll say next.'

'Whoever designed that feature clearly failed to grasp the infinite unpredictability of humankind.'

I looked around the salon.

The lighting was dim, presumably better to show off the incandescence emanating from the four large fish tanks against the back wall. They were positioned at floor level, just in front of a strip of raised black leather seating.

Each of the tanks seethed with a mass of small fish, each around the size of a large stickleback and the colour and lustre of a fresh horse chestnut. The restless, twirling, intertwining shoals they formed within the tanks looked like silk scarves waved in interpretative dance.

Duke beckoned me closer.

'You mean you haven't found an actual location yet?'

'We're on it,' I said, confidently. Though to be honest, it was proving a near-impossible task. We needed an address that wouldn't ring alarm bells with the delivery man (Barnie was only diverting the *delivery*, not the order, so as not to ring alarm bells with the supplier). Somewhere the police wouldn't check that was secure and large enough to house several huge pallets of bingo books. I reached into my handbag and brought out a plain beige mug enclosed in a sandwich bag. I passed it down to Duke at hip level, extremely discreetly, and he took it with a subtle nod. We made no eye contact. When Duke realised he had nowhere about his person to conceal it, he simply placed it on his knee as he sat in the waiting area.

It was time to get down to the business of foot care.

'I've paid the lass,' said Karen, staring with some apparent trepidation at the row of tanks. Neenie, as you may recall, had given us the ten pounds each it would cost for a ten-minute treatment.

'Good,' I said. 'Duke, are you joining us?'

'I'll just watch,' he said.

'Isn't it meant to give yer HIV, or somethin'?' said Karen, her brow incredibly furrowed. 'I read it in the news when I got me last fish and chips. The water or the fish or whatnot, they can give yer HIV, if someone who's had HIV has had their feet in there.'

I shook my head.

'That's just scaremongering.' I paused. 'Scare fish-mongering, if you will.'

Karen seemed appeased.

Just then, a middle-aged woman appeared before us. Up until then, I realised, she'd been excellently camouflaged against the Egyptian Blue wallpaper, by virtue of her Egyptian Blue top and the low lighting. She held a portable foot spa in front of her like a votive offering.

'You's next, then?' she asked, even though we were the only people in the salon.

'Yes,' I said, 'us next for the aquatic pedicure.'

So this was the Bastard Fish Woman (henceforth BFW) who was stealing all of Neenie's trade. She did look a little like a fish, in the face department. Her lips were large and fleshy and her face was vaguely scaly with what might've been mild psoriasis. I noticed the ring and middle finger on her right hand both ended in smooth stumps at the first knuckle joint, and the thumb, index and middle finger of the left were entirely missing. I hoped this was not the result of testing out her own treatments.

'I need to check yer feet for cuts and stuff,' she said, bending to place the foot spa on the floor just in front of us and revealing, in the process, a sweaty, possibly bottomless cavern of cleavage.

'Shoes and socks off.' Her demeanour and facial expression seemed relaxed, but every other word she spoke sounded cracked and painful, as though she were, in actual fact, terrified.

I toed off my black chandelier rhinestone sandals and peeled off my pop socks with a flourish. I'm rather proud of my feet. Today I was wearing a glossy single-coat nail polish in Fandango purple. Karen was somewhat more reluctant (her feet are not her best feature), but nervously, and with some difficulty, rolled up her leggings to the knee and slipped off her flat black pumps. The hems of the leggings left red raw indents around her chubby ankles.

After submitting to a foot-check and a quick, bubbly dousing in the foot spa for each of us, we were escorted to the fish tanks and told to take a seat on the raised chairs. It was something of an achievement hoicking myself up without dropping the water-filled sandwich bag of fish currently clenched between my soft thighs, but I managed it.

'Before yers put yer feet in, I'll warn yers.' Ignoring the look of terror on my face, she went on. 'It'll feel weird. Really weird. But don't tense up, or it'll feel weirder.'

I nodded mutely.

The BFW waggled her abbreviated fingers encouragingly.

'Go for it,' she said.

Simultaneously, Karen and I lowered our bare feet into the tank.

'What's it like?' asked Duke, observing wide-eyed from a chair in the waiting area.

It was quite unpleasant.

'It's quite unpleasant,' I said.

I looked at Karen, to see her eyes wide and her mouth hanging open like a dead guppy.

Yes, it did tickle. In fact, it sent ribbons of tingling, electric sensation from my toes, where the fish were nibbling, up my thighs, past my abdomen and all the way up to my earlobes. I must admit that I was so arrested by the sensation that I completely forgot about the mission at hand. Before I knew it, our allotted ten minutes had expired, and the BFW was helping us down from the seats.

My feet felt like they'd been eaten entirely off. I was relieved to look down at them and discover that they were still intact.

As I was pulling on my pop socks, I wondered how on earth I was going to complete my side of the bargain. The BFW was now hovering, assisting Karen with her shoes, and there was no way I could get the bristlenose plecos into the tanks unnoticed.

I quickly formulated a Plan B.

'Execute Pattern 21A,' I whispered quickly into Karen's ear. She gave me a knowing look, and a brisk nod.

52

Danny La Rue

'Oy,' said Karen, beckoning the BFW over towards the window.

'Yeah?' asked the BFW.

'Yer mam's a lesbian,' said Karen.

'Yer what?'

'Yer mam's a lesbian.'

'What?'

'Yer. Mam. Sa. Lesbian.'

'No she isn't.'

'Yeah she is.'

'But she isn't.'

'I know she is.'

'How?'

'I've shagged 'er.'

'Yer don't even know 'er.'

'Yeah I 'ave.'

'What are you on about?'

'Me shaggin' yer mam the lesbian.'

'Me mam's straight.'

'Yer wha?'

'She's heterosexual. Me mam. She was married to me dad for fifty-seven years before 'e died. She's ninety-two now, and she's in a care 'ome.'

'Yeah, well, she's a lesbian, and I've shagged 'er.'

'Are you tryin' to be funny?'

'Well, I 'ave.'

'Well . . . doesn't that make you a lesbian as well, then?'

'Yer wha?'

'Well . . . if you've shagged me mam, doesn't that mean you're a lesbian as well?'

'Yer mam was just a one-off. Anyway, I don't mind bein' a lesbian and yer mam does.'

'I don't get it.'

'Yer dad was there as well.'

'I told yer – me dad's dead.'

'It was before 'e died. 'E wanted to watch.'

'What?'

''E watched while I used a dildo on 'er.'

'Right. That's not on. Gerrout. Alleryers.'

The conversation gave me more than ample time to reach beneath my skirt, detach the sandwich bag from my knickers, undo the elastic band and deposit one bristlenose pleco in each tank. Karen was still going strong.

'Yer sister was there as well.'

'I don't even 'ave a sister.'

'Yeah, well, they must've lied to yer, because she was there.'

'If yers don't gerrout, I'm callin' the police.'

'She was well into it. She was in crotchless knickers.'

'Do yer want me to bat yer?'

'She was watchin' while I teabagged yer dad.'

'Teabaggin'? I know what that is. I've got the Internet. Yer askin' fer me to bat yer?'

'I was teabaggin' 'im, and then I gave 'er a cream p—'

I crossed to the window and took Karen by the hand.

'Certainly we'll leave your establishment,' I said, already moving towards the door. 'I've heard one can catch HIV in these

places, anyway.' We left the BFW on the verge of a violent
outburst, her fists clenched at her sides ready to swing.

'Well done, old thing,' I said to Karen once the three of us
were safely outside.

Then we lingered for a while by the window to watch the
carnage. I took out my phone and dialled the salon's number
(emblazoned on the sign above the door). We watched the BFW
walk to the reception desk and pick up. Putting on a Swedish
accent, I asked to book an appointment for next Thursday.

The BFW thus otherwise engaged, we were free to watch the
bristlenose plecos – ravenous after two days of starvation – go
for the Garra rufas with grim efficiency. Some minutes later,
they were neatly reduced to a collection of tiny, delicate white
spines precipitated at the bottom of their tanks like a light dust-
ing of snow.

'*Adjö!*' I said into the phone. 'And by the way . . . *din mamma
är en lesbisk.*'

We scarpered. All the way, Duke laughed his evil-genius laugh.
The one that sounded like he was planning to take over the world.

'Mwahahahahahaha!' it went. 'Mwah. Mwahaha. Ha.'

Neenie would be over the moon.

53

Stuck in the Tree

In the dark, the magnificent rigging of HMS *Rosielee* looked like the half-finished home of a gargantuan spider, silhouetted as it was against a flesh-coloured full moon. Karen and I cut through the car park of the Historic Quay Heritage Museum, over neat new cobblestones as pink as babies' bottoms. Here, on this expanse of friendly coloured, pastel paving, is where they hold the Farmers' Market every first Sunday of the month. We rounded the corner to the long walkway by the harbour where the boats were moored, and strolled along between the water and the strip of abandoned office buildings, their 'FOR RENT' signs held up hopefully on the brickwork. To our right the wind churned the water into black, choppy waves, tall and distinct as meringue peaks.

Karen and I supplemented our income every so often by pilfering pennies from the bowl in the monkey statue. A ticket for the coach trip to the Stockton Octagon, including the bingo entry, cost ten pounds fifty – three weeks of visits to the monkey statue and we'd nearly amassed enough to cover the excursion. One more haul should do it.

I ventured forth on to the lock. Karen remained behind a little to keep a lookout. This late at night, the lock master would have left his post – no boats pass into or out of the Marina between 10 p.m. and 6 a.m. My high heels made the metal floor of the bridge reverberate impressively, like the distant industrial clanging you hear from edge-of-town steelworks. When I reached the centre of the bridge, I assessed the situation. As luck would have it, there was a boat moored just five feet or so to the left of the monkey statue.

It was the *Deerpool Maiden*, the boat that takes people on tours of the coastline, to Seaton Carew and back again.

Why anyone would pay for such is beyond me.

Her hull was long and yellow, her mast was thick and white, and her rigging was white as well. Easy enough to see in the dark.

I looked back to see Karen standing beside a stack of blue and red cans of Calor Gas by the hoist. She was amusing herself by performing a small improvised dance – restrained, but still entertaining. For musical accompaniment, she drummed the cans of gas with a twig and a stone.

'Careful,' I shouted.

'Fuck off,' she replied.

It was a particularly frigid night. A layer of tiny ice crystals clung to the statue.

It would be slippery; harder to grab.

This would be tougher than usual.

54

Clean the Floor

I planted one high-heeled shoe over the middle bar of the barriers and heaved myself up until I could plant the other shoe on the top bar. Then, with extraordinary acrobatic skill, I launched myself forward onto the thick white central mast of the *Deerpool Maiden* and clung to it for dear life, my legs and arms wrapped around it in something akin to a mad lover's embrace. Immediately, I shimmied down and, letting go just a beat too soon, dropped heavily to the deck of the boat, jarring the bones of my ankles.

Regaining my balance, I clambered over various oddments and fittings – three large white funnels stuck up from the deck, thick as big tree trunks and curved at the top like periscopes or creatures from Tellytubby Land. I peered into the dark round 'face' of one and saw that it was hollow. I resisted, however, the urge to put my arm into it.

Stepping over a candy-cane-coloured lifebelt, I reached the prow and prepared to swing myself up on to the statue. The best way to achieve purchase, I reasoned, would be to lean forward, jump, and wrap my arms tight about the monkey's neck and my legs tight about his crossed legs.

This was easy enough to contemplate, somewhat more difficult to actually perform. I found myself clinging for dear life to the cold metal neck, my legs flailing in the night air, a small, sudden icy breeze shooting up my knickers and reducing my balls to shrivelled, frozen snails. One shoe fell off and breached the surface of the water with a resounding plop. After several tries, I managed to swing my legs around with enough momentum to encircle the monkey, hooking my ankles tightly to keep them in place.

I peered into the money trough cradled between the monkey's legs.

Oh dear.

'It's frozen.'

'Wha?' shouted Divvy Karen.

'It's frozen,' I repeated, through exhausted, almost-panicked panting breaths. 'The bowl's full of water and the coins are all frozen solid. Shit and buggery.'

It was true. At least six inches of thick ice lay between me and the money in the bottom of the trough.

'Can you hack away at it wi' summat?' shouted Karen, her voice shrill and resonant in the still, freezing air.

'With what?'

'I dunno. Yer elbow.'

Had I not been otherwise occupied, clinging on for dear life, I would have shot her a withering glance.

'Toss me your lighter,' I shouted, breathing out billows of snowy white vapour into the monkey's face. Seconds later, a tab lighter hit me on the side of the head and bounced off into the trough, landing on the ice with a resounding crack and creating a quite attractive spider-web shatter on its surface.

With a supreme effort I shimmied my weight up the statue, wrapped my right arm tight about the neck as though joshing with an old drunken friend, and with my left hand grabbed the lighter, flicked my thumb over the flint and held the long, steady flame against the ice. It began to melt.

Just then, I became aware of voices other than Karen's, booming from over near the Calor Gas cans.

55

Snakes Alive

I craned around with some difficulty to see two rather dubious-looking youths in replica Burberry shouting imaginative insults at Karen.

'Yer meff,' said one of them. 'Yer mam's a lezzer.'

The other, who was pushing an Almart shopping trolley, using it like a scooter to launch himself forward every few steps, sang a self-composed song:

> *Divvy Karen, Divvy Karen,*
> *Yer mam's a lezzer and you stink.*
> *Divvy Karen, Divvy Karen,*
> *You smell like other mingers' twats.*

To my astonishment, he sang this to the theme tune for *University Challenge*.

I gripped the monkey more tightly. They hadn't seen me. I was largely obscured, I realised, by the boat hoist and the rigging of the *Maiden*, and they were in any case rather focused on their persecution of Karen. As concerned for her as I was, I knew I could trust her to keep them occupied until my mission was complete.

I held the flame hard against the ice, gnawing impatiently at my bottom lip until it bled. After ten seconds or so, the ice began to thaw in earnest.

Karen had begun to dance. Good girl. I saw that the youths had taken out their phones and were busy filming her with their in-built video cameras. I knew that this was Karen's intention. Certain townsfolk take uncommon pleasure in capturing Karen and me, separately or together, on video and uploading the films for people to watch on their Pads and Pods. I hear that they're rather popular, and receive in excess of one thousand 'hits' a day (this, Karen tells me, does not mean that people strike, cudgel or flagellate the videos – but to me 'watch' and 'hit' seem like the two least interchangeable words one could think of). You may imagine that I find the existence of these videos mortifying and degrading. In truth, though, I've always been of the mindset that no publicity is bad publicity. And I'd far rather receive 'hits' on a website than the more conventional and painful hits I used to receive far more frequently, before the unenlightened contingent found this new outlet for ridicule and abuse.

At last. The ice had nearly melted.

56

Was She Worth It?

I ruined my fresh manicure on the remaining few millimetres of ice, cursing until, finally, I was able to prise out the first few coins – mostly coppers – with a sense of satisfaction akin, I'm sure, to an archaeologist unearthing fragments of brontosaurus bone. I held the lighter flame against the ice again, and before long had reduced it to a soup of freezing slush, from which I fished out the remaining coins like unwanted croutons.

I had no time to count it. I stuffed it down my bra, shivering and convulsing at the nitheringly glacial temperature of the coins, and stretched out a tentative leg to reboard the *Deerpool Maiden*. The tip of my unshod, stockinged foot made contact with the prow. I used my arms to push myself away from the body of the monkey and plant my other foot on the boat as well, and at last I fell hard onto my knees on the deck.

I waited until the youths had tired of their taunting and retreated. Then I shimmied back up the mast, climbed back down on to the lock gates and hopped back onto the lock, wobbling to Karen's side on shaky legs.

'Are you all right?' I asked, taking her by the shoulders.

'Yeah,' she said, as though I'd asked her if Pinocchio had a wooden penis.

'Good,' I said.

Then I gave her a fierce hug.

'Fuckin' 'ell,' she said, 'yer tits are freezin'.'

Over her shoulder, I had a perfect view of the monstrous structure on the small island in the centre of the Marina waters. Smithson's Landing, it had been called at one time. It was a deserted and derelict building of enormous size. Something of a factory-warehouse type structure, it began life as an indoor shopping complex dedicated to high-end designer clothes outlets. Unable to scrape up enough of a customer base, the enterprise floundered and quickly sunk – both figuratively and literally as it happens for, owing to a slight structural error on the part of the architect, part of the north-west end of the building had descended into the waters. Karen and I had occasionally taken refuge at Smithson's Landing on particularly cold nights, when I was between tenancies and Karen temporarily expelled from sheltered accommodation due to some or other misconduct.

The skeleton of the old shopping mall remained – large, sun-bleached androgynous spectres of stick-thin clothing models gazing grimly from Prada and Ralph Lauren billboards; the hollow cavities of River Island, Jack Wills and Edinburgh Woollen Mill yawning soullessly into the great wide space of the main concourse. The two central elevators were forever stalled. And in the far left corner, at the very back of the place, a section of the flooring had fallen away to reveal a small pool of cold, dark water, connecting the inside of this synthetic cavern with the wider waters of the Marina without. The foundation had collapsed in such a way that this area of water was somewhat sectioned-off by timber and debris (I had attempted to take a bath in there before). I had little idea what size a zebra shark would grow to, but I would suppose there'd be enough room in there for at least one of them fully grown.

And as for the shipment of bingo books – well. There was room for five hundred shipments of bingo books, as well as an adult elephant and a double-decker bus, should our scheme suddenly require the latter two objects. It wasn't out of the question. I'd never have anticipated that a zebra shark would enter the mix, but there you go.

This was it. Our Base of Operations. Our Hideout. Our Headquarters.

The nerve centre of the whole darn scheme.

57

All the Beans

The coach was grumbling and heavy-breathing at the front of the building, hogging four disabled parking spaces. A substantial crowd of regular customers had set up camp just outside the vehicle's doors, and were eyeing the driver intensely, attempting to guilt-trip him into letting them on early. Neenie was heading the troop, much like a power-crazed general.

Fixing the driver with a stare, Neenie drew herself up to her full height and said, in a loud, clear voice, 'It's cold. And we are old. This woman is ninety-five.' She gestured vaguely over her shoulder to no one in particular. '*Do you have no feelings?*'

One lady with a pink rinse used the head of her walking stick to rap on the glass of the bus doors. The driver wasn't budging. The coach sighed loudly, spicing the early morning air with poisonous fumes, but the doors didn't open.

Dawn had not yet risen. I refer to the sunrise – not Neenie's second niece, Dawn Carruthers. She had evidently risen, as she was sitting quietly on the bench beside the ash tree on the right, chain smoking and touching her own face self-consciously, as if examining for blemishes by feel.

'All right, Dawn,' I said.

'All right, Maurice,' she said. 'You all right?'

'Yeah,' I said.

She continued to prod her own right cheek.

'Not coming off, then?' I asked this in reference to the unsuccessful spray tan she had recently acquired, gifting her of late with the moniker 'Spray Tan Dawn'. Or, amongst the crueller of the populace, 'Oompa Loompa'.

'You're comin' to Stockton, then?' she asked.

'Yes,' I said. 'Do you like my ensemble?'

Today's outfit comprised a S'NOB de NOBLESSE oriental-print blouse, a slate-grey ponte pencil skirt and a Linea Weekend cardigan in sky blue. Underneath I wore my Elle Macpherson Intimates jade lace contour bra.

'Yeah,' she said, 'it's all right.'

'Ta,' I replied.

I became aware of Karen scampering across the car park. She'd insisted on sleeping in an extra half an hour, much to my chagrin.

58

Make Them Wait

Barnie chugged into the car park in his battered green Reliant Robin, parking in his usual spot near the hardy perennials with a worryingly violent, jolting halt. His enormous form unfolded from the tiny ramshackle vehicle like so many clowns pouring from a clown car. I tried to imagine him flying a light aircraft. I couldn't. As he approached, I noticed that he was holding a large Almart bag stuffed to the brim with Something Or Other.

'Mornings, all,' he called to the assembled crowd. Barnie pluralises his greetings and farewells, should there be more than one person present. To one person, he might say, 'Good morning'. To two, he would invariably say 'Good mornings'. It seems to me to make grammatical sense, and I have often thought of adopting the habit myself.

Barnie drew a clipboard from the Almart bag and, reading from the paper attached to it, began hollering out names and ushering us one by one on to the coach, whose doors had grudgingly hissed open during the pantomime of his arrival. As we were called aboard, I fished in my handbag for Duke's doctored condom, and as Barnie ushered me up the stairs I passed it to him with astounding legerdemain. (I'd enclosed it in a sandwich bag, of course, to keep it moist and preserve the delicate fingerprint etching.) Barnie slid it quickly into his trouser pocket.

Karen and I chose a seat somewhere in the middle, in case there was a crash and the front or the back of the bus got dunched in. We ended up right behind Neenie and Sheila. I motioned for Barnie to take a seat behind us, so that we could discuss important matters.

Before long, we were merrily under way.

'You remember our task once we get there,' I whispered to Karen, as she stuffed an entire Snickers bar into her mouth, deep-throating it like a pro. 'We find a seat close to the caller's podium. Just as the game starts, we create a commotion – just as we planned. Barnie thus gains access to the podium and notes down the username and password for the RNG.' Karen nodded.

I leaned back to see whether Barnie was awake. Thankfully, he was.

'Barnie,' I whispered, 'we've found a location to divert the books.'

'Oooh,' he said, a little too loudly for discretion.

'Shhhhhh,' I told him.

'Sorry. Where is it?'

'Smithson's Landing.'

'The old shopping centre?'

'No one would think to look there. It's not even checked by the police – it's too structurally unsound for them to go in. And there aren't any squatters, I've checked it out. People are too scared of the floor falling through.'

'The floor might fall through?' He looked a little concerned.

'It probably won't,' I said. 'Or not all of it. I'm going to text message Duke tonight to let him know.' Karen shot me a stern look. 'Or Karen will text message him,' I said. 'I don't seem to be able to master something called "Predictive Text".'

'When we get back, then,' said Barnie, 'I'll sort out the diversion with the delivery company.'

'Good man.'

We lapsed into silence.

Feeling boredom lick at the edges of my consciousness, I leaned forward and poked my head between the seats in front. Neenie was looking intently out of the window, while Sheila lounged half-asleep, her neck braced in a horseshoe-shaped air cushion.

59

Brighton Line

'Hello, Neenie,' I said, quite loudly. Sheila's eyes popped open. She looked down at me and shrieked.

'Yer bastard,' she said. 'I nearly shat meself.'

'Bit of fun, this excursion,' I said, 'don't you think, ladies?'

'Yeah,' said Neenie. 'All together like the folks of Shields. Whoever those bastards are.'

Karen interrupted with the matter-of-fact demand, 'Bag,' dragging me out of the range of stimulating conversation.

I whipped a sick bag from the cardboard box and handed it to her. No sooner had she peeled open the top than she lurched forward, made the most unpleasant and guttural sound I'd ever heard and filled the bag with rancid and watery vomit.

'Are yous two goin' to that Monkey Night next month?' asked Neenie, with a note of disapproval in her voice.

'Hmm . . .' I said, attempting nonchalance, 'we might, I suppose. The prize they're offering is certainly an incentive. You never know, do you? Are you going?'

'Nah,' said Neenie. 'I don't like special nights. Too many people. Someone always takes me seat. Besides, there'll probably be some bugger dressed as a monkey jumping out on folks that'll scare the bastard shit out of me.'

I nodded.

'Still,' she said. 'A monkey made of solid gold.' She shivered and let out a small moan. 'What yer could do with that, eh?'

Karen remained silent, hunched over her sick bag.

I dozed off for a while, only mildly distracted by the wafts of stomach-acid stench from Karen's general direction.

When I woke, it was to the reedy strains of an off-key campfire song.

'There was a farmer had a dog,' everyone shout-sang, *'And Bingo was his name, oh!'*

The only passengers not singing were Neenie and Sheila. Karen was singing as well, waving the sick bag around rather danger-ously. I snagged the bag from her grip and held it safely away from her. It felt warm, fleshy and malleable, like a breast.

Neenie and Sheila were talking loudly enough to compete with the racket.

'I saw a documentary last night,' said Neenie. 'It was fascinat-ing. It was about this lad. And 'e 'ad this thing growing inside of 'im.'

'Really?' said Sheila.

'Yes,' said Neenie. 'It was this thing. And it was growing. Inside of 'im.'

'Was it?' said Sheila.

'Yes,' said Neenie. 'Inside of 'im. Growing.'

Sheila paused contemplatively.

'It was probably a growth,' she reflected.

'All together!' shouted Dot from the back of the bus, half-cut. 'Like the folks of Shields!'

'B-I-N-G-O, B-I-N-G-O, B-I-N-G-O and Bingo was his name, oh!'

I succumbed to the mob mentality and joined in as we careened round the roundabout towards the Stockton turn-off.

'What a stupid fuckin' name for a dog,' said Neenie.

60

Three Score

The Stockton Octagon is one of the forerunners in the New School of Bingo.

You see, there is something of a Renaissance taking place.

You'd be forgiven for thinking that bingo is inextricably inter-linked with seaside piers, working men's clubs, toaster and microwave giveaways and rhyming calls about pairs of clinically obese females.

Oh no. Not so. No longer.

Bingo is moving into the twenty-first century. True, it took a little longer for this revolution to reach the North East of England – we're a little more attached, perhaps, to our traditions and our inventive wordplay than the rest of this Green and Pleasant Land. But reached us it has.

The initiative is entitled:

TOP OF THE HOUSE

It is the brainchild of the enterprising conglomerate which owns sixty per cent of the large chain bingo halls in the country. This super-power, in fact, owns a fairly substantial chunk of all the gambling, gaming, holiday and entertainment centres in Great Britain.

Until early last year, they conceded that the North East was a little too set in its ways to accept their new master plan to . . . 'Jeooge Up' bingo.

So they introduced new ideas gradually. Peripherally.

Touchscreen slot machines. UniBooks (flip-books of all the session's bingo, attached in order. No need to shuffle the main, early and late session books around – it's already done for you), and so forth.

Eventually they thought, well, maybe these folks are ready for something bigger. We got them to give up coal fires, after all. Maybe, just maybe, they're ready for TOP OF THE HOUSE.

The Stockton Octagon was the guinea pig.

I'd never visited the Stockton Octagon before that day. I'd imagined it. I'd heard it mentioned in hushed, reverent tones – awed references to 'After Dark Neon Bingo', 'Pop Classics Bingo' and 'Hosts' who actually *walked amongst the customers* while calling, wearing *microphone headsets*.

As soon as I clapped eyes on it, I could tell that everything I'd heard was true. Even from several hundred yards away, as we careered around the roundabout in front of the building, the bingo hall shone like a beacon of tantalising, glistening Progress in the midst of a grey and featureless landscape. It was truly enormous – an expansive, flat structure the size of an aircraft hangar – and looked as though it might've been hewn from a block of lime-green Perspex. There was not a strut, a window or a beam in evidence. It looked like a giant Saharan lizard with its eyes closed. Quiet but not sleeping. Alert and listening, sensing, feeling through every pore in its skin.

We pulled into an area of the car park designated for coaches. There were five there already. The one closest to us read 'PANSIES SUPPORT GROUP' in large purple cursive lettering. From the motley collection of stricken-looking geriatrics spilling from its innards, I supposed it was the vessel of conveyance for some sort of bereavement group and not an organisation of troubled homosexuals.

'Right!' said Barnie, in a voice that sidled up and tapped nervously on the shoulder of Commanding. 'Exit the coach, passengers in the front seats first, please. WAIT by the entrance to the hall until all the party is assembled. NO ONE is to go inside until we are all together. Is this clear?'

After a vague murmur of agreement, the passengers in the front seats began to stir and, eventually, tumble out on to the pavement. There was some palaver with Dolly, a ninety-nine-year-old Alzheimer's sufferer, but at length she was hoisted through the doors and deposited into her wheelchair, and Karen and I dismounted the vehicle, breathing deep of the car park's petrol-tinged air.

'Are you coming?' I said to Karen. 'I'm buggered if I'm waiting around here.'

61

Baker's Bun

We lingered in the foyer of the Octagon. It was similar to the Pentagon's Front of House, but brighter, bolder and bigger. Even the customers looked strangely equivalent to our regulars. I recognised the Octagon's version of Teddy Boy Bob – a young man with curly brown hair clutching a small blue cushion embroidered with a grinning face. He was talking intently to the club's receptionist over by the admissions desk. From what I could hear, he seemed to be explaining to the young lady that he considered the cushion his adopted child. Over at the fruit machines was a print-bloused, be-trainered woman feeding tenners into her game at a rate of knots, a smaller, squatter lackey clutching a coin tub at her side. 'Just like Neenie and Sheila,' I thought, just a second before realising that it actually was Neenie and Sheila. Christ. They'd made a beeline for the fruit machines pretty sharpish.

'There you are,' said Barnie, chuffing to a red-faced halt beside me. He was clearly exasperated. 'If you would, please, remain with the party from henceforth,' he said. I turned to see the rest of the Pentagon crowd milling in a restless, amorphous cloud, examining their surroundings with barely contained astonishment. 'Put these on, if you please, if you would,' said Barnie. He handed me and Karen a pair of sparkly purple and silver deely-boppers each. I don't know how I'd failed to notice before, but I then saw that all the other members of the Pentagon party were also wearing identical deely-boppers, as casually and humourlessly as one might wear a scarf on a chilly day. 'Please keep your deely-boppers on at all times,' intoned Barnie, sombrely. 'That way we can easily identify all members of our group.'

The group nodded, setting off a glittering cascade of purple and silver ball-bobbing.

'We meet back where the coach dropped us off, 9.30 p.m. sharp,' said Barnie to the rest of the party. With that, the deelys dissipated into the crowd. Barnie then turned to me, a little furtively. He reached into his pocket and removed a small something clutched tightly in his fist.

When he unfurled his fingers I saw that his palm contained a tiny, green-haired, wrinkle-faced creature.

I snatched it from him.

'What is this?' I hissed. 'This isn't Chunky's troll. His had . . . dirtier hair. Its nose was scuffed.' I sniffed it. 'And it smelled of tobacco and Murray Mints and *front bottoms*.' This specimen smelled of nothing so much as Toys R Us.

'I know,' whispered Barnie, 'but I can't find Chunky's. I really can't. I've turned the whole blasted Lost Property cupboard upside down and inside out. We're going to have to distress this one to convince Chunky it's his.'

I wasn't too convinced of the wisdom of this plan. Still, it seemed there was little else we could do. I stuffed the troll doll into my handbag.

62

Turn of the Screw

The main hall of the Octagon was magnificent. Barnie had mentioned to me once that it was, in fact, a perfect octagon – eight walls, all of precisely the same length. It was also roughly three times the size of the hall at the Pentagon. Instead of the uniform rows of shabby upholstered chairs and sharp-cornered tables one expects of a bingo hall, this place was furnished more like an up-to-the-minute, sophisticated coffee house. Large circular tables were placed at intervals around the hall, and the chairs – capacious, plush affairs with tall backs and tapered dark wooden legs – weren't even nailed to the floor. You could *move* them around. The whole thing was startlingly casual. The lighting was dim enough to be acceptable in a bar, and there was *music* playing in the *main hall* – a high, wailing song in which some young androgynous-voiced individual was offering something to a wifey named 'Matilda'.

The bingo books had all been included in the price of the trip, and we'd collected these from Booksales without incident. Now came the problem of where to sit. This was always a tricky thing in a new bingo hall. The odds of accidentally taking someone's regular seat were high, and should this happen – well, it was a consummation devoutly *not* to be wished, to put it in Shakespearean terms. Once, in my novitiate days at the Pentagon, I'd accidentally sat in the regular seat of a heavy-set lady called Ethel who worked at the train station café. The resultant furore culminated in the arrival of several law enforcement officers.

We chose a table directly behind the caller's podium – an optimum spot for our planned commotion-causing. It didn't seem to be anyone's regular seat. At least, no one set off the fire alarm or came over with a knife, so I presumed we'd chosen wisely.

From our vantage point we could see both mainstage and Neenie and Sheila's chosen table over near the bar (they hadn't been quite as savvy in their seat selection as we). They were engaged in a heated conversation with two middle-aged women in skin-tight leopard-print dresses. Their deely-boppers were jiggling madly with their agitation. I thought briefly about going over and trying to calm things down, but with everything that had been going on lately I hadn't the energy. I left them to it. Barnie slid into a seat at our table just as the main session started.

'All systems go?' he asked. He had a pen, I saw, poised to note down the information from the RNG.

'All systems go,' I echoed.

63

Tickle Me

Their jingle was different to the Pentagon's. This one was revamped and rocky, with a heavy bass line and some clichéd electric guitar licks. It had lyrics, too, sung in a strained male voice far too high for the singer's range:

> *There's nothing like a game of bingo*
> *To take your blues away,*
> *So come along and take your seat,*
> *And play with us today,*
>
> *You could be a winner,*
> *And take away a prize,*
> *Or purchase from our bistro,*
> *For half-price pea and pies . . .*
> *At the Octagon.*

Aha. There was the Octagon's mainstage caller. I'd expected a clone of Leonard Overall, but this man was somewhat more slender and unintimidating, and he mounted the tall flight of stairs to mainstage in three artful bounds, like a gazelle.

'**Good evening, Ladies and Gentlemen.**' He was far more softly spoken than Leonard. I wasn't sure how he asserted any authority over the crowd, but sure enough a hush descended. **'Good to see you all here. And welcome – a thousand times "welcome" – to our visitors from other regional clubs today. We're thrilled to have you with us.'** I could swear I heard a low murmur of disapproval from the regular customers. Bingo clubs don't take kindly to influxes of strangers – no matter how eerily familiar they might be. **'Of course, it's not long until we'll be visiting you at the Pentagon, for Monkey Night,'** a slightly more approving murmur, **'and we're sure you'll extend us all the same warm hospitality.'** I wouldn't have banked on it.

'We're putting on something a bit special tonight,' continued the caller, **'in honour of our guests. After the final house is won, we'll let loose the RNG and bring out three more lucky numbers. If you win on any of these numbers, you'll take away one of our three outstanding chimeneas, as displayed on the stage-area behind me.'**

He pressed a button on his console, and the large, deep-purple curtains behind him parted slowly with a low, insistent whirr.

'What the fuck's a chimenea?' asked Karen.

I nodded towards the stage.

'*They're* chimeneas.'

Karen looked at them, utterly baffled.

'Sort of . . . miniature stoves-slash-chimneys-slash-ornaments you put in the garden,' I explained. 'There are thousands of them in IKEA.'

Karen nodded, seeming satisfied.

'I have a chimenea,' she muttered rhythmically, 'I got it from IKEA, I have a chim-e-ne-a, I got it from I-KE-A.' She continued to repeat this for a while, until I slapped her round the back of the head.

I opened my bingo book to the first page, and went to give Karen her dabber, when I noticed that she'd fallen silent and sat rigid in her seat.

'Sorry,' I said, 'I didn't mean to hit you so hard. You were having one of your "moments".'

She didn't respond. Her eyes were fixed on something behind my left shoulder. From their focus, this thing was over twenty or thirty feet away, though from their sheer glazed terror, this thing was undoubtedly horrifying.

A strange, tickling sense of surveillance crept across the back of my neck, much like a money spider that's fallen gently from the ceiling. And as with a money spider, I began to wonder how long it had been there, crawling around, before I noticed its presence.

A little warily, I turned my head to look.

At a table about fifty feet away, right next to a quietly glowing Cola machine, the artificial panel lights glinted horribly off Chunky's morbid cranial artwork. From a distance, the rendering of the exposed brain looked even more realistic. My stomach heaved. My blood turned to ice. I could see that the other patrons were giving him a wide berth, perhaps unnerved by his tattoos, or possibly deterred by his smell. He wasn't a regular here. They didn't know him. They were clearly and understandably frightened.

'Do you think he's seen us?' whispered Karen, nervously palming her upright bingo dabber as though trying to work it to orgasm.

'He must have,' I said. In any case, he'd see us as soon as we caused our deliberate commotion. 'He must've come by himself on the 95 bus. Just stick close to me. We'll be all right. He can't do anything while we're around people.' I glanced down at my handbag in desperation. 'There's nothing for it. We'll have to prepare the troll.'

64

Red Raw

There wasn't much I could do until the interval arrived. If I got up now, in the middle of a game, all eyes – including Chunky's – would be on me. I only hoped we could make it to a safe haven such as the toilets or the smoking shelter to sort out the troll doll before Chunky noticed us. Besides, we needed to execute our plan of action to get the RNG's username and password.

Divvy Karen's hoarse whisper crept unannounced into my ear, scaring the living shit out of me.

'Have you seen that show *House*?'

She was still marking her book while she talked. I knew she'd have glanced at the page and memorised the precise position of each number before the game started. She could probably mark them off with her eyes closed.

'No,' I said, my breathing slowly returning to normal.

'That telly show. *House*. That one about the doctor. Dr House.'

'No,' I said. 'Who's in it?'

'That one,' said Karen. 'That one who used to be gay with Stephen Fry before 'e ran away to America.'

'Oh,' I said, 'you mean . . . Actually I don't think he—'

'I was just thinkin',' she went on, ignoring me.

'What?' I asked.

'He'd get dead confused in a bingo hall, wouldn't 'e?'

'Who?'

'Dr House. He'd keep thinkin' everyone was shoutin' at 'im.'

I pressed my fingertips to my brow.

'Hush,' I said. 'I'm concentrating.'

'Soz,' she said.

'Nay bosh, mosh,' I replied.

The caller paused for a moment, spun around and fixed us with a cold stare. I was gaining more of a sense of his quiet command over his audience. I mouthed an apology, and he continued to call.

I wasn't even playing my book. I was monitoring Chunky carefully. I daren't keep my eyes on him for long stretches, in case he sensed me, but I kept him in my peripheral vision. So far he hadn't moved an inch. This did not make me feel any safer.

We were nearing the end of the first page, and it was time to act. I nudged Karen in the ribs. With that she slid out of her chair, trotted up the stairs on to the podium and tapped the caller on the shoulder. He looked a little startled and stopped calling, which gave her the opening to take the microphone from his suddenly slack hand and raise it to her lips.

'Next,' she said, 'we have Karen Cholmondeley, with her rendition of "The Summer of Sixty-Nine".'

All around me, patrons squirmed and protested, baffled and impatient. They seemed not so much concerned with *what* was interrupting the bingo – more incensed that *anything* should interrupt it at all. A distinct shout of 'Get her down!' surfed above the crowd like a rock star across a mosh pit.

Karen got halfway through the first verse before I noticed two members of staff – one of them managerially suited – hurry through the doors at the back of the hall and make tracks towards her.

Barnie took this as his cue to climb up on stage and intervene. He went to grab the microphone from Karen, and they staged a bit of a struggle for its ownership – Karen seemed to get a little caught up in this wrestle actually (perhaps she was method acting).

Eventually, though, Barnie prised the mic from her grip and gave it back to the caller, apologising as he did so and offering some detail of Karen's 'difficulties'. To hammer home the point, Karen removed one of her shoes and threw it out into the crowd, where it hit an elderly lady smack on the head, knocking off her knitted tam-o'-shanter. I kept my focus on Barnie. Sure enough, as the manager wavered indecisively between restraining Karen and comforting the clobbered customer, Barnie scanned the array of buttons on the mainstage console. He must have quite quickly located the one Leonard had described as the System Shutdown button, because a moment later the screens on the podium and around the hall went white, and then black.

The caller clocked the blank screens and sighed in exasperation. The manager made to mount the podium, but Barnie held out his hand in warning. 'She'll be all right once we've given her her medication,' he said. He gave Karen a Tic Tac from his pocket, which she scarfed obediently. Meanwhile at the podium, the caller tried to reboot the screens. He typed the username and password into the console. Barnie watched each finger like a hawk as it hit the keypad. The manager waited at the bottom of the podium stairs. Barnie led Karen down and back to our table.

'Is she . . . all right?' asked the manager. 'She won't do that again, will she?'

'No, no,' said Barnie. 'She's medicated now.'

'So sorry,' I added.

The manager knelt down between Barnie and me and said, in solemn tones, 'She can stay. But she can't be throwing shoes.' I nodded.

As the interrupted game eventually resumed, Barnie scribbled down the username and password on the back of his bingo book. Success.

I turned my thoughts to retrieving Karen's shoe – it seemed impossible to keep her shod.

What with both the shoe and the troll, I'd sunk into a troubled contemplation. Consequently, I was scared shitless when Karen shouted 'House!' loud enough to make my arse temporarily separate from my seat by a whole five inches.

'Will you shut up about Hugh Laurie?' I said. She clipped me round the ear.

'You divvy. I've got the house.'

It was then I noticed a claim-checker scurrying to our table. Oh.

Shortly thereafter, the caller announced rather grandly, **'Congratulations! You've won Chimenea Number Two.'**

Karen beamed. I was less thrilled.

'What the hell are we going to do with a chimenea?' I said. Karen shrugged and beamed some more.

And with that, the interval was upon us.

65

Old Age Pension

Karen and I huddled behind a large artificial yucca plant in the corner of the smoking shelter. It was actually more of a smoking *terrace*, come to think of it – vast and quite luxurious, with thick raw floorboards underfoot like a sauna, and a liberal application of artificial tropical foliage. Some tables, a few scattered chairs, and a hell of a lot of ashtrays. Although we were outside and un-covered, the air was hot and thick with tobacco clouds and fierce radiation from several outdoor heaters.

Karen was sucking hungrily on a cheapy tab. I fished the troll out of my bag, coughing as she blew smoke into my face.

'That soil in the plant pot,' I said. 'Is it fake or real?'

Karen stuck her hand into the yukka pot and felt the silty material cradling the plant's plastic stalk. She studied her finger-tips, and then reached back for another feel.

'I don't know,' she said. 'It's dirty.'

'That'll do,' I said. 'Give me some.'

She clawed her fingernails through the dirt and proffered a decent amount. It looked more like magic sand than anything else – slightly sparkly. I scooped some from her palm and rubbed it into the troll's hair. It tempered the pristine newness of the bright-green fibres, but it wasn't grotty enough. After a moment, I had an epiphany, brought the troll over to an overfull ashtray and dipped it in head first, stirring it around as though coating a basting brush with olive oil. That killed two birds with one stone – now it was filthy *and* smelled like tobacco.

A scuffed nose was easy enough – I rubbed the troll's face against the patch of rough brick wall just behind the plant pot. I then fished a Murray Mint out of my handbag and scrubbed it over the face and torso.

Adding the third layer of scent would be more problematic. After a moment's thought, I gave the troll to Karen and looked pointedly at the front of her leggings.

'Wha?' she asked, her mouth hanging open like a dead trout.

I looked again at the crotch of her leggings. Then I looked at the troll, and nodded meaningfully. She must've got the idea, because she shrugged, peeled away the elastic waistband from her stomach flesh, stuffed the doll down there and left it to . . . *absorb*. After a few seconds, she reached in to retrieve it, and I took it reluctantly by the end of the hair, between finger- and thumb tip, wrapped it in an aloe-vera-scented tissue and tucked it into my handbag.

'I hope it convinces Chunky,' I said. I was dubious.

We made our way out of the smoking shelter via a fire exit, intending to sneak around the side of the building and re-enter the hall by another fire exit near our table. That way, we reasoned, gave us the best hope of avoiding bumping into Chunky.

It was a futile endeavour.

We hadn't got twenty feet before I felt my arm twist behind me, and my face was slammed brutally against a brick wall. Now my nose was as scuffed as the troll's. Karen shrieked, and I heard a muffled thump to my right, though I couldn't see to determine what had happened to her.

And then, inevitably, that rancid breath against my right cheek.

I felt Chunky tighten his grip on my arm, and introduce another powerful restraining hand on my opposite shoulder. A bony kneecap connected painfully with the soft flesh at the back of my own knee.

I heard a scuffling and a shifting of gravel, and realised that Karen was regaining her feet – she must've been knocked off them with some force. Then I heard a voice, squeaky and indignant.

'Oy!' it said. 'We've got yer troll, yer meff.'

66

Clickety Click

For a barely perceptible moment, Chunky's grasp on me loosened. In the half-second reprieve, I took an opportunistic lungful of air, and then his fingers were around my throat again.

'Show us it,' he demanded.

'Karen,' I wheezed, 'get the troll from . . . my handbag.'

I heard her scuffling madly in the background and then the squeaky fart of my handbag zipper.

''Ere,' she said, standing on tiptoes to thrust the nude homunculus between Chunky's face and my own. Its hair ruffled slightly in the foul wind tunnel of Chunky's panting breath.

I was close enough that I could see his pupils expand and dilate, morphing like the autofocus on a camera lens, until the troll came into focus for him.

Then, quite suddenly, he released me and snatched the troll from Karen. I slumped back against the wall, weak from abating adrenaline. I watched as he relaxed his grip on the little plastic totem, cradling it with the same tenderness one might use to tame a frightened hamster. He studied it closely, and then from further away. Ran his forefinger over the scuff on its nose. Finally, he brought it to his nose and sniffed, long and deep, closing his eyes like a wine connoisseur testing a bouquet and stretching his eyebrows up towards his brain.

His eyes opened again, just the tiniest bit. He looked at me for a moment with something that might be forgiveness. Then he opened them fully and peered down at the troll again, turning it over to study its little bare bum cheeks.

Oh shitballs.

I braced for bollock impact.

Chunky took the troll by its hair, regarding it as though it was a hamster that had just bitten him. Then he crushed it in his fist and dropped it to the concrete just beside his left foot. Next, he took me by the hair, and forced my chin against my chest, angling my head so that I was looking directly at the troll. Then he slowly brought his Nike down upon the tiny naked creature, increasing the pressure until his foot was nearly flat against the ground. He worked his ankle left and right several times, slowly grinding the troll into the rough, unyielding surface of the car park.

Without removing his foot, he said, 'Where's the teeth marks?' He twisted his foot one more time. Oh *crap*. What an oversight. Chunky kept his troll clamped between his teeth when he played – incisors on buttocks – part of his strange ritual to ensure good fortune.

'I'm gonna be there on Monkey Night,' said Chunky. 'And if yer 'aven't got me troll, I'm gonna hang yers by the neck.'

He began to quietly whistle a familiar tune. It took me a moment to place, and then I realised that it was the Deerpool Monkey song. The one I'd taught Karen's class. The one she'd mentioned in her terrible essay. Apparently more teachers than I, over the years, had used it to spice up the syllabus.

In response to Chunky's threat, I could only nod mutely.

And as quickly as he had appeared, he was gone, slinking around one of the building's eight sharp corners, dissolving into the night.

67

Made in Heaven

By the time we made it to the designated meeting place, the rest of the Pentagon customers were already ensconced on the coach, and the driver looked as though he was seriously considering driving off without us.

Karen had graciously offered to carry the chimenea. They hadn't kept the box it came in (one of the cleaners had apparently thrown it out, the arsehole), so we had to take it home 'as was'. I felt a little guilty as I watched Karen stagger along behind me clutching its huge ceramic form, her arms wrapped tightly round the thing's neck, its stove belly compressing her own in a way that looked painful.

The coach had no luggage hold, so it was necessary to heft the chimenea on to the vehicle with us. Upon trying to leave it in the aisle, we were told quite sternly by the driver that it was a safety hazard. In the end, we had to transport it on Karen's lap.

The atmosphere on the coach was tense. With some gentle probing, I discovered that some unpleasantness had transpired between Neenie and Scruffy Maureen. Apparently, disoriented by the strange new atmosphere, Scruffy Maureen had accidentally hit Neenie in the right eye with one of her deely-bopper balls while getting up from her chair. In retaliation, Neenie had called her a 'Stupid Fat Cow', and there had followed a bitter confrontation, during which certain long-pent-up feelings about Maureen's colostomy bag had surfaced.

For the first ten minutes, I was somewhat on tenterhooks, and couldn't help looking around to check that Chunky hadn't slipped on to the coach alongside us. Eventually, though, I tired myself out with worry, and fell asleep.

When I woke, we were passing the end of Duke McGee's street.

I heaved myself out of my seat and tottered down the aisle to the bus driver, Karen behind me. As I passed Barnie, I nudged him awake with my elbow and muttered, 'Our stop.'

When I reached the front of the bus, I bent down to speak into the driver's ear.

'Let us off here, if you would, my good man.'

68

Saving Grace

Duke McGee thrived in ambient light. He could only truly comprehend information beheld at close range on back-lit LCD screens. His living space was as dank, hot and neon-lit as a tropical lizard's tank. There were wires as thin as hair, tubes as thick as a wrestler's bicep, strung around his skirting boards, crawling over his carpet like tapeworms clinging to the gut walls of an enormous infested organism.

There were more worms, in the form of streams, strips, shreds, swathes of paper, everywhere, strung in tangles over disused, archaic television sets, protruding in tongues from relics of gaping-mouthed dot matrix printers, drinking from month-old cups of mould-skinned, room-temperature coffee.

All of this you could only see in snatches, in the intermittent, flickering light from the screens of his pets, his children: his computers.

His flat hadn't changed in the five years since I'd last been there.

'Oooh!' I said, hurrying to his DVD shelf – a monstrosity that covered the entire back wall behind his foul green sofa. 'You still have *Ma Mère*. I thought I'd borrowed and lost that one.'

'Bought it again,' he said. 'Loves me a bit of French incest.'

'Damned right,' I said. 'Oooh! The full series of *Big Train*. Can we watch it?'

'Later, marrah,' said Duke. 'We've got actual business to attend to. Is Leonard on his way?'

'Karen just texted him,' I said.

The machine Duke sat at was a thing of beauty. Even I, who have never seen eye to eye with technology, could appreciate the aesthetic grandeur of this hybrid beast (tri-brid? Quad-? Quint-?). I'm afraid I will struggle a little in describing it. It looked like he'd taken a food processor, a retro 1960s television, a set of stereo speakers and a pan of linguini, piped in some Barry White and let them go at each other. And nine months later . . .

'Isn't she grand?' he asked, in his expansive Geordie tones. 'She's got components from a second-generation Apple Mac, amongst other things. She's literally like one of them animals they used to sew together from bits of other animals. In olden days. The ones they claimed were newly discovered species. Only this one is *real*. She works. She's *alive*.'

He sounded worryingly like Gene Wilder in *Young Frankenstein*.

He fell silent then, typing away solidly for at least three minutes. Not being fluent in computer speak, I can't reproduce exactly what he wrote. It was something eloquent:

A^%We0(t///shr34785klh3j)./////// 9(v

'I've been constructing a program that simulates the Random Number Generator on the Octagon's computer,' said Duke. 'Once I insert the correct algorithm, Karen can begin to determine where we need to be in the number sequence. From there we can find out our winning set of numbers. All we need to do then is find the right book to match them.'

He bashed at a few more keys, and up sprang an array of colours and numbers much like the one I'd seen on the screens of callers' podiums. A large black space for each number to appear as the caller pressed the 'Generate' button. To the right, a light-blue box with all the pertinent game information – the name of the book (early, main or late), the game being played (line, two lines or full house) and the number of numbers called. Beneath all this, what looked like a red brick wall, made up of ninety bricks in total. I knew from watching the callers that each of those bricks hid a number from 1 to 90, and as each number was called from the RNG, the pertinent brick would disappear to reveal the number. This way, the caller could keep track of which numbers had been called and which hadn't.

Barnie gave Duke the torn piece of bingo book from the Octagon upon which was written the username and password. Duke grinned, pushed himself on his wheelie chair until he arrived in front of another screen three feet to the right, and began to type again.

69

Your Place or Mine?

When Leonard arrived, the party really got started. We put the French incest in the DVD player and let it flicker in the background as Duke typed and worked and hacked and Leonard regaled us with The Memoirs of a Bingo Caller. Duke's horrible green couch was large enough for all four of us, if Karen sat on my knee.

'Has anyone ever died while you've been calling?' I asked. Leonard winced.

'Two people,' he said. 'Hazard of the job. I've been calling for eleven years now, so statistically there should probably have been more. About eighty per cent of our clientele are over sixty, after all.' He was distracted momentarily by Isabelle Huppert thrusting her tongue into her son's mouth on the television, and then continued. 'The weird thing is – we have to keep calling. That's the procedure. The first one, I was young – only twenty-five. The woman coughed up a lung. All over the table. I knew we were meant to keep calling, but I stopped – I was shocked. Did the announcement for the first aider, and just stood there. And then I realised.'

Karen's mouth was hanging open and her eyes were wide. You would think Leonard was telling a ghost story around a campfire.

'They tell us to keep calling,' he went on, 'because when you stop, there's chaos. About fifty people crowded round the woman trying to help. The rest were sitting too far away to see what the matter was, and started chanting for me to restart the game. Hundreds of them got out of their seats and blocked the aisles trying to see what the problem was, so when the paramedics arrived they couldn't get through to help her. She was pretty much a goner by the time they started CPR. So the second time it happened – five years later, or thereabouts, when a woman had a heart attack during the late session – I kept calling.'

'I'm not sure . . . I'm not sure I could've done that,' I said.

'Aren't you?' asked Leonard. 'I kept calling and while the medics were resuscitating her the room were dabbing off their numbers and shouting on the lines and houses. When it comes down to it, it's really all you can do. Because when you keep calling, people don't want to miss the bingo. They don't want to miss the chance to win. I looked over, and the dying woman's friend was – and I still think about this – she was marking off her friend's bingo book, while the paramedics were pounding on her friend's chest. She didn't win, and her friend died.'

'An unlucky evening all round,' said Duke quietly from the computer.

He launched himself across the floor on his wheelie chair, crushing stray salted nuts and fossilised Monster Munch beneath the casters, until he was before another computer console – this one smoother, friendlier-looking and less Frankensteinian.

'I think,' said Duke, pressing a few more keys on this machine and then wheeling himself back to the first one, 'that I might be *in*.' He studied the screen closely. 'Yes,' he confirmed. 'I am *into the system*. Karen! It's time to calculate!' Karen leapt from my lap to stand at attention at Duke's side.

I looked at Duke's wheelie chair.

'Do you know,' I said, 'that if you sit on one of those wheelie chairs and you're really obese, there's a small chance that the internal mechanism will break and the steel pole in the centre will shoot up your bum hole?'

'Really?' he asked, looking vaguely worried.

'Yes,' I said, 'but don't worry yourself. You look to me just under the Body Mass Index that would qualify you as medically obese. How much do you weigh?'

'Twenty stone,' he said.

'How tall are you?'

'Five foot nine.'

'Ah,' I said. Throughout this last exchange, I'd noticed a persistent sound, a little like a drop of water falling into an empty sink, emitting from a smaller laptop computer sitting on the floor to Duke's right. *Bloop*, it went. *Bloop. Bloop . . . Bloop.* 'Your laptop is leaking,' I said to Duke.

'What? Oh. That's just Bronya.'

'Who's Bronya?'

'I told you. I met her on Plenty of Fish.'

'The marine biologist?'

'Yep. Two secs.' He slid off the chair and knelt in front of the laptop. As he looked at the screen, evidently perusing Bronya's message, his features softened, and he huffed out a tiny, affectionate laugh. He looked genuinely in love. I was happy for him.

70

Three Score and Ten

'What am I drawing on your back?' I asked, tracing a pattern on the small of Karen's bare back with the tip of my right index finger.

After a week or so, Karen and I had found the vast hall of Smithson's Landing a little overwhelming as a living space. Consequently we'd moved into a modest bungalow that I'd built entirely from bingo books at the foot of the escalators. The house had one room, roughly eight feet square and three feet high. The roof had been achieved by laying several MDF cut-outs of fashionable under-sixteens from the children's clothing section of River Island lengthways across the top of the walls.

It was cosy.

It was nice to have a fire. The chimenea sat just outside the bungalow's front door and went quite well with the understated decor of the place. I'd relocated bags of old documents from my flat that I'd been intending to shred, if I ever acquired a shredder. Burning them seemed like an ideal solution – they made very good kindling, and there was a near-endless supply.

'A cat,' said Karen. She always guessed 'a cat' first in the 'What Am I Drawing On Your Back' game.

'No,' I replied. I was drawing high up on her back, between her shoulder blades (she said it felt best there), though I couldn't stop my gaze from straying down to the angry scar left by the point of

Chunky's pen. The gash was healing, but slowly, and though we'd cleaned it as best we could, there were remnants of ink still trapped beneath the healing epidermis. It would be as permanent as a tattoo.

'A . . . shoe,' guessed Karen. 'You're drawin' a shoe.'

'No,' I said. 'It's not a shoe.'

In the dim orange light from the chimenea, the skin of Karen's back looked warm and edible. I traced the pattern again, more slowly, with the very tip of my French-manicured fingernail. No one else in the world can see it, but Karen's sex appeal shines as bright to me as the embers of burning debt-collection letters. She, too, is completely oblivious to her sex appeal, and this, to me, is what makes her so attractive. I've always thought that being sexy must be like living in the Garden of Eden. The minute one gains knowledge of one's sex appeal, one is out on one's ear.

'A skyscraper,' she guessed.

'No.'

'A trolley.'

'No.'

'A pack of tabs.'

'No.'

'A condom.'

'No.'

'A willy.'

'No.'

'A phone.'

'No.'

'A beefburger.'

'No.'

I ran my fingertip firmly over the flesh of her back one more time. It gave easily, like a sponge.

'A . . . a . . . a . . . a egg sandwich.'

'No,' I said. 'It's a smiley face.'

'Oh,' she said. 'I'll do you now.'

'Okay,' I said, scrambling to change places with Karen, lying down on my front on the collection of Florence & Fred winter coats we'd liberated from the cobweb-strewn Returns Storeroom of BHS. I hoicked up the back of my Windsmoor rose-pattern nightdress and laid my head on my folded forearms. Karen ran a small, cold finger across the flesh of my lower back, leaving a trail of goosebumps in its wake.

'Is it a cat?' I asked.

'Yeah,' she said, with an annoyed exhalation. 'How did yer guess?'

'A hunch,' I said, 'merely a hunch. Isn't it time to feed young Herb?'

She immediately withdrew her hand, which had been tapping out the rhythm to Herb Alpert's 'Spanish Flea' against my waistline. She scuffled and shuffled around until she was on all fours and squeezed herself through the little 'door' in the front of the bingo-book bungalow.

After a moment of ennui, I too bestirred myself and crawled out into the open.

'Herb' was Duke's zebra shark.

Karen was squatting near a hole over in the far corner near Adams children's clothing store. She was peering into the dark area of confined water where we'd housed the creature. I can't say I'm a massive shark fan, but as sharks go, I must admit, Herb was rather endearing. Three of the four shark eggs had perished, but Herb was a strong little bugger, and from the moment he'd wriggled out of his egg sack it had been clear he was a survivor. He wasn't very big yet. About four feet, give or take an inch. A pale, attractive beige, with a pattern of darker spots arranged into broad stripes. He had tiny white inquisitive eyes, and a boisterous, playful demeanour that reminded me of nothing so much as a youthful golden retriever.

He'd certainly bonded with Karen.

It would be a shame to have to part them when it came time to ship Herb off to Duke's beloved marine biologist, Bronya.

Karen bent down to tickle his blunt nose, and then tossed a reduced-price Almart bun into the water. He would humour her with the buns, nosing them about until she went elsewhere, but I'd never seen him actually eat one. I suppose he found plenty of smaller sea creatures in the depths beneath the shopping centre to satisfy his appetite.

Our worldly belongings were piled to the left of the escalators – several dozen cans of Almart beans and sausages, the black bags full of clothes and my tape player and shoebox full of Herb Alpert cassettes. A meagre collection. To our right, beside the twenty-pence children's ride – Budgie the Little Helicopter – were piled the remainder of the diverted bingo books (the ones we hadn't used to build the bungalow). We'd identified and noted the serial number of the winning book. All that remained now was to get into the right place in the Booksales queue on the night to purchase it.

Just then, something caught my eye through the dark, filthy window of River Island. At once I pulled away from Karen and scurried over to the window, my stockinged feet slipping and sliding wildly on the beige and blue concourse tiles. I wiped my palm in a circle across the store's grimy windowpane. Peering through to the interior my suspicions were confirmed.

'Give me some assistance here, Karen, I've seen something you'll like,' I called, and she skidded to my side, her limbs flailing in all directions like a dog on a skating rink. She mirrored me as I hooked my fingers under the bottom of the metal grille barring the entrance to the shop. We began to heave upwards with all our might. Inch by inch, the grille started to lift open, releasing from the dark space within a gust of cool, stale air, heavy with the scent of festering organic moistness. Like a lover releasing a waft of morning breath into one's face after a long sleep.

I dived into the cavernous void of River Island.

And I emerged soon afterwards dragging my prize with me triumphantly.

71

Bang the Drum

'A trolley!' shrieked Karen. 'A trolley a trolley a trolley!'

'I thought that might perk you up,' I said, gesturing for her to jump in.

I rummaged through my cassettes, keen to choose precisely the right song for the occasion.

I had it. 'Zorba the Greek'.

When I turned back to Karen, she was already perched inside the trolley, squirming to get comfortable as it wobbled and skidded precariously on the slippery floor.

'Zorba the Greek' starts with a lively tambourine beat, segueing fairly swiftly into several bars of lightning-fast bouzouki plucking. In short order, the trumpet starts up, buzzing along faster than 'Flight of the Bumblebee'.

Smithson's Landing was the ideal venue for Herb Alperting. Once I got the hang of skidding along the slippery floor, I found I could use it to my advantage, building up a good head of steam and then leaning most of my weight on the trolley handle and letting our momentum carry us for several smooth yards, the soles of my feet sliding effortlessly along the tiles.

As the music slowed its pace, so did I, moving the trolley in smaller, more measured bursts, until I was almost waltzing with it. I spun Karen once, releasing the handle and letting the trolley revolve under its own steam for three dizzying circles, then I caught it again, this time by the other end, so that I came nose to nose with Karen, drawing the trolley towards me enough to plant a kiss smack on her smiling lips. Then I extended my arms, pushing it away from me smoothly and letting her slide apart from me, before dancing forward and clasping the handle again as the pace of the music picked up once more.

'Yeah! Yeeeeha! Yip! Yip! Yip!' shouted Karen along with Herb. She clapped along with the track.

At that point, I rather lost control of the vehicle and careened into the bottom of the right-hand escalator with some force. Karen spilled out like a sack of onions, sprawled face-forward over the bottom few steps. I shoved aside the dented trolley and came down on top of her, dragging her leggings down over her hips to her knees and marvelling at her incredible arse. I worked apart her buttocks, briefly considering going through the 'back entrance', though Karen hadn't been keen on it the last time we tried, and I was too worked up to stop and have a sensitive conversation. So I pulled down my knickers and nudged my cock forward to her front hole, moving myself in and out of her, just a little at first, in time to the music. Then a little more, and a little more. Until I was sheathed inside her completely, pounding away with shallow thrusts, panting hot breath on to the back of her neck and then licking away the condensed moisture. Herb Alpert set a blinding pace, and I must admit I struggled a little to keep up. But it was oh, so very good, and Karen was beginning to make little endearing yelps in time to the beat.

As the final trumpet blast of 'Zorba' echoed from the walls of the hall, coinciding perfectly with my ejaculation, I pulled away from Karen and turned back towards the warmth of the fire, yanking my knickers back up. Just the restorative shag I needed prior to the stress of the Monkey Night Heist.

72

Par for the Course

Barnie and Duke arrived around twenty minutes thereafter, and Leonard five minutes later still. Barnie sat primly on the bottom step of the motionless left-hand escalator, his legs crossed tightly. Barnie always sat, I realised then, as though he was afraid someone was going to steal his penis. Leonard sat on the floor near Barnie, on Barnie's coat, which he'd purloined to make a rug, and Duke sat in the driver's seat of Budgie the Little Helicopter, angled to the side so that he could dangle his feet out of the cockpit door. I sat beside the chimenea, with Karen nestled between my legs and leaning back lazily against my chest.

'People,' I said, to formally begin proceedings, 'I'd like to welcome you all to our official Eve of Heist Meeting. We have most of the elements in place. All we need to do now is to make sure everything runs without a hitch tomorrow night.'

The chimenea smouldered half-heartedly. There was more light and heat emanating from the glowing ends of the tabs we'd shared out before we sat down. Only Karen amongst us was a dedicated smoker, but it seemed somehow appropriate that we all lit up for this. I took a long drag on my duty-free Marlboro, rolling the acrid smoke around in my mouth until it coated my tongue entirely.

It would be a shame to dismantle the bingo-book bungalow. Still, Karen and I would have to do that tonight, and stack all the books back neatly into the pallets they'd come in, in order of serial number.

'Barnie,' I confirmed, 'you're opening up the bingo hall tomorrow at oh-eight-hundred hours. Duke's hired a van – you'll both have plenty of time to sneak the bingo books in the side fire door and swap them for the ones in the Booksales cupboard.'

'Yes,' said Barnie. 'Duke, be at my place for oh-seven-hundred. The Booksales staff start at 10.45 a.m. We'll have plenty of time.'

Duke had used his technical expertise to loop ten minutes of the club's CCTV camera footage (stolen by Barnie) into an innocuous-looking hour of tape. Barnie would replace the morning's tapes with this doctored footage. He assured me that the management seldom checked the CCTV reel, but we weren't taking any chances.

Duke looked at his cigarette with mild distaste.

'I prefer Mayfair Menthols,' he muttered. Then he lowered his tab to burn a series of juicy brown holes in Budgie's dashboard.

'Has anyone got a pen?' I asked the assembled company. Barnie immediately produced a silver Parker from his breast pocket.

I just needed something to write on. I scrambled to my feet and ducked into the doorway of River Island. Hurriedly, I undressed the top half of a male mannequin and carried the plain white t-shirt back to the group. I spread it on the tiles between us, and sketched a quick blueprint of the Pentagon.

'At nineteen-hundred hours,' I said, 'Karen and I will be here,' I pointed with the tip of the biro, 'in Front of House. Barnie – you'll be working, of course, but you'll need to keep an eye out for signs of Chunky. Do everything you can to stop him from entering the building.'

'I'll be in the gorilla costume, remember?' said Barnie. 'I'll be in and out, doing my "Fun and Theatre" bit.'

'Try to stay in Front of House as much as possible. Even if Chunky does get in, he can't do much to us in the Pentagon, with so many people around. He's probably planning to knack and kill us afterwards. We'll just have to be on our guard, and elude him on our way out.' I ran a sweaty palm through my hair. 'The Chunky Problem aside – at precisely 19.15 p.m. I will call Duke on my mobile phone to ensure he's hacked into the system successfully.'

'I will have,' said Duke. 'I worked out precisely how to do it the other night.'

'Still,' I said, 'we need to keep in touch. Communication is key. At this point, Karen and I will move over to Booksales, where we will linger by the change machine and survey the queue. Karen counts the exact number of people that buy books, allowing us to work out precisely when to jump into the queue and buy the winning book.'

'We have to be fifty-eighth,' said Karen. 'Fifty-eighth.'

'Leonard, you have the link key?'

Leonard produced a tiny silver key from his pocket. It was no more than three-quarters of an inch long, and flat, like a Yale key. I could scarcely believe that such a tiny thing could unlock such incredible possibilities.

'Excellent,' I said. 'So. We've won the full house. On the number 49.'

'Yep,' said Duke. 'You'll win on the forty-seventh number called.'

I nodded.

'While a member of staff is checking our claim, I text Duke – that's his cue to hack into the system and disrupt the link. Leonard turns the link key. No one else knows that the game is now in-house and in Leonard's control. He types in our Super Number. The number 39. It's ours. We shout. We win the golden monkey.'

'Then you get out of there as fast as you can, before Chunky can get you,' said Duke. I nodded. 'We should meet at the lock gates at midnight. I'll need help to get the shark into the tank in the truck – I'll have it parked beside the lock gates ready.'

'Duke, you said you knew someone who'd get the gold converted into cash for us?'

'Yes – actually some guys from a place called BullionBoys. I've used them before, when I needed . . . stuff melting. It's all basically above board. No questions asked. Won't draw any attention from the law. They'll meet us at Smithson's Landing at ten-hundred hours the following morning with the cash in duffel bags. We share it out, and go our separate ways.'

Without prompting, our thoughts clearly in perfect synchronicity, we all joined hands to make our Pentagon of Power.

'Good luck,' said Duke.

'No!' said Barnie. 'No. You never say that in bingo. It's bad luck.'

'What do you say?' asked Duke.

'May all your wins be big,' chimed in Karen.

Duke's massive fingers closed quite tightly over ours.

'May all our wins basically be big, then,' he said.

'May all our wins basically be big,' we echoed Duke as one voice.

Under the Tree

The mirrors and the Oranges were festooned with strings of green crêpe paper chopped messily into leaf shapes. They were supposed, I surmised, to give the impression of jungle foliage. The fruit machines were topped with larger paper leaves, and tied to their top boxes were bunches of brown balloons, coloured with darker brown felt-tip scribbles. It took me a moment to realise that these were supposed to be coconuts.

I'd never seen so many customers in Front of House. The place was heaving. Whether the tropical heat was emanating from their bodies, or management had cranked up the boiler to simulate a humid jungle atmosphere, I could only speculate.

I suspected the latter, for Karen and I were standing just inside the main doors, and the heater was certainly on full blast. A thick sheet of bone-dry hot air was draped across the threshold of the club, billowing slightly in the freezing draughts that invaded the outer doors. I was amusing myself by stepping backwards through it and then forwards again, like a child playing in a water-fall, taking some small thrill in the shivering full-body wash of sensation that enveloped me whenever I passed through it.

Through the undulating crowd, I could make out Neenie and Sheila on their usual perches before the fruit machines. So they did come after all. Neenie was trying her best, it seemed, to shut out the horrific clamour and kerfuffle, and the fact that 'Oobie Do, I Wanna Be Like You-Hoo-Hoo' from *The Jungle Book* was blasting over the speakers rather than something classy, like 'MacArthur Park'. She looked constipated with dissatisfaction. For a start, people were watching her play. Newbies. Non-regulars. Curious bingo virgins, lured by the atmosphere of *Fun!* and *Theatre!* that spilled from the front doors into the car park, where indeed more coconut balloons bounced on their strings in the icy wind to the faint strains of Louis Prima. The 'THIS CAR PARK IS FOR PATRONS ONLY' sign had, for now, been covered with a large paper banner which read, in huge, green and brown letters:

MONKEY NIGHT!!!!

WIN HALF A **MILLION** PONDS!!!!

It was clear that no one had noticed the typo, and I wasn't about to correct them.

I felt nauseous. The edamame-bean salad and two reduced-price wholemeal buns I'd eaten an hour ago sat uneasily on my stomach. Karen clung to me, looking a little lost. She didn't like large crowds. I squeezed her hand in an attempt to comfort her as we made slow and arduous progress through the squash of strangers towards the admissions desk – a condensed odyssey of frightening bodily scents, oblique conversational snatches and unwanted physical contact. (My elbow in someone's cleavage. Smell of wee. '. . . *You should've seen his face at the jumper!*' Whiff of cucumber. '. . . *Didn't he play a paedophile?*' A hip bone in my stomach. Stale sweat. '. . . *Wheat gluten what did it to me.*' Gasoline and pipe smoke. A large, soft bum cheek pressed up against my groin. '. . . *Had all her nerves removed last April in a ten-hour operation.*')

I pulled Karen aside for a rest by the fruit machines.

'Can you see Barnie?' I whispered, fishing out my phone from my handbag and thumbing a button to illuminate the screen. 19.05.

Two feet to our right, Neenie was approaching boiling point, rage practically radiating off her.

'Watchin',' she mumbled. 'All watchin'. Vultures. *Vultures.*'

'There were vultures in *The Jungle Book*, weren't there?' Karen said.

'Yes,' said a muffled voice from behind me. 'I believe they sang the "We're Your Friends" song.'

I span round, and nearly shat myself when I came face-to-face with an enormous, glowering, red-eyed gorilla.

74

Candy Store

'Jesus H. Christ,' I said.

'What's the "H" for?' said Karen.

'Shitballs, it's hot in this thing,' said the gorilla.

Recovering now from my shock, I remembered that this was Barnie. I was a little astonished at his language. 'I've never heard you swear before,' I said.

'I've never been inside a two-stone gorilla costume before,' he replied.

'Point taken.'

'And I've never been this warm in my life,' said Barnie. 'I'm expected to jump out on customers and scare them. I can barely walk. I'm about to collapse.'

'I'm sorry.'

'Not to mention the fact that about seventy per cent of our clientele is over eighty. I've nearly caused twelve coronaries in the last half-hour.'

'Oh dear.'

'Listen,' said Barnie. 'I've told the management about Chunky's threats. You don't have to worry. They don't want any trouble – not on a big jackpot night like this. They're not going to let him in. If he turns up, he'll be refused entry.'

This was an immense relief. Though it didn't eliminate the

possibility he'd be waiting outside for us after it was all over. In fact, it probably increased it.

Barnie reached out with one enormous, hairy arm towards the ledge beside the fruit machines.

'Give me my Sprite,' he said, like a surgeon demanding his forehead cloth.

He gestured towards a litre bottle of drink just beside Neenie's elbow, a long black straw poking out of its mouth like a periscope. I handed it to him. He poked uselessly at the front of the mask with the straw for a few moments before it seemed to dawn on him that there was no mouth hole. He peeled up the bottom of the mask, exposing his sweat-shiny chin and wide, red mouth, which he immediately stabbed with the straw. He proceeded to suck voraciously.

Handing me back the bottle and gulping for breath, he let the mask drop back into place.

'Right,' he said. 'I have to run about the hall for a while beating my chest with my fists. See you in a bit.' He thumped his chest. 'Fun and Theatre. Make 'em laugh.'

And with that, his large dark form was swallowed up by the crowd. A ripple of shrieks followed his blundering course towards Booksales.

'Fuck this for a game of chess,' said Neenie, snatching the chameleon brooch from the front of Sheila's M&S cardigan. She flicked open the catch to expose the pin. Then she stood up, burst every one of the coconut balloons tethered atop the fruit machines, and took her seat again, much pleased with herself. 'They were putting me right off me game,' she explained.

75

Strive and Strive

There was already a sizeable queue in Booksales. I counted eleven people. We took up position by the drinks and snacks vending machine opposite the desk.

Pretending to peruse the comestibles on offer, I identified the furry shadow of Barnie's masked head beside the Booksales computer. As the queue shifted, I saw that he was arranging tiny monkey key rings along the edge of the counter, ready to give to customers with their books.

Beside him, Trish-Who-Worked-On-Booksales reached under the counter, tugged out the rolling keyboard platform and started typing something into the console. It was then that a flash of green caught my eye.

Affixed to the platform, standing knee-deep in a generous blob of grubby Blu-Tack, was a disgustingly tooth-marked, smelly-looking green-haired troll doll.

Well, I'd be buggered.

'Barnie,' I hissed. Barnie turned. I gestured towards the troll. He angled his head carefully – it must've been difficult to see out of those eyeholes – and when he spotted it he actually jerked a little in surprise. I could imagine his face slack with wonder behind the mask. I motioned him forward. He waited until Trish's back was turned and then lunged forth, peeled it from the

Blu-Tack and tossed it in my direction. I caught it expertly and stuffed it into my handbag.

Euphoria quickly wore off. Trolls were the least of my worries.

Right now, it was all about the queue: we had to be fifty-eighth in line at the counter to nab the winning ticket.

I fired off a text message to Duke to check that he was all set to hack.

Are you all secateurs?

Bloody predictive text. He'd know what I meant.

Five minutes passed, and eleven more people joined the queue. Still no answer from Duke. I checked my phone every three seconds as Karen crouched clumsily, fisting the mouth to the vending machine. She was evidently attempting to reach the lowest rack of goodies via this unconventional route, and miserably failing.

'Karen,' I whispered, hoicking her up from her kneeling position.

'Ow!' she said, looking at me pitifully.

'Sorry. Do you think this text message has sent properly?'

She snatched the phone from me.

'Looks like it.'

'Then why isn't Duke replying?' I took back the phone.

I decided to call him. By the fifth ring, the symptoms of my anxiety were intense enough to be physically painful. I was sure I could feel an ulcer sprout and throb on my stomach lining. My calves were sweating inside my second-hand Debenhams hold-ups.

Finally, the line clicked and opened.

'Duke!' I said, quite loudly. Then, remembering myself, I hissed, 'Are you all ready? Is everything prepared?'

There was a muffled thump and some scrambling. Then Duke's voice, strangely reedy and slurred.

'I'm not *bashicly* ready. I'm . . . I'm sort of . . . well. Yeah. I'm not *quite* . . . getting there.'

Oh shit. Oh shite shite shite shite shit-balls.

'Duke, are you pissed?'

'Ha! What? Mr Vodka and Mr Brown Ale have been round to visit, it's bashicly true, but pished? What's that?'

'Oh CHRIST!' I shouted. I thrust the phone upon Karen, took her by the shoulders and looked her straight in the eye. 'Listen to me. I have to go to Duke's. Wait here. Watch the queue. Get in there and buy the fifty-eighth set of books.' I pressed a fiver into her hand (courtesy of Leonard. It was strange not having to buy free books, for once). 'Call me on Duke's number when you've bought them.'

Karen gave a brief, stunned nod, and looked around with mild panic, evidently realising she was to be left alone for a period of time.

'Karen,' I said, squeezing her biceps, 'you can do it. You'll be fine.'

She nodded again, though I could see her faith in herself was weak. No more time to reassure her. I had to go.

I pushed my way through the hot press of bodies, fell frantically through Front of House and burst out into the sting of the freezing night air. Duke's place was three minutes away, if I ran like a fucking cheetah. I kicked off my high heels somewhere near Wilkinson's traffic lights, dimly aware of them clattering across the pavement into the gutter. Shit. They were my favourites.

By the time I reached Duke's flat, I was encased in that awful variety of sweat you excrete in intense exertion combined with extreme anxiety on a cold day, and my lungs felt full of termites.

I leaned on the buzzer to number seven, until Duke's voice exploded from the speaker.

'Who's it?'

'Fuck! Fuckit, Duke, it's me. It's Maurice. Let me up, you arse of a twat of a shitting divvy.'

'Well, if you're gonna be mean to me, I bashicly dunno if I should.'

'DUKE!'

The buzzer sounded for the door release, and I shouldered my way through, taking the grotty concrete stairs three at a time.

Duke's door was standing open – oh so wonderfully discreet and secure for someone in the midst of a highly illegal defrauding plot – and I slammed it behind me as I stumbled over old food cartons and snagged my stockinged feet on bunches of tangled wires.

Duke was slumped over the keyboard of his modified Compaq, the backs of his knuckles brushing an incriminatingly empty bottle of Smirnoff. To his right were five more empties, of Brown Ale.

I hefted him up until he fell back against the swively chair.

'D'you know,' he said, 'if you're morbly obese and yer shit on one of these, the shentral pole can go up yer arse?'

I shook him once, and slapped him hard on each cheek.

'Listen,' I said, 'I haven't got time to find out why you're off your face, but rest assured we'll discuss that later, at length. Right now, I need you to wake the hell up and get with the programme.'

'Wha? Ah. Hacking. Pentagon mainframe,' he said, slowly and thoughtfully. 'Pentagon . . . pelican mainframe. Moving scwiftly . . . scwiftly . . . on from that. You know the shark?'

'What?'

'The shark. You know it?'

'What about it?'

'She didn't want it. She didn't want the shark. Bronya. It's all been for . . . bashicly . . . nothin'.' His eyes glistened with unshed tears. 'She wanted the shark, I got the shark. Now she doesn't want the shark. She ses . . . she ses she doesn't think it's gonna work between ush. She'sh met "Rodrigo". He'sh a marine biologisht too. She called . . . coupla hoursh ago. Been drinkin' shinch.'

'I'm sorry, Duke. I'm really, truly sorry. But you have to focus.

You have to hack into the Pentagon mainframe to disrupt the link game. It's nearly seven o'clock. We need you to do your stuff in less than half an hour.'

'Doesn't matter now. Just – doeshn't matter. Was gonna go 'way – go to 'merica – with her with my share. Don' wan' go on my own.'

'You'll meet someone else. You can't fade on us now. You need to go through with the plan!' I punctuated this sentence with four more sharp slaps.

I looked at the screen. A jumble of numbers that meant nothing to me.

'What does this mean?' I asked him. 'Is it set up to hack into the mainframe?'

'Main *frame*,' said Duke. 'Frain mame. Frainnn maaame.'

What was I going to do? I needed to stay here with Duke. Sober him up somehow. Make sure he hacked in at the right moment. But I knew Karen couldn't manage on her own. Karen couldn't cross the street on her own, let alone carry out one half of a golden monkey heist. She needed me there.

'Duke,' I said, taking him by the shoulders, 'I'm going to make you some of the strongest coffee in existence.'

Trombones

As I sprinted across the Pentagon car park, my right heel bleeding in the wake of a brutal encounter with a broken Bulmer's bottle, I was startled to find myself staring down the headlights of an angrily honking white Skoda, a blue flashing light atop its chassis.

Shit.

This was it. We'd been caught. Well. I supposed there was heating and occasional hot water in jail.

Another loud honk, and then the muted whirr of an automatic window being lowered and the head and shoulders of a policeman, popping up with the comic suddenness of a Punch puppet.

'Sorry, love. You all right?'

'Oh,' I fought to look innocent. 'Yes. I'm fine.'

'Watch where you're going, yeah?' He glanced at my injured foot. 'And get that foot looked at.'

'Ah. Yes. I will. Thank you, officer.'

And the car swung sideways into a parking bay.

It was only then that I noticed the commotion. There was shouting. Lots of it, coming from the Pentagon foyer. None of it intelligible. My stomach twisted at the thought of Divvy Karen in the centre of it all. What had she done to the queue? Or had she further provoked the lady at Booksales? Had Barnie been caught doing something surreptitious? What if they'd detected that the mainframe had been hacked? In that event, would they send for police officers in the first instance? It seemed unlikely.

But possible.

The police officers secured their vehicle and preceded me into the building in a neon-jacketed flash, and it was then that I saw Chunky, restrained by the upper arms by Barnie Gorilla, twisting and writhing like an ugly fish in a tangled net.

'You are not permitted to enter the premises!' said Barnie (though muffled by the gorilla mask, it came out as a disappointingly unthreatening '*Yournushpermtedtoenthpremses*').

A crowd of onlookers had gathered, and the two officers – I saw now that they were respectable-looking men in their mid-twenties – forged their way through the spectators as politely as they could.

'Stand back!' shouted Neenie from her perch on her fruit-machine stool. 'Fucking vultures.' The younger and more freshly scrubbed of the policemen gave her an odd look.

'He's barred,' said Barnie to the policeman.

'They've got no reason to bar me!' shouted Chunky.

'He's made violent threats against two other members,' objected Barnie.

'I never!' shouted Chunky. The whole exchange was made somehow more sordid by the *Jungle Book* soundtrack still playing in the background.

I saw the way to diffuse this. With a fearlessness born of proximity to triumph, I strode forward in my stockinged feet, reaching into my handbag.

'Chunky!' I said, loudly enough to be heard above the din. 'I've got something of yours.'

The men froze in a tableau of faint astonishment as I approached, holding out the object of our salvation before me at arm's length.

When Chunky caught sight of the troll dangling by the tip of its peaked hair from my thumb and forefinger, he lurched forward out of the loosened grip of his captors and snatched it in his right fist. All eyes were on him as he cupped it in his hands, raising it to his face to study it intently. He sniffed it. He licked it. And then, in a disturbing display I'll never quite be able to wash from the canvas of my memory, he kissed it full on the face.

'Is the situation under control?' said the taller of the officers. 'Because we've got better things to be doing, to be honest.'

'He's *barred*,' reiterated Barnie. 'He's flouted club policy more times than I've found abandoned trolleys from Almart.'

Chunky seemed deaf to the continuing exchange – he was cradling the troll gently, whispering sweet nothings into its tiny plastic ear.

'*You're home now,*' he crooned.

'Aren't you going to escort him off the premises?' asked Barnie, loftily. 'He's a threat to the peace of this establishment.'

The shorter officer looked at Chunky making love to his tiny friend.

'He doesn't look like much of a threat to me.'

Chunky seemed to become aware of the room again. He looked around like a disoriented lobster just emerging from a tickling-induced trance. There was something rather creepy about the way he allowed himself to be led to the doors by Barnie, no excessive force required. I slipped through the doors behind him, passing through the warm bath of blast heating and into the freezing cold. I had to know.

'Chunky,' I said, 'are we . . . We're all right now, then?'

It seemed he'd been waiting for me to follow him, loitering in the smoke-shrouded shadows beside the smouldering cigarette bins. I saw that his right fist was clenched, as if simultaneously to protect his lucky charm and prepare for a punch-up. He lowered his voice, though his diction was so clear and biting that I could hear it beneath the clamour around us.

'I know you and Karen's the reason I got barred. And the only fuckin' reason I needed the troll was so I'd win Monkey Night. Now I can't even get in to win. So, no. We're not all right, you and me.'

There was really very little I could say to that. As I turned to go back inside, his parting words slithered after me frenziedly like an irritated venomous snake.

'I'll be waitin' for you when you get out.'

77

Umbrellas

Karen, bless her wonderful, amazing, foul-smelling, value Almart nylon-cotton-blend socks, had found our proper place in the queue. She hadn't been served yet. When I joined her, she was fifth in line.

'No problems getting into the line?' I whispered.

'Nah,' she said.

'Excellent.'

As soon as we'd paid, I thumbed through to the fifth page and examined the back. There it was. The tiny, almost invisible mark that Duke had made – a smear of purple dabber ink in the bottom-right corner.

We had the right set of books.

All that was to be done now was to find our seats, play the game and shout at the correct time.

I'd never shouted for a win at the bingo before. All told, I'm a spectacularly unlucky person. Which made me wonder, thinking of it, why on earth I'd thought I could get away with this whole insane plan in the first place.

I'd practised my winning shout in front of the mirror in the women's dressing room in the derelict River Island at Smithson's Landing. For a while, I was fairly confident I was going to go traditional, and say 'House!' I'd briefly considered 'Here!' and fleetingly entertained the notion of 'Oy!' though this seemed a little impertinent. Then I'd branched out a little. Thought perhaps something more unconventional. Maybe 'Get in!' or 'Who's the Daddy?!' Or a little more surreal. 'Keylime!' or 'Tampon!'

In the end, I'd decided just to make Karen do it. She was well practised, the lucky bugger. Her regular wins were the only thing that kept her in cheapy tabs.

I shifted in my chair, capping and uncapping my lucky dabber, restless with nerves. I glanced at my phone. 19.27. The hall was heaving. Nearly at capacity. They'd be turning people away now. The noise of human interaction was nearly ear-splitting. I felt a little claustrophobic. I also felt an insistent, repetitive poking against my right bicep, and turned to find Karen prodding me with her dabber.

'Oy,' she said to me, 'Maurice.'

'What?' I ground out through clenched teeth. I wasn't in the mood to talk. I felt that if I opened my mouth, my tea and that last Toxic Avenger might leap out on to the tabletop.

'It'll be all right,' she whispered. She seemed remarkably calm.

I snatched the dabber from her and dropped it on the table. Then I enfolded her hand in mine.

'I know,' I said.

And with that, the opening music began.

78

Heaven's Gate

Leonard Overall mounted the caller's podium.

He climbed the steps with a sense of purpose, the expression on his face vaguely constipated. As exuberantly confident as he was, I could tell that he, too, was feeling slightly jittery. He was dressed, appropriately enough, as Napoleon. French military jacket, eighteenth-century tailoring. Glistening gold epaulettes. Intricate golden threading around the cuffs and buttons. An enormous tricorn hat. Shining black boots. No doubt it all looked incredibly cheap close up. He'd have got it from Pirouette Costume Shop in Stockton-on-Tees. He pulled the mic from its holder, having to tug rather hard to dislodge it.

'**Good evening, Ladies and Jellyspoons!**' he announced. A hush fell over the crowd. '**I said: "Good evening, Ladies and Jellyspoons!"**'

'Goovning,' we responded, in a half-hearted murmur.

'**I said: "GOOD EVENING, LADIES AND JELLY-SPOONS!"**'

'GOOVNING!' we responded.

'**That's better!**' said Leonard. '**Welcome, welcome, welcome. Welcome to this night of monkey-based Fun and Theatre here at the Pentagon Deerpool. We have twenty-five thousand pounds worth of in-house prize**

money to play for tonight. And of course, let's not forget the reason we're all here. The chance to win that golden monkey. Worth five hundred thousand pounds, Ladies and Jellyspoons. Five. Hundred. Thousand. Pounds.' He adjusted his hat, which had fallen forward to cover his eyes. **'Would you like to see it?'**

'Yes,' came the reasonably enthusiastic response from the crowd.
'Not good enough. Would you like to see it?'
'YES!'

'Barnie,' said Leonard, **'the golden monkey, if you please.'**

Barnie appeared from the shadows of the stage, still in costume. He was holding the statue. It looked very heavy, and he'd clearly had difficulty gripping it with the paws of the monkey suit – opting instead to cradle it in the crook of his right arm. It was about the size of a newborn baby, and holding it Barnie looked for all the world like a simian parody of the Madonna and Child.

I'd never seen a chunk of solid gold before, let alone one so large. It was paler than I'd expected. Beautiful, though. It managed to look at once delicate and impervious – it was heavy and solid enough to brain someone with, but you could scratch it with a fingernail and the detail of the design was astounding. Barnie mounted the caller's podium and turned thee hundred and sixty degrees to give the entire hall a good view of the statue. As he turned in our direction, I noticed it was modelled after a chimpanzee standing up straight on its back legs, arms hanging low so that its hands brushed its knees. Around its neck was an intricately crafted piece of golden rope, tied in a noose.

'Thank you, Barnie,' said Leonard. And then to his audience, **'Barnie's going to bring it back to the safe in Admin now. So don't get any ideas!'** He guffawed heartily, though the club's management had most probably told him to drop that in there – they were clearly being careful. Leonard paused for a moment, evidently looking at a small piece of paper he'd drawn from his pocket. **'Anyway. What do you call an orang-utan that likes dipping biscuits in its tea?'**

'Dunno,' rumbled the audience.

'A dunkey monkey.'

I laughed along with the crowd, a little too loudly.

I barely heard the routine introduction to the game. **'Yellow page, nice loud shouts – stop me, not the people around you. Last number called must be on the winning ticket. Please turn off all mobile phones. We're playing for the full house only.'**

I came to my senses only when the voices and movement around me abruptly muffled, as though someone had put a lid on a jar of canned chatter, and Leonard called the first number.

'Four-and-two, forty-two.'

I thought about what Duke had told me about algorithms. What must be happening now, inside that tiny box in front of Leonard on the stage. I tried to imagine it – the alluring equation planted there, tempting 'four-and-two, forty-two' to join it for a quick bonk behind a microchip, causing it to swell and multiply to:

'Six-and-seven, sixty-seven.'

And before the equation's mother even sensed the first flush of shame, 'six-and-seven, sixty-seven' was all grown up, hanging out with a new algorithm and a slutty equals sign, together rampantly making:

'Eight-and-nine, eighty-nine.'

Before I knew it, there were forty-three numbers out. We would win on the forty-seventh call: number 49.

Three more numbers.

'Seven-and-four, seventy-four.'

From the far wall to our right, there came the angry growl of a shout.

'House!'

I turned and, to my astonishment, saw Barnie in the gorilla costume, holding a book and a dabber aloft in triumph.

One More Time

The shout set off a chain of hurried, haphazard actions. A claim-checker with a large bald spot and incredibly small nostrils dashed over to Barnie's side and took the bingo book from him, followed in short order by a second claim-checker who took the book from the first one and whispered something sharply into his ear. Leonard Overall then raised the microphone to his lips and spoke with an uncharacteristic nervous waver.

'**We should . . . ah. Check the claim. I think.**'

What in the name of . . . What was Barnie playing at? This wasn't part of the plan at all. How could he *possibly* have won the full house?

The first claim-checker raised a radio mic to his lips, but before any sound escaped his mouth, there appeared a petite, impeccably suited man who looked to be in his mid-thirties. His hair was spiked in the manner of a singer I remember Karen was once obsessed with – Gareth Gates, I believe he was called. He gave off an air of corporate confidence as potent as his Thierry Mugler aftershave, which could be smelled from our seats three rows away. I didn't need to be close enough to read his badge to know it read: 'General Manager'. He looked as confused as I was. He too, of course, knew that it was Barnie in the gorilla costume, and I knew for a fact that he didn't allow his staff members to play bingo at the Pentagon. It would lead to accusations of rigging.

I craned my neck to take in their heated exchange. It seemed that the general manager was giving Barnie a sound telling off for playing bingo in his own place of employment, and that Barnie was protesting . . . and then . . .

The gorilla's right hand gripped the tufty hair on top of the mask and tugged – twice with little success and then once again, harder, to reveal the beet-red face of Chunky.

The crowd, feeling uneasy, grew restless and confused. People at the very fringes of the hall stood up to better determine what was happening. Gentle mutterings of 'What's goin' on?' and '. . . blimmin' 'eck's happenin'?' emerged from the hubbub.

Then it became more volatile. After three seconds of restless impasse, an elderly woman near the bar stood and shouted, 'Get the fuck on with it!' This triggered an immediate swell of applause, which at first seemed likely to dissolve, but instead mutated into a regular and ominous rhythmic clap.

I saw a flash of panic in the corporate eyes of the general manager. There was evidently no section in the Handbook that covered 'What to Do When a Violent and Potentially Murderous Customer Has Been Unofficially Excluded but Miraculously Wins a £500,000 Golden Monkey'.

How? How could Chunky have another winning book? One that won *three* numbers before we were due to win? We'd checked every single one of those books for a duplicate full-house winner. Every. Single. One.

Gates muttered something to himself, then to Chunky, and then, more loudly, to Leonard.

'We'll check his claim.'

Leonard was visibly relieved to finally have a course of action.

The rhythmic clapping ceased with startling alacrity, and much of the hall erupted into a frenzy of shouting. It was indecipherable, but it had the tone of protest about it. Claim-checker Number One seemed frozen with terror. After a pause, Gareth

Gates strode over to him, snatched away his mic and returned to Chunky's side. There, he grabbed the contested bingo book and peered at it for the serial number.

'TDJ 183726455502,' read Gareth out loud, a little too loud (he obviously wasn't used to using voice-amplifying technology).

I saw Leonard typing with unsteady fingers, and a moment later, on the numerous LCD screens around the hall appeared an image of Chunky's ticket, all numbers illuminated in green, the number 74 flashing merrily, and underneath, in black words against a stripe of mocking pink, the words 'VALID CLAIM'.

There You Go, Matey

The audience, fickle as pre-pubescent boy-band fans, erupted into applause and cheers of triumph.

Until now fiercely defensive of their chance to win big (and thereby to get out of this dead-end ditch of a life in which they were stuck), the moment someone in close proximity (even if that someone was Chunky – who I happened to know a good two-thirds of them hated outright) was gifted the very thing they longed for, all of those intense feelings transmogrified into a species of awe so powerful they could almost feel the success as their own.

I was filled with a white-hot, raging indignation. *Somehow* Chunky had got hold of that winning book.

I looked at Leonard. Only someone who was deliberately and carefully watching him would have noticed him reaching into the left cuff of his shirt, bringing out the tiny silver key and concealing it in his right palm.

Unless.

Oh God.

Leonard.

Stop and Run

That dirty, low-down, no-good, double-crossing bastard.

How could I have been so stupid as to let him in on the plan? I'd had no choice. I'd needed him. And I'd wanted to trust him. The arse was going to bring out Chunky's Super Number, and they were going to bugger off with the monkey. Five hundred thousand pounds split two ways is far more than five hundred thousand pounds split into five. You didn't have to be Divvy Karen to do the maths on that one.

Only Leonard didn't know Chunky like I did. The complete and utter idiot.

As I watched Leonard slip the key into the hole on the console, keeping it carefully concealed from the CCTV camera, I took a small measure of cruel satisfaction at the thought that Chunky would most likely knack Leonard to a pulp and take off with the monkey all to himself.

Leonard pressed the button to generate the number.

'Thirty-nine,' I mouthed.

'Both the sevens, seventy-seven!' called Leonard.

'Here!' shouted Chunky.

It was all over.

Straight on Through

At least Chunky would leave us alone for a while now. He had his troll *and* an arse-load of money. He might even take his loot and disappear off the map completely. It would make life a little more bearable. A *little*.

Who was I kidding? Nothing would make bearable the knowledge that Chunky had snatched away our fortune.

I had to be strong, and turn my mind to Barnie. In the midst of all the drama, I felt a little guilty for forgetting about him. If Chunky had hijacked his gorilla costume – where was *he*? I had to make sure he was all right. Then we could go round to Duke's, watch some French incest and commiserate.

Now. If I were a psychopathic chav and I'd beaten up a rotund receptionist to gain access to a bingo hall in order to win an enormous jackpot, where would I stow said receptionist's bound-and-battered hulk?

Around the side of the building? Possibly. But whether lure him there and cosh him round the head, or drag him there post-cosh, it wouldn't leave much time to return to the bingo hall in time for the game.

In the manager's offices? No. Gareth Gates had emerged from the direction of the offices after Chunky's claim. Barnie would've been noticed.

No, there could only be one option: the Front of House cupboard.

The arcade and Front of House were eerily quiet except for the fruit machines trilling away to themselves like garrulous, lonely toddlers chattering to imaginary friends.

'Breep-boop! Bad a-bah! Bing!'

'Lucky, lucky, lucky!'

'Diddly-dee, dah-dah, diddly-diddly DEE!'

'Help me! I'm in the cupboard!'

Okay. That definitely didn't come from a fruit machine.

He wasn't gagged, then.

I made haste to the admissions desk and threw open the cupboard door. Inside, it was pitch black, and I scrambled along the wall with desperate fingers for a light switch.

'To the right! To the right!' yelled Barnie. Finally, I found the switch and flicked it, illuminating Barnie in the far corner between two sets of shelves, hog-tied, his face half-squashed against the grubby linoleum floor, his white undervest smeared with dust and blood and his white boxer-brief-clad arse thrust in the air, gleaming like a swollen full moon. He was lying in amongst a messy nest of membership forms and promotional leaflets – he'd no doubt brought these down like rain from the shelves above as he struggled against his bonds.

As I picked my way through 2-4-1 Sunday flyers and temporary membership cards I noticed that his wrists and ankles were secured with thick blue rubber bands. Also that the blood on his vest stemmed from a nasty gash above his right eyebrow – evidence of blunt-force trauma.

'He used the good rubber bands,' he wailed, as I clawed them from his wrists. Christ, they were tight. Barnie's hands and bare feet were stained an inky shade of indigo. 'I was saving these ones for the rolled-up Tenner-Tacular Tuesdays posters. The thin bands just snap . . .' He was sniffling slightly. His cheeks weren't wet, but his eyes were blotchy. When I'd freed all four of his extremities, I began to massage the blood back into them. Only then did it seem to dawn on him to ask about the game. 'What's happening?' he asked, fingering the cut above his eye with the hand I wasn't pummelling. 'Where's Chunky? Have you won?'

'No,' I said, not without resentment. 'I'm so sorry, Barnie. I'll explain when we get to Duke's place.'

As he scrambled into his clothes, Barnie filled me in on the details of his ordeal.

'He dragged me back into the cupboard and hit me over the head with that Brand Standard poster pole. I don't think I was out for long. I've been shouting at the top of my lungs for the past twenty minutes. I can't believe no one heard me.'

'Everyone's in the hall. Plus, there's the *Jungle Book* music.'

Suddenly there was a frantic hammering on the outside of the cupboard door. A pause. The handle rattled. Then Karen fell through the door, hit her head on the shelves opposite, recovered quickly and ran to Barnie and me, hyperventilating.

'Come quick!' she said. 'Chunky's claim's been declared false!'

83

Time for Tea

I grabbed Barnie (his modesty now protected) and we barrelled through the doors into the hall just in time to see Gareth Gates handing a small scrap of paper to Leonard on mainstage. Gareth whispered a few words into Leonard's ear, and then beat a hasty path back through the hall towards the offices. Whatever his decision, he clearly didn't want to be around to see the crowd's reaction.

'**Right,**' said Leonard. He coughed loudly, directly into the open microphone. '**Shit.**' He turned his microphone off and took a deep breath, seeming panicked and short of oxygen. Then he began to speak without turning on the mic. I could see his lips move, then pause, and then move again to issue another silent but unmistakable 'Shit'. A moment later, he spoke audibly into the open mic. I'd never seen him so discombobulated. It was unnerving.

'**Right, Ladies and Gentlemen. The managerial staff have made a decision. It seems that we can . . . *not* allow the current claim to stand as valid. The claim was made by . . .**' he squinted slightly at the paper, '**. . . a member whose membership is no longer in a state of validity . . .**'

His voice lowered to a mumble, '**Well, that doesn't sound right.**'

He spoke again in a normal tone, **'And therefore we cannot validate it. There's – I can't even read this bit. Something about . . . Oh. For a claim to be valid, the member's membership needs to be valid, and as such – the gist of this, Ladies and Gentlemen, is that all of this is invalid, and we're carrying on with the game.'**

There was a cacophony of shouts at this. A strange, dissonant mixture of continued hope, impatience and anger.

'Shambles,' I heard one person exclaim, amidst the racket.

'ANY OBJECTIONS, please address them to management. We are now CARRYING ON WITH THE GAME.'

I looked to the back of the hall. Chunky was nowhere to be seen.

'This is a farce!' screeched a genderless voice.

'If you'll please calm down and keep the noise to a minimum . . .'

The ruckus continued.

'Oh SHUT UP!' shouted Leonard. **'It's only fucking BINGO!'**

That strangled the dissent like chicken wire around a windpipe. It wasn't the command itself that did it – it was the incredible shock of the unprecedented sacrilege. I mean. The Pope might as well have stood up in the middle of Mass and shouted, 'Oh, arse off with your stupid warbling – it's only fucking JESUS!'

Chaos ensued. At least a hundred people stood up from their seats and began to hurl profanities at Leonard. Some were demanding his immediate dismissal, others proposing the visitation of violent acts upon his person.

I, however, had just one thought: two more numbers, and we would WIN.

'Karen,' I whispered, 'where's our ticket?'

'Oh,' she said. 'Cleaner took it.'

'WHAT?'

'Cleaner took it. I let her. We didn't need it any more.'

'Crap. Crap. CRAP! Where's the cleaner?'

I scanned the hall for anyone with a black bag. No one. It had already been taken out to the bins, then, lost in a slag heap of crumpled tickets, dried-out dabbers and snotty tissues.

In the midst of all this insanity, a kind of peace came over me. At once, I knew what to do.

'Karen,' I said, 'remember when we were building the bungalow in Smithson's Landing? You saw all the books, didn't you? And you'll remember the numbers on those books?'

'Yeah,' said Karen.

'So if the game carries on now, you could tell me which book will win the full house?'

'Yeah.'

'Karen?'

'Yeah?'

'Which one would it be?'

'Errr . . .' She closed her eyes. 'It would be the one with 11, 67, 39 on the bottom line. Serial number TDF2305955567. It'll win on the number 57. Three more numbers called – then it'll win.'

'And was that book bought before us in the queue?'

'Ten before us. Sheila's book.'

'*Sheila's* book?' I looked over to Sheila's regular seat. She'd evidently retired to the arcade, but her book was still on the table. The cleaner hadn't done that part of the hall yet.

There seemed to be no sign of play resuming any time soon. Several staff members were physically restraining some more violent customers and Leonard was sitting on the edge of the podium with his head in his hands.

I dashed into the arcade, making sure my route took me by Sheila's table. As I passed it, I snatched up her book. I glanced at it. Her Super Number was 90.

Predictably, there was Sheila on her stool watching Neenie feed coins into two bandits at once. The deflated brown husks of coconut balloons still hung from the top of one of her machines.

'Sheila,' I said, 'I need you for a second.'

'Er – hang on,' said Neenie. 'She's helpin' me. You can't just steal 'er.'

'Sheila,' I said, 'do you want to sit and watch Neenie win and lose for the rest of your life? Or do you want to take a gamble and come with me? I promise you, it'll be worth it.'

Sheila wavered for a moment before she nodded, and followed me over to the dark corner of the arcade near the Deal or No Deal machines. Neenie shot her a furious gaze, but was soon distracted by a merry, hypnotic trilling from her machine. She'd got the Pots.

'I don't have much time,' I told Sheila, 'so you'll have to decide quickly. We have a way to win the golden monkey. But we need your ticket. In three more numbers, you'll win the full house. But you won't have the Super Number. We can make it so that your Super Number comes out. Then we'll cash in the monkey and share out the money. There are six of us in on the plot, including you. Are you in?'

'Errrrrrr . . .' said Sheila. She licked her lips. I could see the turmoil on her face as she tried to process this new information at lightning speed. She looked again towards Neenie. Then looked me directly in the eye. 'I . . .' She grew decisive. 'I left my ticket on the table.'

I held it up, grinning.

We ran back into the hall, weaving through the tables and bowling past disgruntled, arguing customers, until we reached Sheila's table.

'Stay here,' I instructed Sheila. 'And get ready to shout.'

I made my way to the podium, where I found the despondent Leonard. When I said his name, he startled and uncurled.

'Hi there,' I said. 'I know what you've done. I know you're a double-crosser, and I know you're in league with Chunky. Your plan's fallen flat on its face. But you can still get something out of it. It won't be half the money, but it'll be a sixth of it. All you need to do is to continue the game, turn that link key, and call 90 as the Super Number.'

He thought about it for all of a second. The opportunistic shithead.

And so the game continued. And when her moment of bingo fame came, Sheila yelled, at the top of her lungs, an explosive, exhilarated:

'Yabadabadoooo!'

84

Seven Dozen

'We're getting the monkey out of the safe now,' said Trish on Booksales. 'It's heavy, mind. Will you be able to carry it?'

'I should think we'll manage,' I said.

Leonard brought it out.

I'd never handled solid gold before. It was soft – smooth as skin. And heavy. Stunningly heavy for its size. Its surface was shimmery, but contrary to so many poetic depictions, it didn't glitter. The tiny eyes of this monkey were less bright and alive than those of the bronze one mired in the Marina.

'Thank you.' I opened my handbag and nestled the monkey in amongst my Kleenex, softmints and spare silicone breast forms. I slung the strap across my chest to distribute the weight across my torso.

'I need yers to sign this prize winner's receipt,' said Trish, thrusting a small slip of paper and a pen in my direction. I signed it with the largest, loopiest version of my name I could muster.

'I'll walk you out to the car park,' she said. I must've looked puzzled. 'In case you get mugged,' she explained. 'I've ordered you a taxi.'

This seemed reasonable. And also wonderfully convenient, in light of the Chunky situation.

'Give me two seconds, Trish,' I said. I peeked through the

doors to the hall and signalled to Barnie, who was helping the cash bingo staff to tidy, picking up scattered counters from the floor and folding up the fixed seats around the tables.

'Pssst,' I said, and he heeled like an obedient puppy. 'Duke was pissed last time we spoke. When you get off, would you go round and check on him? Think he's had a bit of a romantic disappointment. Me and Karen will join you soon as we can.' Barnie nodded, gave me the double thumbs-up and then ducked back down to resume collecting counters. Three rows away, he popped up again and declared, 'Hey. It all worked out in the end, didn't it, Maurice?'

I smiled. Then I saw Sheila, waiting patiently by Neenie's usual fruit machine. Neenie was nowhere to be seen – it seemed she'd opted for an early night. I gave Sheila a warm smile.

'I promise,' I said, 'I'll have your share of the money for you tomorrow.' I gave her a slip of paper with directions to Smithson's Landing scribbled on it. 'Be there at ten o'clock tomorrow morning. Thank you, Sheila.' I hugged the breath out of her. 'You do something amazing with it. *Don't* put it in a bandit,' I said firmly. She nodded.

Trish accompanied us out to the car park and we jumped into the waiting cab. As soon as we were under way, I instructed the driver to take us round the corner to the lock gates – our old haunt. The weight of the golden monkey, resting substantial and comforting in my lap, was squashing my penis slightly, but not at all painfully. Though it was only a hundred yards or so, the driver asked for two pound fifty. A shocking rip-off that no longer mattered.

I stood with Karen for a while on the gate bridge, her small hand clasped in mine, looking out over the sluggish swell of the freezing sea. I turned towards the Pentagon. Seagulls wheeled overhead in the dome of light that cocooned the building. Brilliant white, like desiccated coconut in a snow globe.

I was still a little shell-shocked, I think. Of course I'd known all along about the possibility – the probability – of winning, but I guess I hadn't *really* believed we'd manage to pull it off. It was unreal.

I looked back out at the sea, my eyes resting on the bronze monkey statue.

'What was the last wish you made when you threw a penny into that thing?' I asked Karen, and tugged my hand away.

Karen smiled.

'Years ago. Wished you and me would get together.'

I laughed, loud and hearty.

'You?' she asked.

'I wished . . . for a Dolce & Gabbana handbag.' I blushed in the dark. It seemed lame now, compared to her wish. Still, I wouldn't have wished it if I hadn't really wanted it. I beckoned Karen closer, turned her so that she faced open ocean, and shucked up her top at the back. 'What am I drawing on your back?' I asked, tracing a pattern with the tip of my index finger.

'Erm . . .' She fell quiet for a while, her breath hitching when I used my fingernail to form the curves of my invisible picture. '. . . A cat.'

I huffed out a breath of laughter.

'Yes,' I said. 'Yes. It's a cat.'

I'd been drawing a monkey but I couldn't tell her. I couldn't find breath for the words. In fact, I couldn't breathe at all.

A large, dark, hairy figure had a tight hold of me. I felt a rubber mask brush against my neck. Its wearer started to speak, leaking rancid breath close to my ear.

'What do you call an orang-utan,' it asked, in a quiet, sibilant voice, 'that cuts people into pieces?'

'I don't know,' I said, reflexively, though I suspected I knew the answer.

'A Chunky monkey,' it said.

And at that, it spun me around, seized me quickly by the shoulders again and kneed me hard in the testicles.

I bent double, a small string of bitter sick dangling from my bottom lip onto the gravel. A powerful weight grasped me from behind. I could smell plasticine.

Even in the face of peril, I laughed. It didn't escape me that in that moment there was, quite literally, 'a monkey on my back'.

'Hey, ho and away we go,' trilled Chunky as he threw me down on to the concrete in front of the boat hoist. 'Now. Where would a fuckin' radged pervert like you 'ide a golden monkey?' I groaned. Searing strands of pain shot up from my groin, and I clutched my handbag closer to my chest, instinctively protecting the treasure. Chunky let out a mirthless laugh. He took hold of my handbag, dragging the strap from beneath my arm and pulling until it supported my neck, right against my Adam's apple. Then he held the handbag still and kicked me once between the shoulder blades. I thought for a moment that he'd successfully decapitated me – the strap sliced into the most sensitive part of my neck with such ferocity that I gagged and saw stars. When he let go of the handbag, I flopped heavily and helplessly on to the tarmac like an injured sea lion, landing face down in a splodge of fetid seaweed.

I could hear the crunch of Chunky's Nikes moving closer across the grit and cockle-shell strewn ground, until they squelched in the seaweed just before my face.

'Fuck you,' I said with what little breath I had left, and bit him hard on the ankle. His sock tasted like Peperami. He howled and bent to slap me away, and in that moment I rolled to the right with all the strength I had and forced myself to my knees in one quick wrench. There was no way I was escaping this. Still, Karen was nowhere to be seen, so perhaps she'd managed to get away. Thank God. I tugged the handbag from around my neck, swung it with some effort – damn, the thing was heavy – and hurled it overarm like a shot-putter. My aim was true. It hooked around the beefy shoulders of the monkey statue. Perhaps Karen would be able to sneak back and get it, after this whole horrid mess was finished. Small hope but still . . .

Just then, I heard the low grumble of a car engine and the scrunch of tyres on gravel. Then came the pop and slam of a car door opening and closing. Suddenly a pair of firm hands – one clutching each of my wrists – yanked me to my feet. A chuckle reached my ear, and a pervasive and instantly familiar smell reached my nostrils. *Lynx Chocolate*. The yanker was none other than . . .

Leonard Overall!

The absolute *arsehead*.

85

Staying Alive

Leonard held me, my back tight against his barrel chest, as Chunky began to strip himself free of the gorilla costume.

'Leonard,' I said, 'think about this. You seem like a decent guy.'

'I am,' he said, 'more or less. Still, I look out for number one. Nearly went along with your little plan, actually. But you have to agree that a two-way split is much better than a six-way split. Chunky seemed like the obvious choice. And he wouldn't attract your suspicion by hanging around and monitoring you. After all, you thought he was all hung-up on that stupid chewed troll doll.'

Slowly and rather laboriously, Chunky peeled away the monkey mask to reveal his face, red and squashed as a stepped-on cherry tomato. Next he struggled out of the huge hairy jumper top – it was like watching the slow-motion replay of a televised wrestling match between a stick insect and a tarantula. Lastly, the trousers came off – he rolled them down his legs and hopped on first one foot, then the other as he dislodged the cuffs from his trainers.

There then ensued a struggle to get the costume on to *me*, which was as awkward and painful as you might imagine.

The inside of the mask smelled like Chunky's breath: horrible. Plasticine, naturally, but something else, too, even more horrible and deliquescent – something like a jar of olives you've left open for a year in a malfunctioning fridge, ripening, oxidising and slowly decomposing, until you finally remember – damn, I left that jar of olives in there – and much to your immediate and desperate regret you open the fridge to release a nauseating blast of pong.

At first it was mercifully warm inside the costume, but the warmth soon thickened into an unbearable, stifling heat. Streams of sweat began to flow freely from my armpits to my waist. How real gorillas survived in this get-up, and in the jungle at that, was frankly beyond me.

After that, things seemed to happen fairly quickly – as things do when all control is wrested from one. It was as though my consciousness was edited to include only the vital moments. A little as though a director had taken this long, onerous episode and carved it into a movie trailer. A hairy and organic-looking rope – hemp, probably, or possibly flax – was slung over the top bar of the boat hoist. Chunky made short work of tying a hangman's noose – a skill undoubtedly acquired at the University of Hard Knacks – and looped it loosely around my neck. I felt its weight settle impertinently on my shoulders like an awkward hug from someone I disliked.

I could hear Chunky's voice, over the low hum of the car's engine, still running.

He'd started to sing.

> *It 'appened in Old Deerpool in the Napoleonic War,*
> *An 'airy little monkey was washed upon the shore,*
> *The people of the town were a little bit confused,*
> *And the innocent primate was 'orribly abused.*

Through the inadequate eyeholes of the infernal mask I could just about see Leonard standing by the bonnet of the car, watching. I noticed he was still dressed as Napoleon. There was a look of mild concern in his eyes, as though he hadn't quite expected it to be like this.

'Oy!' barked Chunky, gesturing wildly for Leonard, 'Mush. Gerrover 'ere and 'elp me 'oist 'im.' Leonard stood impotently, presumably unable to translate Chunky Speak.

'Hhhere,' I intoned, 'hhhelp, hhhoist,' my words bouncing back at me hot and moist in the confines of the mask. I immediately wondered why on earth I'd spoken. Something about being a teacher, I think, compels one to ensure people pronounce their aitches.

At that, Leonard waddled to stand behind me again, and I felt him swiftly undoing the ties at my ankles and wrists, a mere split-second before he and Chunky grabbed the end of the rope they were using for leverage and pulled, pulled, pulled, heaving-ho like sailors.

In time with their heaving, Chunky began to sing again. This time, Leonard joined in.

> *Siiiiiiingin . . .*
> *All yers lads and lasses, get yers to the dunes,*
> *Come and see the radgie man what's gone and been marooned,*
> *The mayor says it's a monkey*
> *But we say 'Is 'e 'eck',*
> *It's clear that 'e's a Frenchman*
> *So we'll 'ang 'im by 'is neck.*

At last, I was dangling helplessly in the air, halfway between the boat hoist and the water it straddled. They tied off the rope around a mushroom-shaped bollard.

They had untied my hands and legs, I realised, so that they could watch my limbs flail. And flail they did, for the several seconds it took me to realise that my panicked movements were making me die twice as quickly. I'm sure it was quite a spectacle.

I was horribly aware that I was clawing at nothingness in the empty air, like a non-swimmer doggy-paddling at sea. Hopelessness deepening as little by little my breath abandoned me.

At last, I dredged up enough presence of mind to stop struggling and instead raise my arms to clutch at the rope around my neck, insinuating my fingers underneath to loosen it a fraction. I made some attempt, too, to tighten my neck muscles – I'd heard somewhere that this prevents one from dying quite so quickly in such situations.

It's funny how one doesn't really appreciate oxygen. I'd never before had occasion to think, 'By Jove, this is some tasty oxygen I'm sucking down.' But at that precise moment, I knew that I'd like nothing more for an early Christmas present than a great big bottle of the stuff.

It didn't help at all with the oxygen acquisition when I saw Leonard disappear behind the rack of Calor Gas cans and re-emerge hauling a limp and pitiful bundle of dark hair and podge.

Karen.

Between the Sticks

She was bound, quite innovatively, in Sellotape, from her shoulders to her ankles. They must have used at least three whole rolls. More office supplies stolen from Barnie's cupboard, no doubt. Karen's fat bulged out between the tight bands of translucent tape. She looked like a grub gone into hibernation. And, like a hibernating grub, she was unconscious, sleeping quietly – no doubt due to an earlier clock on the head.

For a few desperate moments I assumed that she was to meet the same fate as myself, until, through quickly blackening vision, I saw a heated exchange between Leonard and Chunky. It ended abruptly with Chunky snatching Karen from Leonard, lifting her bodily and throwing her face down into the water beneath the boat hoist, below my helplessly dangling feet.

I wondered, dimly, where Barnie and Duke were. Had Chunky and Leonard caught them and knacked them, or worse? And if not, why in the arseing hell weren't they here?

Oh well. Not really worth worrying about that now. My brain seemed to be losing the capacity to care about very much at all.

Torquay in Devon

'This may well be *it*,' I thought to myself.

Things certainly looked pretty bleak, from where I was hanging.

What had brought me there – they called it a 'game of chance'. Rubbish. Bingo isn't a game for gamblers. It's a game for fatalists.

They say every number called in a game of bingo is random. I know now that this is a lie.

They used to paint the numbers on little white balls and toss them about in a big glass globe, a tube popping one out at a time like a fertile chicken in constant labour. Now they use a computer – a series of sums, algorithms and codes to aspire towards randomness, calculating each apparently random number from the last, engineering what they think is infallible unpredictability.

There is no such thing as a Random Number Generator. Now I think about it, you don't have to be a computer whizz or a maths genius to work that out. Only a philosopher.

Every event, however bizarre, is always the sum of the events that have gone before. Therefore the culmination of events that led to this was entirely pre-determined. When your number's up, your number's up.

And if this was the final number in the game of my life – number 90, Nine-Oh, King of the Castle, Top of the Pile, Last in the Bag, Top of the House – then . . . Well. At least it had been a damned exciting game.

I comforted myself with the knowledge that if I was to die, at least I would do it alongside Karen. It seemed fitting. Right. And meant to happen. In the great RNG of our lives, all algorithms evidently added up to our tragic and humiliating death.

Karen floated so silently, so still in the water. One moment I could see her clearly – her distinct, small human form bobbing on the black water – and the next I wasn't sure she wasn't just a piece of flotsam or jetsam, a large bag entwined with seaweed, perhaps, twisted into the vague shape of a person.

She was slipping away by degrees. As was I. I cared about her more than any person alive on this earth. And as we drifted further and further away from each other, I begin to realise that I was wrong. Each of us was going to die alone. One. It's the loneliest fucking number.

88

Two Fat Ladies

My vision was blacking out. The most worrying thing was that I didn't feel frightened. Just vaguely uneasy, as though I was nodding off to sleep in a public place. Strange, half-formed scenarios drifted into my consciousness. One moment I was hanging in a gorilla costume from a boat hoist at midnight, the next I was painting a bedroom in eggshell blue. I could smell the paint, sweet and chemical, feel it caked on my hands – it had splashed on to my face, and it cracked as I smiled, standing back to look at my work. It was important that I finish this room, because Karen would be coming to stay. This would be her room, and she loved eggshell blue. Mum would make edamame-bean salads, and we'd all sit together in the kitchen, in the small, detached house in the Fens. Mum would say, 'It's all right, Maurice. You tried your best. Most of us in this life are adrift in a freezing sea without an anchor. Just let yourself drift. I'm out here waiting for you.'

A myoclonic jerk snapped me back to the boat hoist. Cold sweat wormed its way in a trickling, tickling line, from my groin, down the inside of my right leg, to my ankle.

And then a thought occurred to me.

Of course in the great RNG of our lives, all algorithms add up to our tragic and humiliating death. But why shouldn't we rig the game?

Perhaps I was delirious from lack of oxygen. It was insane, and near-impossible, unlikely to work. But. But.

We managed it once.

Why shouldn't we manage it again?

I relaxed all of my muscles. It is exceptionally difficult to force one's body to go limp. Especially when one is half-hanged and trying desperately to resist succumbing in this very way. Somehow, however, I managed it – and then I waited, slipping further and further away from reality, from breath, from life. I waited for them to cut me down.

And at last . . . at last . . .

I felt a tug on the rope. A sharp tug, and a series of smaller reverberations, transmitted through the rope to my neck. They were untying it!

All of a sudden I was falling, so quickly and so briefly that I hardly had time to acknowledge the powerful, astonishing tug of gravity that dragged my stomach up my oesophagus and into my mouth, before I felt the slap of impact with the water and, be-latedly, its icy cold seeping through the costume to chill my skin.

My first instinct was to make a grab for Karen, though I knew that if I so much as twitched – if I seemed anything less than stone dead – they would hoist me back up and finish the job properly.

So again I waited. I waited while the foul, freezing water leaked in through the sockets of my mask. I took two or three desperate, surreptitious breaths – all I managed before I was drowning again, my mouth and nose filled with trout-flavoured pollution, the gorilla costume thirstily sucking up all of the water it could hold until, gradually, I was tugged beneath the surface. Down, down, further and further still, silent and cold, limp and heavy. Forgetting that anything ever mattered. Anything. Rigging a game of bingo. Making it to Tijuana. People pronouncing their aitches. A girl called Karen, her lips eggshell blue. Forgetting it all, until . . .

Until something nudged my right foot.

Insistently, eagerly. Like an excited dog wanting to play.

Go away.

Go away. Get out of it. I don't want to play.

I . . .

89

Nearly There

Herb!

The half-grown shark thudded into my right leg yet again, this time with more force – startling me back into awareness. Awakeness! I'd woken only to find that my whole body had gone numb. I had to concentrate harder than I'd ever concentrated before to flex my fingers, coax the nerves back into life, reach up and tear the sodden mask from my face, letting it float away from me in the darkness; to open my eyes, to see through the murk and the gloom the indistinct form of Herb, his face directly in front of mine, his wide mouth curved at the edges in something resembling a satisfied smile.

I struggled out of the monkey trousers. I couldn't get out of the jumper – even after all those swimming lessons in which we were taught to undress from our pyjamas underwater. Fifty Metres Fully Clothed, the certificate said, and I never achieved it – yet still I fought against the weight of the sodden fur until, with a breath so enormous I felt I might inhale the entire Marina, I breached the surface of the water and began to thrash my legs to keep myself afloat.

Three feet from me I saw Karen, still floating face-down, but stirring a little. Herb was flapping around her, bumping and buffeting her from all angles. The Sellotape was coming loose in the water. Great strings of it snaking out into the water around her like the tentacles of a Portuguese man-of-war jellyfish.

I thrashed to her side, grabbed her shoulders, flipped her over and started banging her between the shoulder blades.

She spluttered, twitched like a corpse convulsed by lightning, and vomited a great spew of seawater into my face.

I was delighted.

I propelled us both through the water until we reached a small, rusted ladder extending out of the water to the tarmac above.

Then, without warning, a heavy sack of something descended upon us, shoving us below water again. I surfaced, clawing for Karen. Having dragged us both clear of the bloated missile, I squinted to make out what it actually was. I issued an involuntary sound of disgust when I realised that it was, in fact, Leonard Overall, his eyes wide with shock, his throat slashed cleanly and steadily pumping blood. His tricorn hat was floating beside him, upside down and dented, like a miniature wrecked boat. The gold of his epaulettes looked startling against the inky sludge of the water around him. Napoleon was dead.

Then came the faint crunching footsteps above me.

Cradling Karen's small cold face to my chest (less pillowy now that my silicone breast forms were lost to the deep – maybe some jellyfish would find them and try to mate with them?), I watched as Chunky's face appeared grinning above the ladder. As his arms and torso came into view, I saw that he was clutching the knife he'd evidently used to dispatch Leonard.

Just as I let myself be grateful that Karen wasn't fully conscious for this, the expression on Chunky's face altered to one of amazement. A few uncertain seconds passed, in which time he swayed slightly and loosened his grip on the knife. It fell to the water with an unremarkable plop. Chunky followed shortly afterwards, albeit with a much louder crash.

Thankfully, this body didn't hit us – I'd doggy-paddled to the right the moment I saw him start to waver.

Then on the harbour appeared the faces of Duke and Barnie,

pale and concerned. Barnie put down the Calor Gas can he had used to brain Chunky, and Duke held out his tree trunk of an arm to hoist us up on to the rungs of the ladder and from thence to dry land. I lay on my back in a wet puddle of exhaustion, feeling Karen stir slightly beside me. A groan bubbled and leaked from her lips, along with another good half a pint of seawater.

Barnie spread his arms wide, looked up in wonder at the night sky, and let out a *whooooooooooooop!* of glory.

'This might be the best night I've ever had,' he said.

'Why the *fuck* did it take you so long?' I wheezed harshly, breathless from the cold. Barnie didn't answer, he didn't even seem to hear. He was too high on adrenaline.

I peered back over the side into the water – I'd been through enough to have learned that Chunky had a nasty habit of rearing his head just when you thought he'd gone for good.

No chance of that this time, though. He was face down in the water and I watched, nauseated but unable to look away, as Herb began to toy with the lifeless body much as a Labrador might play with a large, meat-flavoured animal toy. At first he simply chewed on the right leg above the knee, getting a mouthful more of sodden jeans than any flesh. Then he grew a little overexcited, lurched towards Chunky's top half and bit off his right ear.

At this point, I looked away.

Duke, still a little dazed from his drinking binge, tugged at my sleeve.

'Maurice,' he said, gravely, 'where's the actual golden monkey?'

For a moment, I panicked. Nothing quite compares to that awful lurch of the stomach when one's brain registers the lack of familiar weight over the shoulder – the pinch of patent leather strap and the comforting heft of handbag against the hip, like an infant clinging to its mother.

Then I remembered.

I turned, squinting into the biting wind.

There it was. My knock-off designer handbag, in it a hunk of pure gold, the strap hooked around the glistening wet shoulder of the huge bronze monkey, its bulk sitting in the bowl between the creature's legs where children and poor people aimed their coppers and threw and wished for a stroke of luck to carry them far, far away from this two-bit town.

90

Top of the House

Whenever I'd thought of Tijuana, I'd pictured its colours, its music, its heat. But I'd never imagined its smell. It's funny, but the smell turns out to be the best thing about it. Fajitas. Yes, they're in there somewhere. But money, too. The chalky, warm scent of money, flitting by like banknote birds on the breeze.

'Turn it up a little, my good man,' I shout to the taxi driver. He'd been a little reluctant to play my CD when we set out, but a fifty peso tip had sweetened him somewhat.

'What this music, anyhow?' he asks, as he screeches recklessly past a red convertible stuffed with what I assume to be drug dealers sunning themselves in the early afternoon light.

'You've never heard it before?' I ask, incredulously. I turn to Karen. 'He's never heard Herb Alpert before. Can you believe that?'

'Fuckin' radged,' says Karen, with feeling.

'Radged,' I affirm. 'Radged indeed.'

Karen had been keen to leave for Tijuana on the night of our win, though I'd pointed out that there was no rush. Chunky and Leonard were gone. And it's not like we were *criminals*, though of course we had originally intended to be. No, now we had time. Time for Duke to delete all evidence of our plot from his computers, and for Barnie to compose an eloquent letter of resignation to the Pentagon. (This time I was more than happy to proofread.) In the end, I took the monkey to Cash Converters, as the whole BullionBoys thing had sounded a bit shady, and paid the money into a brand-new bank account (do you have any *idea* how many benefits you get from the bank when you deposit that much money? And gains from gambling are *untax-able*, too!) and from there transferred Duke, Barnie and Sheila's shares to their accounts. I paid off all the rent I owed, and squared things with npower, which was something of a relief. Three days later, we set off for Tijuana.

For the moment, Karen and I are staying in a rather luxurious hotel, though I suppose at some point we'll get an apartment. In the meantime, it's just good to bask in the glory of a working fridge and a double bed.

Sheila, apparently, is planning to start up her own beauty salon, just across the road from Neenie's. She's going to offer pioneering rejuvenation treatments involving sterile maggots applied directly to the dry skin of the feet. She gave Neenie ten thousand pounds, which, over the course of five days, Neenie fed into a fruit machine.

Duke is planning to take a degree in Marine Biology.

Barnie I haven't heard from. Though I did read on the Internet this morning (Karen's teaching me to make better friends with technology) that a new bingo hall is opening in Bristol. It was particularly newsworthy, as it intends to operate a revolutionary and generous employee-benefits scheme, based on the principle that entry-level employees are as valuable to a franchise as the most high-powered managers. The article didn't name any names, though there was a picture of a beaming prospective employee modelling the intended uniform design. It took me several seconds to look past the neatly combed hair and tasteful moss green waist-coat to recognise Teddy Boy Bob.

I reach into my brand-new acacia cross-body and pull out a

bundle of banknotes. The bag is Dolce & Gabbana. *Real*. Though the rest of my outfit belonged to Mum. My hands, when I look down at them clasping the bag handle, look just like I remember hers to be.

'Drive us by the Plaza Río and the Plaza Monarca,' I say to the driver. 'Then along La Coahuila. Drive us around until nightfall.'

'You no want to get out anywhere, Madam?' asks the driver, lighting a filterless cigarette.

'Just keep driving,' I say.

With a flourish, I toss the notes through the gap between the front seats. They flutter in the air like doves released in a magic trick, coming to settle on the front passenger seat, the lap of the driver and the floor at his feet.

I don't make a wish. I don't need to.

'On the floor,' I say, reapplying my lipstick, 'to the door.'

Karen pokes her head out of the open window. Her hair flies in the wind like a shimmering, silken flag.

I am the luckiest man in the world.

Acknowledgements

With thanks, above all, to my family – most of all to my Mum, Dad, Granny, Nana, sister Amy, brother Jonathan and brother-in-law Garry. Enormous thanks to my agent Georgia Garrett, her assistant Emma Paterson, and editors Sarah Castleton, Tamsin Shelton and Olivia Hutchings, and to James Gurbutt at Corsair. Thanks too to my former tutors Andrew Cowan and Trezza Azzopardi, and my fellow students on the Creative Writing MA at UEA, class of '07, especially Tat Usher, K.J. Orr, Sarah Hesketh, Jenny Thompson, Stephanie Leal and Melanie Mauthner. A big thank you to my good friend James (Max) Finch, and my friends at Hart Gables, in particular, Jack, Deanna, Dakota, Xander and Jenny, for all their support. A heartfelt thanks, as well, to everyone at the bingo.